Jade Knew What She Wanted

She knelt at Morgan's side and unlocked one of the chains, loosening it enough for him to slip his hand free with little difficulty. She was overwhelmed by how small she felt next to his great size. No one had ever made her feel so dainty. So feminine . . .

As she moved to his other side, Jade thought of all the problems that had been piled on her shoulders: the loss of her mother, her servants and friends, her home, her father's incarceration, her cousin's high-handedness, and now Morgan Frazier . . . the prisoner who refused to escape.

Praise for *Amber* by Sue Rich

"Filled with a cast of splendid characters who capture the reader's heart from the start. A delightful read."
—*Rendezvous*

Books by Sue Rich

Jade
Amber
Aim for the Heart
Wayward Angel
The Silver Witch
Mistress of Sin
Rawhide and Roses
Shadowed Vows
The Scarlet Temptress

Published by POCKET BOOKS

Sue Rich

Jade

POCKET BOOKS

New York   London   Toronto   Sydney   Tokyo   Singapore

This book is a work of fiction. Names, characters, places and incidents are products of the author's imagination or are used fictitiously. Any resemblance to actual events or locales or persons, living or dead, is entirely coincidental.

An *Original* Publication of POCKET BOOKS

 POCKET BOOKS, a division of Simon & Schuster Inc.
1230 Avenue of the Americas, New York, NY 10020

ISBN: 0-671-00045-4

First Pocket Books printing September 1997

10 9 8 7 6 5 4 3 2 1

POCKET and colophon are registered trademarks of Simon & Schuster Inc.

Cover art by Mitzura Salgian

Printed in the U.S.A.

To Dianna Elaine Crawford,
Stef Ann Holm, and Mary Lou
Rich. For your friendship,
loyalty, and valuable input.
There aren't enough words to
express my appreciation.

To Caroline Tolley, my editor.
For always being there to pick
me up when I fall down.
Thank you.

And to my husband, Jim Rich.
Just for being you.

Chapter
1

London, England
Spring 1785

It was just lying there. *The damn thing was just lying there.*

Morgan Frazier froze in place. Several thoughts whirled through his mind as he attempted to understand what was happening. He couldn't. This had never occurred before, and it shouldn't be happening now. *Especially not now.* Not when he'd finally convinced Belinda Gates to share his bed last month.

He tried to gain control of his growing panic. He was only twenty-eight. Things like this didn't develop in people his age.

He peeked over at the woman lying in bed beside him—the one waiting for him to make love to her— then back down at his lower body. It was happening. *To him.*

"What is it, ducky? Is there a problem?" his voluptuous companion asked.

He couldn't think, much less speak, with Belinda's bold gaze fixed so diligently on the part of him that should have been alert.

It would have been easy to blame her for his lapse. He found that most women blamed themselves for a man's failure in the bedchamber. Not that he'd ever failed. *Before*. But he knew she wasn't the cause. Belinda was pretty, with full curves in all the right places. She was a large-boned woman, only twenty and six last fall when a duel plunged her into widowhood. She hadn't caused this.

In fact, there wasn't a single thing that could have. He sat up abruptly. Or was there? Could his father have . . . ? It wasn't possible.

Yes, it was.

Morgan didn't know whether to be furious or laugh that his father had bested him so well. He relaxed, certain now that it was a passing inconvenience. One his father would pay dearly for.

He inhaled the heavy scent of Belinda's perfume and cast her a warm glance. "There's no problem. I'm just . . . overly tired, that's all." The lie stung. He'd had so much rest lately, he shouldn't need sleep for a month.

Morgan had made plans to go to the Colonies with his friend, Christian Stanfield, this week, but Christian had been delayed on his return from France, and he wouldn't be here for a fortnight, possibly longer. Since Morgan had recently merged his fleet of ships with the British East India Company and hired a manager to oversee schedules and goods, he was now at loose ends. His investments in cotton and metalworks were stable and in the capable hands of his solicitor.

He smiled inwardly when he thought of the ships he'd purchased from his brother, Clay. Since Morgan's days in knee britches, he'd envied the life his pirate brother had led. Morgan had longed to take the sea for his mistress, just as Clay had. But, after only a month on the rolling, nauseating ocean, in a coffin of a cabin with only one window, and food that even the gulls wouldn't eat, he'd had his fill of sea life.

And, as of today, he'd had his fill of pranks.

Rising, Morgan walked to the window, avoiding Belinda's gaze as he did so. He needed to find out what his father had used to cause this, and he couldn't do that in the Widow Gates's house. "I hope you'll forgive me, but I've had a lot on my mind lately, and it's probably another cause of this . . . situation." He returned to the bed and drew her into his arms, holding her warm body next to his, hoping to feel *something*.

A breeze from outside feathered over his naked rear end, and the cushiony warmth of Belinda's skin enveloped him, but his body didn't stir in the least.

Damn his father's rotten hide.

With a disappointed sigh, Morgan turned away. "Why don't I make plans for a picnic Friday next?" If he was right about his suspicions, he should be fine by then. "Just the two of us by the lake . . . in a very private location." He brushed his lips over hers. "I'll make sure I get plenty of sleep and have nothing on my mind but you."

She moved seductively against him. "I'll look forward to it. But then I *always* look forward to our special times."

His frustration grew by bounds, and he had to steady his voice when he spoke. "I'll make the arrangements, then. So I'd better go."

She ran her fingers through the hair on his chest. "Do you have to?" Her hand slid lower. "Perhaps you just need a bit of encouragement."

3

Was this the same woman who'd been so terrified of his size? The same one he'd paid fifty crown for the first night? Wishing he could respond the way he wanted to, he cursed his father again and eased away from her. "I'm sorry, Belinda, I truly am."

He didn't look at her as he pulled on his breeches and Hessian boots, but he sincerely hoped Belinda wouldn't mention this mishap to anyone. Unfortunately, he knew women too well. In his gut, he was sure that before the day was out, she'd tell someone. Hell, who was he kidding? She'd tell everyone.

As he rode away from her apartments on Oxford Street, he knew as sure as it rained in England that he'd have to find another mistress—and that could take months.

The inconvenience, and the hellishly long ride out to Ainshall to confront his father, would add another pound to the weight he'd level onto Robert Frazier's head.

Ignoring the spring breeze that carried the fragrance of honeysuckle and a trace of smoke from the docks, Morgan mentally went over everything he'd eaten or drunk that day; tea, two glasses of port, and salmon for the noon meal.

One of those had been his downfall.

His prankish father had managed somehow to slip him something. The old goat had to have. Any other explanation was too painful to consider. And it certainly couldn't have been anyone else. Considering Morgan's six-feet-six, two-hundred-pound frame, no one would have dared. Only Robert Frazier would.

Not for the first time did Morgan wish these silly games would cease. But, in truth, he'd been just as much a part of them. With a smile, he remembered one of the last jokes he'd played on his father. Morgan had posted a note in London for the sale of his father's prize stallion . . . for ten shillings—a pittance of the animal's worth. The resulting chaos around Ainshall Manor had been hilarious, and it was due payment for what his father had done to him the previous Michaelmas.

The gelding beneath him sidestepped, and Morgan tightened his hands on the reins, thinking about the stallion his father had presented him. He knew if he searched the world over, he'd never find a more mean-spirited animal than that one. Morgan had been unseated three times before he realized what his father had done. *That time.*

He'd owned Midnight Flame for over a year now and still couldn't fully control him. But, whenever he felt he was up to the challenge, and time would allow, he'd try again.

The only good thing he could say about their pranks was that they'd grown farther apart. Of course, that could be because it was becoming harder and harder to think of new things to do to each other.

But this time his father had gone too far. No one—*no one*—messed with Morgan's manhood.

He nudged his gelding into a faster gait, determined to find out exactly what his father had used—and shove it down his throat.

But, as quickly as he'd kneed the horse, he slowed it. His father would never tell him. Robert Frazier was as stubborn as he was intelligent. If Morgan wanted to find out about this, he'd have to talk to someone with knowledge—like their family physician, Samuel Verde. Most likely, that's where his father had gotten the information in the first place.

Wheeling his mount around, Morgan headed for Sam's residence on the outskirts of London.

He passed coaching inns and a cobbler's shop and several rows of houses stacked close together. Most of them were whitewashed wood. A few of brick.

An oak-lined lane curved away from London, and the houses grew farther apart. Newly planted fields, small compared to Ainshall, began to separate the buildings.

When he saw the physician's familiar brick house with a white rail fence, he drew his horse to a halt and leapt down.

"Morgan? What are you doing here?" Samuel asked as he came out onto the porch. The deep lines in his forehead and grooves in his cheeks gave evidence that his gray hair wasn't premature. "You aren't ailing, are you?"

Morgan sincerely hoped not. "I'd like to talk to you."

"Come in then." He opened the door and motioned Morgan inside.

Morgan followed him into a small, neat drawing room off a wide entry hall. Shelves of salves, ointments, elixirs, and books lined the walls, and a faint odor of liniment lingered in the air.

Samuel gestured to a chair by the window, automatically positioning Morgan where he wouldn't feel so confined. Sam had known for years about Morgan's dread of enclosed places. Hell, anyone who knew him knew about that. It wasn't exactly something he could hide. Even walking down a hall that was any length made him sweat.

"Would you care for a sherry?" Sam asked. "I was just about to have one myself."

Morgan nodded, then sank into the chair, suddenly hating to tell anyone about his problem, even an old family friend. What if his father hadn't done this? What if he really couldn't—Ah, damn.

"So," Samuel said as he handed Morgan a glass. "What brings you here? Not that I'm not happy to see you, but I am surprised. You usually reserve our socializing for dinner engagements."

Morgan took a fortifying breath. "Sam, I've got a problem."

"What kind?"

"Impo—" the word stuck in his throat. "I, er, can't . . ."

"Can't what?"

Bloody hell, he'd never be able to say the most horrifying word he could imagine. He took a steadying breath and spit it out. "I can't perform in the bedchamber."

Samuel didn't move for several seconds, and when he did it was only to set his glass aside so he could study Morgan more closely.

Morgan wanted to sink through the floor. He had never been so embarrassed in his life. A bird chirped outside the window. A child laughed somewhere down the lane. But nothing could ease Morgan's discomfort.

Sam leaned back in his chair and steepled his wrinkled fingers. "When did you first notice this?"

Taking a healthy swallow of sherry, Morgan still couldn't look him in the eye. "Today. What I want to know is what causes it."

"Any number of things. Anxiety, illness, exhaustion, unhappiness, or an injury."

"I don't mean that kind of cause. I think my father gave me something to make this happen. In fact, I was hoping he got it from you."

7

His friend chuckled. "So you two are still at it."

"Some things never change."

"Well, I'm sorry to disappoint you, but he didn't get anything from me." Samuel lowered his gaze to a woven rug beneath his chair. "Still, potassium nitrate isn't that difficult to come by."

"Potassium what?"

"Nitrate. It's an ingredient used in saltpeter."

"What's that?"

"Let's just say it temporarily suppresses some of the normal functions of your body. Like arousal. And more than likely it was ingested."

A weight lifted from Morgan's shoulders when he realized his condition really did result from a prank. "I'd hoped it was something like that. But, other than tea and sherry, the only things I've had today are two glasses of port at Belinda's, and salmon for dinner."

"Where did you eat dinner?"

"At Ainshall."

"Was your father home?"

"Yes." The word came out like a hiss, even to Morgan's own ears.

Samuel picked up his glass and took a drink. "My guess is, because of the saltiness of salmon, he put the drug on the fish so you wouldn't notice the taste."

He was going to murder his father, that was all there was to it. "How long will it last?" If it was more than a day, it would be a slow, painful death.

"You should be fine by tomorrow."

Morgan tried very hard not to slump in relief. Instead, he rose and put his half-full glass on the sideboard. "I hope you'll excuse me, Sam. But there's someone I've got to see."

"Don't be too hard on him, Morgan. The drug is harmless, and the length of time it lasts is relatively short."

"Ten minutes would have been too long." With a sharp dip of his head, Morgan strode out of the room and mounted his horse. He would get his father for this one. Oh, yes, he would.

The sun had set, and the gelding was lathered and panting by the time Morgan drew him to a halt in front of Ainshall and sprinted up the wide steps.

Liberty, his father's aging butler, opened one of the great doors before he even reached it. "Master Frazier," he greeted formally, as if he hadn't known Morgan his whole life. "I did not expect you back so soon."

"I'll wager my father did," Morgan grated as he stormed past the servant and threw open the door to his father's study.

"Where is he?" Morgan asked in as calm a voice as he could muster.

"If you are referring to the viscount, Master Frazier, he is not here. He left shortly after dinner for Bath and said to tell you he would return in a few days."

Morgan glared at the servant with a fury as impotent as the rest of him. His father had gone away to give him a chance to cool down. "You tell him," Morgan managed through clenched teeth. "I'll get him for this. If it's the last thing I ever do, *I'll get him for this."*

"You can't be serious," Jade Wentworth voiced incredulously. She stared in disbelief at her eldest cousin, Sedgewick. Even though, for all intents and purposes, he was now her guardian, he'd been more like her brother her whole life, and it was extremely difficult to see him as anything else—and this matter was far too important to keep her mouth shut. The consequences were too great.

Sedgewick glanced up from stirring sugar into his tea, his short, thick arms bunching as he moved his hand. "Of course I am serious. The man ruined our family. Why should he not have to pay the price for Uncle Fredrick's release from debtor's prison? Taking Morgan Frazier captive and holding him for ransom is a sure way to gain the funds."

A silent groan squeezed the back of Jade's throat, and she shifted her position on the brick hearth. He *was* serious. Sweet heavens, didn't they have enough problems already?

Her other cousin, Wilkison, peeked over a pile of cards he'd been stacking on top of each other at the opposite end of the hearth. "Would we have to tie him up?"

"Tie him?" Sedgewick groused. "We will probably have to *chain* him. He is as big as a bull."

Wilkie frowned in confusion. "How can we make him pay if his hands are chained?"

Sedgewick rolled his eyes.

Jade leaned over and touched her youngest cousin's arm. He was such a joy. The childlike quality about him warmed her heart. "Sedgewick didn't mean for Mr. Frazier to pay the money himself," she explained carefully. "He plans to post a letter to Mr. Frazier's father, telling him to pay the money for his son's safe return."

Wilkie dug his fingers into his thick brown waves and scratched his head, his wide, guileless blue eyes mirroring his bafflement. It was difficult for him to comprehend devious schemes. "Won't his papa worry?"

Sedgewick snorted.

Jade wanted to kick him. "Yes, Wilkie, I'm sure he'll worry. In fact, a lot of people would worry if we did something like that."

Sedgewick stretched out his squat legs in front of him and settled more deeply into one of the few pieces of furniture they had left in the parlor, a worn Queen Anne chair that had once been in Jade's mother's sitting room. The action caused a thin lock of hair to slip from its tie and droop over his hefty shoulder. "You know, missy. We would not have to consider something like this if it were not for you."

"Me? How could you possibly think I have anything to do with this?"

"You know exactly what I am talking about. If you were not so tall and gawky, or if you would at least have tried to reduce the appearance of your height by crouching a bit instead of standing so erect, you could have found a husband to pay for Uncle Fredrick's release."

Embarrassment stung Jade's cheeks. She hated how Sedgewick always had to remind her of her lanky size, as if she couldn't see it for herself. Still, out of habit, she tried to defend herself. "I'm only five-feet-nine, Sedgewick. Not a giant—and how can I meet anyone to marry, when you won't let me leave the grounds?"

"Your virtue, missy, is your only asset, and I promised your father I would see that you stayed intact. Need I say more? And we are getting off the subject of Morgan Frazier."

"I wish we could stay off it," she said more to herself than him.

"Of course you do," he said sarcastically. "After all, the man is so virtuous. Aside from the fact that he is noted to be one of the most ruthless gamblers in all of London, and that he merely destroyed our entire lives, I am certain he is a veritable paragon. Why, I think the man should be commended, do you not?"

Jade winced at his sarcasm, but she couldn't deny his words. Morgan Frazier was all that. But was he to blame? She wasn't sure. For as long as she could remember, her father had gambled and their livelihood had suffered because of it. But in that game five months ago, he'd gone farther than he ever had before. He'd given the deed to Wentworth Hall as a marker. A marker that must be paid before the first day of May, or the property became Morgan Frazier's. In just twenty and four days, they'd lose their home.

Her gaze returned to Sedgewick. "No one twisted Father's arm to force him to use Wentworth Hall as a marker, and he didn't go to prison solely for the money he owed Mr. Frazier. You know the creditors had been after him for months. That aside, I'd prefer not to spend the rest of my life in Newgate for abducting the son of a nobleman."

"I have considered that, and I think after we receive the ransom money and free Uncle Fredrick, we should make for the Colonies. Lots of people lose themselves in that vast wilderness."

"I don't like being lost," Wilkie announced. "I got lost in Hyde Park once, and I was real scared."

Jade smiled. "Sedgewick didn't mean really lost,

Will. He meant we could go to the Colonies and never have to worry about getting in trouble for what we did here."

"Why didn't he say that?"

"I did say that, you bloody idiot!" Sedgewick railed.

Jade glared at her older cousin. "Wilkie's not an idiot. He's bright and kind and sensitive. And when you call him those awful names, you hurt his feelings." She knew it wouldn't do any good to mention that to Sedgewick. He just didn't care. Like her father, he'd always been ashamed of Wilkie. Knowing if she stayed much longer, she'd say something that would probably earn her a slap, Jade hurried out of the parlor.

Sometimes Sedgewick made her angry enough to curse. And that ridiculous notion about abducting Morgan Frazier. She'd never heard anything so ludicrous. She could only hope her cousin wouldn't act on his scheme for a few days so she'd have enough time to think of something not quite so unscrupulous to gain funds.

Making her way to the cookhouse, she opened the door to the lingering scent of porridge and woodsmoke. The shelves that had once been filled with canned vegetables and fruit now stood bare and dusty. The table was gone; sold a week before Father left, and the larder door stood open, its edges swollen with dampness from a leak in the roof. She couldn't even remember the last time her father had ordered repairs.

Her gaze drifted over the shelves in the larder, and she fought to keep despair at bay. There were only two half-full sacks of grain, three of beans, and a tin of tea and sugar. So very little.

She could remember how it was right after Grandfather Hammond had died, and her mother had inherited her father's vast fortune. The cookhouse had been filled with bustling servants preparing for a dinner party or soiree. Oh, but the excitement had been grand, and she'd so enjoyed the gleeful turmoil even though she'd never been able to attend because of her young age.

Well, she was old enough now, but there weren't any more parties, and there probably never would be again, not with Grandfather's money gone. Her father had gambled it all away.

Bitterness clung to Jade like a wet cloak. There hadn't even been money for a doctor when her mother became ill last year. Her mother had died of consumption at the age of thirty and seven.

The pain tightened her throat, and she focused her thoughts on better times. On the times that Grandfather Hammond kept their household from falling into ruin, by paying her father's debts again and again.

But Grandfather wasn't here anymore.

Releasing a long sigh, Jade thought of all the positions she'd applied for over the last months. A governess, a seamstress, a cook, and a maid. For goodness sakes she'd even sought employment as a laundress. But the destitute daughter of a nobleman wouldn't be considered to fill such lowly positions. For all her size, everyone was convinced that she was too delicate to handle laborious work.

It was almost laughable. Since the servants' departure, she'd kept the entire house by herself, tended the garden, cooked the meals, washed and mended everyone's clothes. She wasn't capable of doing laborious work? In a pig's eye, she wasn't! She did *all* the work.

She cringed at the uncharitable thought. That wasn't fair. Wilkie had tried to help. He would do anything for her. But, although she'd never tell him, he usually caused her more work.

Closing the pantry door as best she could, she tried to think where there might be another store of goods she'd forgotten about. The smokehouse was down to plank walls. The wine cellar only had a couple of broken barrels, discarded crates, and an old iron bed Wilkie had taken down there during a game of make-believe. The rear room had served as his military headquarters, and on the feather tick— his miniature battlefield—he'd planned all his strategy for warfare.

She thought about the empty fruit cellar, the nearly barren attic and stables that didn't have even a partial sack of grain for their old mare, Patience.

There was no help for it, she'd have to fix porridge or beans again tonight.

As she went into the yard to fill a water bucket from the well, she tried not to look at the sagging stable roof or the peeling shingles on the house. But she couldn't help it. Everywhere she looked things were deteriorating. Again, anger at her father rose. Money for gambling had been much more important to him than anything else.

Even Mother hadn't been able to reason with him when the money started getting low. His love of cards had become an obsession.

A tear slipped out as Jade stared over the once lovely flower beds her mother had treasured. They were completely overgrown with weeds. With all the other chores, there just weren't enough hours in a day for her to care for it.

Fleetingly, she thought about Sedgewick's idea, but immediately brushed it aside. No matter how dire their circumstances, they could not, *could not,* consider abducting Morgan Frazier.

Chapter
2

Morgan drew a brush through his hair and tossed it on the bureau, then strode across the bedroom in his London apartment and lifted his shirt from the back of a chair. Frustration and anger took turns stretching his nerves every time he thought about his father's prank. And he hadn't been able to *stop* thinking about it. Nor had he been able to stop imagining ways to get even with the old goat. Nothing spectacular had come to mind yet, but it would.

Pulling on his shirt and drawing his hair back with a leather strip, he headed for the door, glad he'd agreed to meet his friends at the club tonight. He needed a diversion to take his mind off his . . . temporary affliction.

Cards had a way of doing that for him.

As Morgan sprinted down the stairs and out to the stables, he thought of his friend, Christian, and his return in less than a fortnight. It would be good to see him again. Two years was much too long a time to spend away from someone as close as a brother. A friend he'd literally grown up with.

17

Morgan still remembered how glad he'd been when he got his friend's letter. Christian had sent word he was returning to England.

Well, not actually returning, Morgan amended. He was merely stopping off in London while en route to the Colonies where his brother now resided.

Taking his gelding's reins from the groom, Morgan led the horse out of the stables and moved to its side. He knew Chris missed his brother. Morgan, himself, had gone for several years without seeing Clay while he'd been away at sea. Now Clay was in the Colonies, too.

Near Christian's brother.

Morgan had decided to make the trip to the Americas with him, not only because of Clay, but also because he was intrigued by the stories of opportunity in the new nation. In fact, Morgan had done a great deal of study on the matter and found that indigo had the potential of making a substantial amount of profit. Second only to tobacco.

Having been raised on an estate which had an income from grain, Morgan had an extensive background in farming. The only thing holding him back was checking into the markets and seeing the Colonies for himself.

Feeling a thread of excitement about venturing into this new land, he smiled as he shoved his foot into the stirrup and grabbed the pommel. Leather creaked as he swung his leg over the saddle and eased into the seat.

The gelding sidestepped, and Morgan tightened his legs, then reined the animal toward the road and the Apollo Club in London's Devil Tavern.

It never failed to amaze him how many people were out this late in the evening. Even though it was after eleven, carriages filled the cobbled streets. Bawdy music thrummed from the open doorways of pubs, and candlelight danced from the windows of coaching inns.

Men and women dressed in elegant finery strolled along Charring Cross as if it were broad daylight.

Glad when London's Devil Tavern came into view, he rode his horse around to the stables and dismounted, then handed the reins over to a young groom by the door. Feeling lighter of spirit now, Morgan headed across the dark alleyway to the rear door.

Hundreds of candles from enormous chandeliers lit the elegant interior of the infamous Apollo Club, filling the red-carpeted room with the heavy scent of smoke and candle wax—and toilet water from the hordes of dandies prancing about the room.

Morgan searched the sea of faces, some at card tables, some standing in groups talking, others lounging on plush settees with drinks in their hands.

Servants in black kept those glasses filled.

He spotted his friends, Percy, Joseph, and Bishop seated at a table at the rear of the room. A chair had been left unoccupied directly in front of an open window.

Morgan smiled as he made his way toward his friends. They never failed to make allowances for his phobia.

"I say, Morgan," Percy piped up, his pronounced Adam's apple bobbing, the front of his brocade vest stained from where he'd spilled his drink. "Didn't expect to see you tonight."

Pulling out the vacant chair, he sat down. "Why not? That was the arrangement, wasn't it?"

Percy glanced at the others for support. Seeing he

wasn't going to get any, he cleared his throat. "Well, yes, but we heard rumors."

"Really. What about?"

Percy shifted as if he were suddenly sitting on thorns. "About . . . Widow Gates."

Belinda had talked. Damn her to hell. But had Morgan really thought she wouldn't? Not likely. Regaining his composure before they realized he'd lost it, he schooled his voice. "What's she supposed to have done?"

Joseph, the youngest of the group and usually the quiet one, spoke up. "Don't beat around the mulberry, Percy. Just tell him."

"Tell me what?" Morgan asked with a sinking feeling in his gut, and wondering how he was going to explain himself. But he already knew.

Percy stuck a finger between his bobbing throat and his cravat to loosen it. "We heard that you couldn't . . . couldn't . . ."

"Ah, hell," Bishop, the oldest and more vocal of the group, injected. "He's trying to say that your lusty widow friend is spreading rumors that you couldn't perform in her bed."

Heat burned Morgan's neck, but he still managed to stare calmly at each of the men seated around the table. He could tell them about the prank his father pulled, but even to him the story sounded like a feeble excuse. Besides, they knew him well enough to know that he wouldn't respond to a statement like that. Nor would he defend himself. He shouldn't have to.

Instead of saying anything, he gestured to one of the servants. "Bring a bottle of brandy." Then he returned his gaze to the others. "Are we going to play cards or repeat some woman's foolish prattle?"

"Cards," Percy squeaked.

Bishop arched a thick brow, but he didn't say a word. He merely picked up the deck and began to shuffle.

Joseph avoided looking at Morgan, which made him want to gnash his teeth. But Morgan wasn't angry at his friend. He was furious with his father.

It was late when the game finally broke up, and Morgan knew he'd had too much to drink when he watched another of his markers slide across the table to Bishop. It had been years since Morgan had lost so resoundingly at cards. But tonight, he hadn't been able to concentrate on anything but another drink and getting revenge against his father. Robert Frazier had pulled a lot of pranks over the years, but this was the lowest—and Morgan would see that it was the last.

"Come on, Morgan," Bishop said as he rose and straightened his waistcoat. "Stop sulking. I'll give you a ride home in my carriage."

"My horse is in the stables." He tried to keep his words steady, but they felt like they were rolling off his tongue and dropping on his shirt.

Bishop shrugged. "Then you'd better hope the animal remembers the way home, because I doubt you will."

"I've never had trouble finding my way home before."

"Then don't start tonight, hmm?" Bishop grinned as he headed for the door.

Morgan had to smile at his friend. Bishop should know by now that Morgan never allowed himself to get so deep into his cups that he couldn't keep his wits about him. Downing the rest of his drink, he pushed from the table and rose.

Several men in the smoke-filled room sent curious glances in his direction as he made his way over the plush carpet toward the entrance, and he was sure everyone in London knew what happened at Belinda's that afternoon.

It was a good thing he was going to the Colonies soon, otherwise he'd probably end up calling out half of the men in England.

When he stepped into the dark alley between the club and the stables, he noticed a lopsided wagon near the end of the path. Wondering what member of the elite club owned a wagon in such disrepair, he crossed to the stables.

The groom sprang to his feet immediately. "The gelding, sir?"

Morgan nodded, then felt in his pocket for a coin. There wasn't one. He'd lost his cash and several markers during the game.

He started to apologize and promise the lad double on his next trip, when he remembered his boots. He always kept extra cash in them, in a leather pocket sewn inside. Cash that a thief would never find.

Kicking free of one boot, he withdrew a shilling and tossed it to the boy.

"Thank ye, kindly, sir."

Relieved that he hadn't embarrassed himself, Morgan nodded, then stomped back into his boot. The scent of manure and urine-damp hay made his stomach curl, and he stepped out the door to wait for the boy to saddle his mount.

Again, his gaze wandered to the dilapidated wagon. He'd never seen it here before, he was certain of it.

A noise sounded behind him.

Morgan whirled sharply.

A thin shadowy figure stood at the side of the stables.

Morgan tensed. He curled his fist, ready for battle.

Something slammed into the side of his head from behind.

An explosion ripped through his skull. Bright spots burst before his eyes. The ground rolled, and he felt himself falling.

Then everything went black. . . .

"You did *what?*" Jade all but screeched. She couldn't possibly have heard her cousins right.

Wilkie shuffled his feet and glanced at Sedgewick.

Sedgewick crossed his arms over his stocky chest. "Are you obtuse, missy? Or were you not paying attention when we spoke of this? We took Frazier."

"Took him *where?*"

"The wine cellar."

Oh, God.

Wilkie nodded vigorously. "We chained him to Grandmother Wentworth's old iron bed."

She couldn't believe what she was hearing. They *couldn't* have done that. But they had. Oh, sweet Providence, *they had.*

Brushing the hair out of her eyes, she sat up on the edge of the bed and massaged her forehead with her fingers. Maybe she was dreaming.

She rubbed her eyes and blinked, then glanced up again.

Both her cousins were standing in her bedchamber, fully dressed, and looking as if they hadn't been to bed yet. A moan slipped up her throat. It wasn't a dream. "Are you trying to get us all hanged?"

"I am merely doing what is best for our family," Sedgewick declared.

"I only did what Sedgewick said," Wilkie defended.

Shaking the last remnants of sleep away, she rose and grabbed her worn dressing robe. "You said he's in the wine cellar?"

Sedgewick stepped between her and the door. "Just what do you think you are doing?"

"Trying to save our necks." Holding onto her fear as much as her tongue, she sidestepped her cousin and headed toward the cellar. Maybe it wasn't too late. Maybe Mr. Frazier would be reasonable and understand what a horrible mistake had been made.

The rusty door groaned as she wrestled it open. Dust and the odor of mildew rose from the opening, and she hesitated to go inside. She turned her head to draw in a lungful of clean air, then started down the rickety steps.

A soft moan drifted toward her, and she froze. Had they hurt him? Sedgewick said Mr. Frazier was as big as a house, so how *had* they taken him.

She didn't want to know.

Lifting the hem of her nightclothes higher, she descended the rest of the way into the depths of the long, narrow room lined with wooden racks. The lingering odor of fermented wine clogged the air.

Someone, Wilkie most likely, had left a small candle burning at the other end of the aisle, in what had once been the room where barrels of wine were left to age. The candle sat on a rock ledge that bordered three of the walls in the small stone-lined room.

Empty wine barrels and crates had collected dust and spiderwebs, and she stepped around the debris that blocked parts of the dirt pathway as she hurried toward the back room.

Her hopes of making Lord Frazier see reason were fading fast. The man wasn't going to be in a very congenial mood after being in a place like this.

She had just stepped through the doorway when she heard another moan and warily glanced at the man sprawled atop the worn feather tick.

His face was turned away, so she couldn't see his features, but she had to agree with Sedgewick about his size. He was huge. His head was against the iron headboard, and his booted feet poked out between the rungs of the footboard. And those shoulders. For goodness sakes, they must have turned him sideways to get him through the cellar door.

Her gaze moved over his long, slim build and snug buff breeches. His hips were trim, his thighs muscled and tight. He looked very strong and very, very big. She really wished her cousins hadn't bothered him. The consequences could be devastating.

She could only pray the man would be reasonable about this awful mistake. Taking a fortifying breath, she gingerly approached the bed.

Mr. Frazier rolled his head toward her, and the breath froze in her throat. He was so handsome it almost hurt to look at him. His nose was long and straight and a perfect fit for his lean, bronze face.

Jade couldn't tell what color his eyes were, because they were closed, but his mouth, even though drawn into a tight frown, was beautifully shaped, with a gently curved upper lip, and a full, sensuous lower one.

Her pulse picked up speed, and she quickly pulled her gaze from his mouth. That's when she noticed the blood. It was caked on the side of his head.

What had her cousins done?

Instinctively, she reached out a hand to brush a black curl away from the injury.

His eyes flew open. Sky blue eyes, that were wide with terror so acute it sparked her own.

"Help me," he rasped in a shaky voice. "G-get me—out of here." The cords in his neck tightened, and he arched his head back, straining to breathe. "The walls . . . crushing me . . . no air . . ."

It took her less than a second to realize the man was in desperate trouble. He couldn't breathe down here. She bolted for the door. "Wilkie! Help me!"

As if he'd been waiting on the other side of the doorway, he tumbled into the room. "What?"

Sedgewick stepped in behind him, his gaze darting around as if he expected someone to pounce on him. "What is it?"

"We've got to get Mr. Frazier outside."

"We most certainly do not."

She didn't have time to argue. "There's something wrong with him. Hurry!" She urged Wilkie toward the bed.

"Leave Frazier be," Sedgewick commanded in a sharp tone.

Jade spun toward her cousin. "Leave him? Is that what you said? Fine." She threw up her hands. "Then you can explain to the viscount why his son died down here! Because if you don't get him out of here, right this minute, that's what's going to happen to him. He can't *breathe!*"

"Always the authority, eh, missy?" He let out a harsh breath and nodded to Wilkie. "We will take the bastard to the stables."

Jade couldn't explain the surge of relief that rushed through her.

The man didn't have the strength to fight as they unlocked his chains and all but dragged him up the steps. The second they were outside, he started sucking in quick, deep gasps, his chest rising and falling with such desperation, her own chest began to labor.

"Come on, let us get him inside so I can chain him before he comes to his senses," Sedgewick ordered Wilkie.

Jade stared at the man lying on his back, fighting for air. His stomach sank deeply with each desperate breath. "I think you should leave all the doors open. I'm certain enclosed spaces have something to do with his ailment."

Sedgewick smirked as he hefted Mr. Frazier's shoulders.

Her cousins had a difficult time moving Mr. Frazier's large frame, half dragging him into the stables. Concerned about his injury, she hurried to fetch a bowl of water and a cloth to clean his wound.

When she returned a few minutes later, she saw that the man had been propped against a stall gatepost next to the open rear doors, his long legs out in front of him, his arms chained behind him, to the post at his back. His dark head was slumped forward. His chest still rose and fell with his heavy breathing, and he looked very uncomfortable.

"Wilkie, fetch a cup of tea. There's a pot on the stove."

Her cousin glanced up from where he was sitting on a crate by the unconscious man. He surged to his feet and ran out the door.

Sedgewick snorted. "By all means, pamper the bloke."

"Pamper him? If giving him something to drink

after he nearly suffocated is pampering, then I guess I'm guilty." Jade jammed her hands on her hips. "Now, at the risk of being overly compassionate, too, would you mind tearing off some strips of a sheet so I can bind his head so he doesn't die of infection after all this?"

"Get the idiot to do it. I have business in town." With a disgusted glance at Mr. Frazier, Sedgewick walked out. A moment later, she heard Patience's hoof beats as he rode away from the house.

She didn't have to guess where he was going. He must have found something of value on Mr. Frazier to wager at the tables. He had nothing else. Thanks to him, neither did she. Sedgewick had sold all of her gowns months ago.

"What the hell's going on?" a rough voice demanded from behind her.

She was sure her heart stopped.

Morgan Frazier was awake.

Drumming up all her nerve, Jade turned to face him, intending to explain. But she couldn't speak. Now that his face wasn't twisted with torment, she could see every gorgeous feature. The man was absolutely breathtaking.

A queer fluttering in her chest snapped her to her senses. "I think what's happening is obvious."

"Who are you?"

"You can't honestly believe I'd tell you that."

"Where am I?"

She simply looked at him.

He gave a disgusted sigh. "Never mind. I think I've pretty well figured what's going on." He pulled against the chain, then glared at her. "Weren't you warned about enclosing me in?"

"I have no idea what you're talking about."

28

His gaze followed the movement of her mouth, but when she stopped speaking, those blue, blue eyes slid into hers. "Of course you don't. But believe this, beautiful. I've never been a forgiving man. The moment I'm free, I'll see that lovely neck of yours stretched by the hangman's noose."

Jade swallowed against the imaginary rope her mind conjured. But she didn't say anything. What could she say? She sank down on her knees beside him and reached for the bucket and cloth, then dipped the material in the water. "I need to tend your wound."

"Wound?"

"On your head." She twisted the cloth to squeeze out most of the liquid, then gently pressed it to the angry-looking cut near his temple.

"Ow." He winced and turned his head to the side, trying to escape her touch.

"Be still so I can wash the blood off."

"I'm *bleeding?*"

"Not anymore. It's mostly dry."

His brow creased into a frown of confusion as she wiped his temple and checked the gash along his hairline. "It's not too deep. But you'll probably have a scar."

Another mark against them.

He turned his head away, then cocked it to one side to look at her. There was an odd expression on his face, almost as if he were seeing her for the first time. "Apparently my summation of this situation was a little off," he said in a more subdued tone. "Would you mind telling me what this is about?"

"We needed money, and my cousin thought this was the quickest way to get it."

"Money for what?"

She wasn't about to tell him their plans. "Food."

He studied her face, as if trying to tell whether she was lying or not. "No one hired you to do this? Perhaps as a prank?"

"No."

He frowned for several long seconds, then his mouth spread into a dazzling white smile. "Well, I'll be damned. You've actually abducted me."

He didn't have to sound so happy about it. "Mr. Frazier, I know you're a gentleman, and if you'll give me your word you'll forget this terrible incident, I'll try to get my cousin to release you."

"No."

"But—"

"I said no. You have me, and you're going to see this ridiculous scheme through. I give you my word, *as a gentleman,* if you let me go, I'll notify the authorities at once."

The sincerity in his voice caused chills to skip along her flesh. Why didn't he want to be released? Surely this gorgeous man wasn't like Wil— No, of course he wasn't. But she didn't know what to do. Perhaps a small threat? "Then, I'm afraid, you leave me no choice but to upset your father by sending him a ransom note."

She thought she saw a flash of triumph in his eyes, but it was gone before she could be sure.

"I'm at your mercy, madam. Do what you must."

Chapter 3

Morgan watched the confusion flitter over the girl's exquisite features. He'd heard her cousin call her Jade. The jewel-like name suited her. Everything about her reminded him of jewels, from her pearl white skin to her shimmering emerald eyes. Even her dark hair looked like the strands were coated with liquid rubies.

He let his gaze roam over her slender figure, marveling at the incredible length of her legs, the pronounced fullness of her breasts beneath a grayish dressing robe that looked like it had been laundered once too often.

She was tall, willowy, and she was stunning.

He still couldn't believe this was real. When he'd first awakened in that cellar, he'd nearly gone insane until she had gotten him out of there—something he would be eternally grateful for. He thought he was going to die in that hole.

Taking a breath, he remembered when he'd regained his senses and heard them talking about ransom. Up to that point, he'd been sure this was another of his father's pranks. It was only when he realized he had a wound and was bleeding that he'd begun to doubt that. His father was rotten to the extreme, but he would never have allowed someone to injure him—*and he would have warned them about confining me.* Morgan's phobia was something neither of them joked about. It was a trauma Morgan hadn't been able to overcome. When he was four years old, he fell into an abandoned well, and the sides had caved in on top of him. He'd spent two horrifying days in that hole, with only a small space to breathe, before his frantic father and his men could dig him out.

The mere thought caused his stomach to tighten, and he forced himself back to the situation at hand. Back to the fact that his father hadn't done this after all.

When he realized his situation was real, he'd at first been confused, then elated. He'd been handed with the means to get revenge on his father. *If* his father believed he'd been abducted, which he probably wouldn't. At least, not for a while. But he would . . . eventually.

He eyed the lovely woman kneeling in front of him. Every time she touched his head with the rag, he caught a whiff of her soft, lilac scent. He could even feel the silky heat of her fingers.

He wondered why he'd never seen her around London before, and he was certain he hadn't. He wouldn't have forgotten. He explored the beautiful face so close to his own, the long, thick lashes, the full lips that begged to be kissed. No, he'd definitely never seen her before. If he had, he would have made it a point to become acquainted.

Shocked by the turn of his thoughts, he glanced

around, trying to focus on something else. He spied the sagging stable roof. Beyond the open door, he could see the rickety wagon he'd wondered about the other night. Everything was deteriorating, probably even the post he was tied to. Escape would be easy once he was ready.

Morgan wouldn't allow this abduction to go far enough to forfeit his family's money, but he would stay until his father was turning gray with worry. He couldn't think of a better way to make sure the pranks ceased forever. Hell, he wished he'd thought of it himself.

"I brought the tea like you asked."

He swung his head around to see the young man walking down the aisle between the stalls, shuffling his feet in the straw as he walked. He appeared to be a little older than the woman, perhaps twenty, with dark hair and a frail build. Morgan could tell by his features that he was related to Jade, but his diminutive size didn't match up to hers by any means. In his hands, the youngster carefully balanced a cup and saucer.

Jade sprang to her feet and quickly took them from him. "Thank you, Wilkie. You did a fine job."

Her curious statement sent Morgan's gaze back to the younger man. There was something different about him. Morgan studied him for a few seconds, then he knew what it was. Wilkie had a child's mind.

Morgan's anger toward him softened. He wasn't the one responsible for this farce and neither was the girl. It was the other one. Sedgewick.

She knelt in front of him again and lifted the cup to his mouth. "Here, take a drink. After your ordeal, I'm sure you could use one."

He watched her over the rim of the cup and felt

another swift tug of attraction. He turned his head to the side.

"Not thirsty? All right." She set the cup aside. "Of course, you do realize, we may not remember to bring you something later. You know how that goes, people get in a hurry, get too busy . . ."

He glanced at her long, slender fingers, still resting on the edge of the saucer, then into those green eyes. With just the smallest effort, he could drown in them. He liked her quick wit, her smile, and her husky voice. Hell, he liked everything about her.

Pulling his gaze from her, he fixed on the corral outside and said the first thing that came to mind. "I'm hungry." And he really was. He hadn't eaten since noon yesterday.

Jade rose slowly to her feet, but he couldn't read what was in her thoughts as she straightened the folds of her dressing robe. She glanced at Wilkie, then turned away. "I'll fix you something." When she got to the door, she stopped. "Wilkie? Would you tear a sheet into strips for me?"

"How big?"

"This wide." She gestured with her fingers, spreading them a couple inches apart.

Wilkie was out the door like a shot.

She avoided looking at Morgan. "I'll set the water to boil, then come back to bandage your head."

Morgan was confused. Where was the spirited woman he was just admiring? This one looked as if someone had struck her.

Not even attempting to understand the female mind, he moved his foot inside the boot to see if his money was still there, or if the cousins had taken it.

A lump pressed into his ankle, and he smiled.

"Here are the strips you wanted," Wilkie said,

rushing through the door. He stopped and looked around in confusion.

"I'm right here, Will," Jade said as she came in behind him.

She took the strips and raised one to Morgan's head.

His head didn't feel bad enough for a bandage. "I don't need that."

That lovely mouth tightened. "Very well, you may die of infection if you wish."

"You sound like a physician."

"I'm not, but I learned a lot about medicine from my grandfather. He was a doctor. I listened to his instructions over the years, and cleanliness was always among them."

So, she was the granddaughter of a physician. . . .

"Humph," another voice grated from the doorway. Sedgewick had returned. Now that Morgan didn't have to pretend unconsciousness, he could see the man clearly. He looked to be about Morgan's own age, with stringy brown hair, and a hefty, squat build. There was a touch of cruelty in his hooded hazel eyes.

Sedgewick leaned a thick arm against the frame. "Grandfather had about as much sense as—" He glanced at Wilkie.

"Don't say it," Jade said angrily. "Don't even think it."

Sedgewick watched the boy trail a piece of straw along a rail, oblivious to the conversation. Then he returned his gaze to her. "I do not have to say anything. We both know."

"I thought you went to town."

"I forgot something."

"What?"

"Your trunk."

Jade threw the strips down. "No. You've sold nearly everything I own. *You're not taking my trunk!*" She walked up to him, literally towering over him. "If you want to sell something for gambling money, this time, sell something of yours."

Shoving past him, she stalked toward the cookhouse.

Sedgewick followed, his steps quick and angry.

Morgan jerked against the chains. What was Sedgewick going to do? Would he hurt her? He swung his gaze to the youngster. "Wilkie. Er . . . would you ask Jade how much longer breakfast will take?" Maybe Wilkie's presence would forestall any unpleasantness.

"Sure." Smiling, he ambled out the door, dragging the straw across everything in his path.

Morgan leaned his head back against the post and listened. He didn't hear any shouting. Any angry words. But a moment later, he did hear a rider leave.

Was it Sedgewick or Jade?

"The porridge has to cook a little longer," Jade said. "I have time to wrap your wound first."

He looked up to see her coming toward him, the discarded strips once again in her hands. Wilkie was right behind her, still engrossed in the straw.

Morgan didn't want to think about how glad he was that it was Sedgewick who left. When she knelt beside Morgan and lifted a bandage to his temple, her delicate scent reached him again, and he fumbled for something to say. "I don't need that. Are they brothers?"

"You do need the bandage. And, yes they are. Although Sedgewick has the misguided belief that he's superior to Wilkie."

"What's wrong with him?"

"With Sedgewick? Everything."

Morgan bit back a smile. "No," he said in a lower tone. "The other one."

Her eyes drifted to Wilkie and softened. "There's nothing wrong with him. In fact, I wish more people were like him. He's so open and honest. So gentle. But in answer to your question, my aunt had a difficult time birthing him, and the physician had an even harder time bringing Wilkie around afterward. My grandfather said the lapse caused damage."

Morgan studied the younger man and wondered what he would have been like if his birth had been normal. Probably like Sedgewick, Morgan thought uncharitably. Maybe the fates had been kind to him, after all.

When Jade finished tying the bandage around Morgan's head, she tucked the ends under the strip. "Is that too tight?"

"No."

"Good. I'll be back in a minute with your breakfast."

That gave Morgan pause. With his hands chained behind his back, how the hell was he supposed to eat?

He pondered the thought the whole time he waited for her to return.

When she finally did, she was carrying a steaming bowl of porridge. "Wilkie? Will you put that crate by Mr. Frazier?"

"I'm sitting on it."

She sighed. "Then would you get another from the wine cellar?"

"All right." He started out the door, but stopped. "Do you want one, too?"

"No. Just one for our guest."

Nodding, Wilkie ambled toward the cellar.

"You're very patient with him."

She pulled Wilkie's crate over and sat down, then lifted a spoonful of porridge to his mouth. "I explain things to him, if that's what you mean. Open."

Morgan stared at the spoon. Ah, hell. She was going to feed him. With a resigned sigh, he parted his lips and allowed her to spoon the watery porridge into his mouth. He swallowed quickly, trying not to show his distaste for the flavorless gruel. "That's not what I mean. You explain very well, but you don't get frustrated or angry when he doesn't understand at first."

"If that's patience, then I must use it all on Wilkie, because I don't have a shred left for Sedgewick."

Morgan smiled around another bite. "I said you were patient, not a saint."

She chuckled, and he was rewarded with a flash of small white teeth and two adorable dimples.

"Here's Morgan's crate. Can I have mine back?"

Still smiling, she rose. "Of course. I just borrowed yours until you returned."

When the crates were switched and Wilkie once again entranced with the straw, Jade took her seat again and picked up the bowl.

"What's the difference in the crates?" Morgan asked before she could shove the spoon in his mouth.

"There isn't any. He just has a fear of someone taking things from him. Sedgewick is to blame for that. He's taken everything Wilkie cherished, from his favorite chess set to the great coat that had belonged to his father."

"A real likable fellow, that Sedgewick."

"Not that I've noticed."

By the time she finished feeding him, Morgan felt like an invalid. Glad the experience was over, he watched her gather the bowl and spoon, then leave him to Wilkie's company.

The straw now discarded, Wilkie dragged his crate over beside Morgan. "You want to play a game?"

"What kind?"

"Draughts. Jade says I'm real, *real* good."

He'd like to do something besides sit here and stare at boards, but . . . "I can't use my hands."

Wilkie studied him for a moment, then nodded. "I'll move your men for you."

Morgan had to close his mouth to keep it from falling open. The boy was remarkably bright. "All right, let's have a go at it."

Wilkie was back within minutes, holding the draught board in one hand and a box of black and white disks in the other.

After the first game, Morgan realized that Jade hadn't been just trying to encourage Wilkie when she'd said he was good at the game. He was.

If Morgan hadn't had age and experience on his side, it would have been a fair match. Still, when he saw how intent the youngster was on winning the game, he couldn't bring himself to disappoint him.

Wilkie won the first game.

They had just finished, and Wilkie was setting up the board for a second game when Jade walked in carrying a tray with a cup and saucer on it. She saw the board between them and glanced at Morgan in confusion.

"Wilkie moves for me," he said, answering her unasked question.

"I see." She smiled at her cousin. "Could you set those aside for a few minutes? Then after you've had your breakfast, and Mr. Frazier has had something to drink, you may continue. All right?"

Morgan was having a hard time concentrating on her words. He'd just noticed the pale green dress she'd changed into. The gown didn't exactly fit. The bodice laced in front across her breast, but the material didn't quite reach. He could see a line of white chemise behind the ties. He could see the outline of her corset beneath the snug midriff. Even in ill-fitting clothes, Morgan was awed by how pretty she was.

Wilkie removed the board, then beamed at her. "I beat him the first game."

"Did you? Why, that's wonderful." Her gaze drifted to Morgan, and he saw a flash of gratitude just before she set the tray down. "There are some scones on the kitchen table, Will, to go with your breakfast."

Wilkie hesitated. "Is it that watery porridge again?"

"I'm afraid so."

"Can I wade in the pond instead?"

"Wilkie, you have to eat. If you don't, you'll get weak. Then you won't be able to wade in the pond, or play draughts, or any of the fun things you like to do."

He considered her words, then climbed to his feet. "I'll wade in the pond after I eat." He glanced at Morgan. "Then we'll finish our game." Satisfied with his plans, he trotted toward the house.

"You let him win the game, didn't you?" Jade asked.

"What makes you think so?"

"Because I've seen the kindness in your eyes."

She had? "Don't underestimate your cousin. He's very bright."

"I know he is. But I also know he's not quite as good at draughts as he thinks he is."

"All right. From now on, I'll trounce him every chance I get."

"Very well. Of course, if you do, you'll have to feed yourself from now on."

"My hands are chained."

She gave him a mischievous smile. "I know."

The little imp.

"Here, drink some tea. It may be the last you'll get." There was a definite chuckle in her voice.

He smiled as she brought the cup to his lips. "You're a tease."

"Ah, so you've found me out." Her cheeks dimpling, she remained silent as she gave him the rest of the tea. Then she rose. "I've got to wash some clothes, so I'll leave you in peace. Wilkie shouldn't be long." With a swish of her worn skirt, she hurried outside.

Morgan watched her go, his thoughts troubled. She was going to do the wash. She'd cooked gruel for breakfast. They needed the ransom money for food.

He leaned his head against the post and studied what he could see. Everything within his vision was in sad disrepair. He began counting boards in the rafters, trying not to think about what dire straits they must be in.

He was still counting when Wilkie ambled in.

As the boy started to set up for another game, Morgan interrupted him. "Do you have any cards?"

"Mmm-hmm."

"Do you know how to play Brag?"

"No."

"Would you like to learn?"

Wilkie thought for a sceond, then nodded. "I like games."

"Good, I'll teach you, but we'll need something to wager with."

"I don't have no money."

"We could use pebbles, or the draughts chips, or perhaps even beans."

Wilkie's eyes brightened. "We have beans. I'll get some."

Morgan smiled at the youngster's enthusiasm.

Wilkie came back within a few minutes, carrying a bag of beans and a worn deck of cards. When he took his position on the crate again, he carefully moved the draughts board to one side and set the cards down to untie the bag. "How many beans do we need?"

"Why don't we each take half the bag?"

That was a mistake. Morgan watched with a resigned sigh as Wilkie began to count each and every bean.

When he at last finished and had set a pile in front of each of them, he was still holding one bean. "What do I do with this one?"

"Put it with yours."

"Why?"

Morgan tried to think of a good reason. "Er . . . because you did all the work, counting the beans. Whoever does the work, gets the extra bean."

Apparently that made sense to him, because he dropped the bean into his pile.

"Now, mix the cards up real well, then give each of us five cards, all faceup so I can show you how to play."

"Wilkie!"

Morgan started at the sound of Jade's enraged voice, and he turned to see her standing a few feet down the aisle, her hands on her hips, her eyes flashing with anger.

"Just what do you think you're doing?"

Wilkie gnawed his lower lip. "Morgan was teaching me how to play Brag."

"And the beans?"

Morgan took pity on the boy and answered for him. "Since Wilkie obviously doesn't have any money, we were using beans to wager with."

If Morgan had thought to pacify her, he was dead wrong.

"Let me get this straight, Mr. Frazier. You were teaching my cousin to wager what little food we have on a game of chance?"

"I was going to give them b—"

"Spare me explanations." She marched over to the crate and scooped up the beans, shoving them into the bag with quick, angry movements. Then grabbing the cards, she whirled around and stormed out.

Wilkie sat there for several minutes in silence before he spoke. "I know what's wrong with her."

Morgan could pretty well guess. "What?"

"Jade didn't have any breakfast. She always gets grumpy when she doesn't eat."

"Well, I hope she eats soon."

"She won't. There wasn't enough food for all of us, so she gave her portion to you."

Morgan felt as if someone had punched him in the stomach. He'd eaten her food, for God's sake! Guilt swarmed him, and his brain worked frantically to find a solution.

If only he hadn't lost all his money at the tables, he could give them some. Damn it, why hadn't Sedgewick sold Morgan's clothes for coin? Surely he was smart enough to know he could get a hefty sum. Or was he planning to do that later?

It didn't matter. Right now, *he* had to do something. After several tense moments, it hit him. But his idea meant he'd have to use Wilkie to do his bidding, and he'd have to wait until Sedgewick came back with the horse. "Wilkie? Do you know how to drive a wagon?"

"Yes."

"Do you know your way into town?"

"Uh-huh. Stevenage isn't very far. I've taken the wagon three times by myself. Once when Sedgewick—"

Stevenage. *They were near Stevenage.* "Er . . . good. Do you think you could go into town for me—later this afternoon?"

"Sedgewick won't be home until almost morning. What did you want from town?"

Morgan studied the youngster. If Sedgewick came in that late, he'd probably sleep most of the day. "I wanted some food so Jade could eat."

His crestfallen look tore at Morgan's heart. "No one will give us food without money. Jade told me so."

"I have money. I'll give you some."

"Truly?"

"Truly. Now, if you'll take my boots off, I'll show you where it is, but this has got to be our secret." He didn't want Sedgewick knowing anything about the money until it was spent.

"Sure, but . . . are you certain I won't get in trouble?"

44

"If you do, I'll take the blame."

Wilkie rose. "All right, but you don't know how angry Jade can get when she's really upset."

"I hope I won't have to find out."

"Me, too," Wilkie said on such a solemn note it made Morgan wonder if he wasn't making a terrible mistake.

Chapter

4

Jade slammed the back door, tossed the beans on the sideboard, and kicked a chair as she walked by the table, her hand in a death grip around the deck of cards.

These were the cause of all their problems. These wretched, filthy squares had destroyed her family! She stormed into the parlor and ripped open a drawer on the small table where her father had kept his gaming paraphernalia.

She'd intended to throw them in, but when she glared down at the dice, the chips, and the dagger her father had purchased to defend himself, her fury increased.

Her gaze shifted from the drawer to the barren room. Enraged, she slammed the deck down on the table, and the cards bounced and scattered. Just seeing those spots, the leering faces of the king and knave, made her want to rip them apart.

Her fingers closed around the dagger, and she stabbed it through the king's face. The knave. The seven of hearts. Again, again, again. She wanted to hurt them the way they'd hurt her. She wanted to destroy them the way they'd destroyed her life.

Finally, in exhaustion, she slumped into the only chair. Her heart pounded wildly, her chest rose and fell from the exertion. But, she didn't feel any better. In fact, her fit of temper had only made her feel worse. Now she had a mess to clean.

"Curse men, and their stupid cards! Curse them to Hades!" Pushing from the chair and ignoring the clutter on the floor, she marched up to her room and kicked the door shut.

Plopping down onto the bed, she braced her elbows on her knees and threaded her fingers through her hair, her gaze fixed on the bare floor. She could feel the tears behind her eyes, but she refused to let them fall. She'd cried enough during the last months. She'd cried enough during the last *years*.

Her gaze drifted over her room, and she saw a lighter square area on the floor where her armoire used to stand. Other spots marked the places where her bureau and desk had been. Everything she held dear was gone because of a deck of cards.

Everything but her sketches.

Sliding to her knees on the floor, she reached under the bed and withdrew two of the canvases she'd hidden away, just to touch one of the few treasured items that hadn't been taken from her.

The first was a charcoal sketch of one of her grandfather's field hands. He was naked from the chest up, his muscles and thick chest vividly portrayed. Even his male nipples and navel. It was a scandalous drawing. One that could have landed her in serious trouble if her parents had ever seen it. When she'd drawn it, she hadn't thought it was terribly scandalous. She'd even sketched bushes in front of the worker's lower half. Of course, that hadn't been for the sake of modesty. She done it because she had no idea what lay beneath a man's waistline.

The other drawing was of Wilkie. She'd sketched him one day down by the pond. He'd been lying on his belly in the grass, his elbows braced on the ground, his upraised hands supporting his chin. His eyes had been filled with wonder as he'd watched the sluggish, erratic movements of a caterpillar.

It was a good likeness of him. One that brought out his innocence and vulnerability. One that caused her eyes to mist just looking at it.

Replacing the pictures, she rose and drew in a deep breath. She had too much work to do to indulge in the foolishness of temper tantrums and melancholy.

She gathered her bedding and nightclothes, then rolling them into a ball under her arm, she headed downstairs, where she left the bundle in the entryway and went to the parlor to right the mess she'd made.

Seeing the scattered cards and the dagger speared through several that had clumped together, she realized she'd managed to mutilate quite a few during her angry tirade. She smiled. At least no one would use that deck again.

Smugly pleased, she righted the room, then put the bag of beans away before heading for the washing tub outside, her step lighter, her spirits considerably brighter.

Jade finished taking down the last of the wash and carried the full basket into the house and set it on the dining table. Brushing the hair out of her eyes, she glanced around, wondering if Wilkie was still in the stables. She hadn't seen him since she snatched the cards.

Her gaze drifted to the building. If he was still there, she wondered if he'd even thought to give Mr. Frazier something else to drink these last hours?

Probably not.

Massaging a kink out of her back, she walked to the cookhouse and got a pitcher, then filled it at the well.

Her stomach rumbled, and she placed a hand over the complaining area as she carried the pitcher and the cup she'd stuffed in her apron pocket.

When she entered the stables, she was surprised to find Wilkie gone, and Mr. Frazier staring out the door with an unhappy look on his face.

She was struck again by how handsome he was. Every masculine angle of his face was set in perfect unison with the rest of his features. Especially that firm jaw, now shadowed by dark stubble.

It hadn't occurred to her that the man would eventually need to be shaved. And she truly wished it hadn't occurred to her now. The notion brought other problems to mind. Like a bath, and using the privy. The man surely had to go *sometime*. A flush burned her cheeks, and she quickly forced the embarrassing thought aside. When Sedgewick returned, she'd make sure he took care of the . . . situation.

"I figured after the way you stormed out of here, that I'd never see you again."

Mr. Frazier's voice startled her, and the water in the pitcher sloshed over her wrist. Gathering her composure, she set it down. "I considered it."

Those heavy-lashed blue eyes crinkled at the corners. "What changed your mind?"

49

"I'm not sure that I have. But, presently, there isn't anyone here to see to your thirst." She withdrew the cup from her pocket and filled it.

She really wished the man had the use of his hands, so she wouldn't have to keep kneeling so close beside him and holding the cup for him to drink—which he did quite greedily.

In awe, she watched the way his tanned throat worked as he swallowed. The way he closed his eyes in satisfaction. The way he arched his head back to drain the cup.

"More?"

He shook his head, and a dark curl drooped over the edge of the bandage.

"If you were that thirsty, why didn't you call out to someone?"

He licked a drop from his lips. "I didn't think you'd come."

"Wilkie or Sedgewick might—"

"Wilkie's at the pond. And he told me Sedgewick wouldn't be back until late."

"Then I apologize for not coming sooner."

He arched a brow. "But not for depriving a man of a little entertainment, eh?"

When she thought of what she'd done to the cards, another rush of heat filled her cheeks, but she wasn't going to feel remorse for the deed. "Mr. Frazier." She gestured toward the stable and house. "This is what *gambling* has done to my home . . . and my family. If I had things my way, I'd burn every deck of cards in England." She set the cup on the crate and rose.

Walking to the rear opening, she crossed her arms and stared out over the broken corral fence and pastures beyond. "I will never understand what gentlemen see in games of chance. In wagering the money that's needed so desperately for their families. I do know what my father wants, though. He's waiting for that one big windfall. The one that will set him for life."

Her gaze drifted back to him. "Sedgewick has the same burning desire."

He studied her for several seconds. "I've heard everyone's dreams but yours. What do you want, beautiful?"

Curse the man for making her stomach flutter. "I want a stable home. One where I don't have to worry about the next meal, where I don't have to worry about creditors at the door, or finding the silver sold to finance another game. One where I don't have to watch someone I love being taken—I just want a normal life. That's all."

"It's been rough on you, hasn't it?"

"It's been rough on all of us."

"Where is your father?"

"In prison, Mr. Frazier. Dragged from our home in the early hours of the morning for debts he couldn't pay." She didn't mention that *he* was one of the men who helped put him there.

Father put himself there, a tiny voice reminded her. No one forced him to play.

"I'm sorry to hear that, Jade. I truly am. I realize now just how hard things are for you. Especially with your cousin following the same path."

The sincere compassion in his voice touched her, and she turned away from him again, not wanting to feel charitable toward a man who was exactly like her father. "Sedgewick can drop off the edge of the earth for all I care. Wilkie's the one I'm worried about. The examples the males in my household are setting for him are frightening."

"You're setting a good example."

"For now. But all too soon, he'll start seeing me as the others do. As an ill-tempered female who has never learned her place."

The corners of Mr. Frazier's mouth twitched as he sought to assuage her. "You're not *that* ill-tempered."

"Yes, I am. And I'll continue to be so until the men in my family gain some sense." She glanced at the post behind him, then headed for the door. "I'll see if I can't find you something a little more comfortable to lean against. Something considerably softer than that post." Then she had to get back to work.

Morgan sighed as he leaned deeper into the pillow Jade had wedged between his back and the post. He hadn't realized how uncomfortable he'd been until she did that. She was a generous, thoughtful person.

Still, he was a little nervous about how she would react if Wilkie was able to get the food in the morning. Morgan was at a helluva disadvantage with his hands tied behind his back. And if that display of temper he'd seen earlier was an example of her anger, he could certainly understand Wilkie's concern.

Morgan really felt for her, though. She was trying so damned hard to keep her family together, to have a normal home. He just wished there was some way he could help.

He'd considered letting this farce continue until the ransom money was delivered, but he knew he couldn't. Not only for his father's sake, but because the gesture would be useless. Her cousin would gamble the money away, just as her father had.

He thought about his own enjoyment of the game, which of late had been quite often because of his lack of commitments, but he'd never gambled more than he could afford to loose, he'd never gone hungry because of it, and he'd certainly never hurt anyone.

That gave him pause. Or had he? A few months ago, he'd taken a man's estate as a marker. Even now, he had the deed to Wentworth Hall in his safe at home, and it would remain there until the man paid, or until the first day of May, when the property would become Morgan's. For the first time, he wondered at the consequences of that game. What would the man's family do? Did they own another home? Or would they become dependent on relatives for a roof over their heads? When he returned to London, he would damned sure find out.

An uneasy feeling moved through him, when he realized that, even though he'd been extremely fortunate at cards, he wasn't that much different from Jade's father and cousin after all.

The uncomfortable notion made him rethink his carefree pastime. If it weren't for men like him, who'd wager for just about anything, there wouldn't be men like her father, who'd forfeit everything they owned.

It was a sobering thought.

A damned disturbing one.

Jade dumped the last of the water into her tub, her arms aching from weeding the garden and carrying so many heavy buckets upstairs. But what else could she do when she wanted a bath? Wilkie was already in bed, and Sedgewick still wasn't home.

She set the buckets aside and began working on the laces of her dress, smiling when she thought of Wilkie. After she'd spoken to Mr. Frazier, she'd decided to have a talk with her young cousin. She wanted Wilkie to understand the reason for her earlier anger. She'd found him at the pond, just as he stepped out of the chilly water.

Her youngest cousin was much, much brighter than she'd given him credit for. He'd already absorbed everything that had happened, and the exact cause. She'd never forget the solemnness in his voice when he promised her he'd never, *ever,* hurt the people he loved the way his uncle and brother had.

She believed him, and that was one pound of crushing weight off her shoulders.

Dropping her dress and undergarments on the floor, she stepped into the tub, shivering against the cool night air lingering in her room. Even though it had been fairly pleasant ouside, it hadn't been warm in the house for weeks. They were running low on firewood, and they needed to save it for cooking and laundry and baths. She'd be so grateful when the summer finally brought its soothing warmth.

As she eased down into the warm water and braced her head on the rim, she thought about how cold Mr. Frazier would get tonight—especially with the doors open. She could imagine him trying to snuggle deeper into the pillow at his back and clenching his jaw to keep his teeth from chattering.

It wasn't a pretty picture.

Briefly, she considered having him brought into the house, but she was afraid being enclosed might affect him. There was no help for it. As soon as she finished her bath, she'd have to take him a blanket.

It wasn't something she was looking forward to, not in the cold, wearing only her nightclothes, and not when she'd have to use a candle to light her way, and literally tuck the man in. Getting close to him in broad daylight made her nervous. She could imagine how much worse it would be in the dark.

Too agitated to stay in the tub long, she quickly washed and rinsed her hair, then grabbed a thread-bare towel and got out.

As she dressed, she wondered what it would be like to kiss a man like Morgan Frazier—or any man, for that matter. She'd never kissed anyone but her parents and Wilkie. She had seen her parents kiss, though, when she was much younger.

But, during the last years, with her father away at the clubs more and more, her parents barely spoke to each other, much less kissed.

Jade wondered why her mother had never gotten angry at him for his foolishness. Or, maybe she had, but was too afraid of her husband's beatings to unleash her feelings.

Shaking her head, Jade moved to the small dressing table she'd taken from the attic and picked up her hairbrush. She could never be like her mother. Being able to vent her anger was the only thing that kept Jade sane.

When her hair was nearly dry, she set the brush aside and dipped her fingers into a jar of lilac petals and water. She'd saved the petals from last summer and had let them seep all winter, adding water every so often. The fragrance didn't last long, not like those expensive perfumes from France that her grandmother had worn, but the flowery aroma made her feel more feminine—and not quite as big and gangly.

After tying her hair back with a frayed ribbon, she picked up her candle and walked to the attic where a couple of old blankets were piled in one corner.

Hoisting the thickest one under her arm, she made for the stables.

A nippy breeze fluttered the flame on the candle as she went across the yard to the open stable door. Moonlight cast a silver glow over Mr. Frazier, and she saw that he was staring straight at her.

"I thought you could use this," she said, gesturing to the blanket she carried.

She saw his lashes move as he shifted his gaze to the bundle under her arm.

"I've never known anyone who was so considerate of others."

"I'm not that considerate. I just know what it's like to be cold." She'd nearly frozen to death last winter, building only small fires to take the icy chill out of the rooms in an attempt to conserve firewood.

Setting the candle on the crate, she unfolded the blanket and spread it out over his legs, then drew it up to his chest. "It isn't much, but it will keep the chill off you." Tucking one side around his shoulder and stuffing it between his back and the pillow, she was assailed by a male scent she'd never noticed before. Something musky and intriguing.

She reached across him to tuck the cover behind the other shoulder, and her fingers trembled at the heat of his skin. Her face came within inches of his, so close, she could feel the warmth of his breath on her cheek. Tingles skittered through her midsection, and she pulled back the slightest bit.

"Jesus, you smell good."

She swallowed, trying not to think about how she'd thought the same about him. "Thank you." Her fingers still shook as she finished tucking in the opposite side, then quickly got to her feet. "That should be warmer."

"I wasn't cold."

She'd noticed. "You would have been before the night was over."

"Then I'm extremely grateful for your thoughtfulness."

"You're welcome. And, now that you're settled, I'll say good night."

"Do you have to go?"

Now why did that simple question make her feel giddy all over? "Yes, I do. Tomorrow's going to be a long day. I have to clean windows." She tilted her head toward the manor. "And there are a lot of windows in that house."

She thought she heard a soft whoosh of breath before he spoke.

"Good night, beautiful. Try not to work too hard. Better yet, get that lazy cousin of yours to help."

She chuckled at that. "Sedgewick? Getting him to work would be about as easy as starting a fire with wet logs." She turned for the door. "Good night, Mr. Frazier."

"Morgan."

"What?"

"My name is Morgan."

Chapter
5

Jade!" Wilkie shrilled from outside her bedroom door. "Come quick. See what I got!"

She blinked into the morning light. "What time is it?"

"Almost eleven."

"Eleven!" Good heavens, she'd nearly slept the day away.

"Come on, Jade. I want to show you. In the cookhouse, hurry."

She smiled at his enthusiasm, and she knew he must have found another insect he wanted her to see. "Go on. I'll get dressed and be done in a minute." Eleven o'clock? She just couldn't believe it. She'd slept so sound. Had such wonderful dreams . . .

Quickly climbing from bed, she pulled on a blue dress she'd had since she was thirteen years old. All of her clothes were at least that old. Sedgewick had sold the others.

After washing her face in cold water and running a brush through her hair, she pulled on her slippers and laced the front of the too-small gown. She wasn't all that thrilled about seeing Wilkie's newest pet, but she'd pretend enthusiasm just the same. Her approval was so important to him.

Mentally preparing herself, she went down the hall, glancing at Sedgewick's inert, snoring form as she passed his open door.

Wilkie stood just outside the cookhouse, anxiously motioning her inside.

Figuring he'd found a small animal and knowing she'd have to give him a gentle scolding for bringing it inside, she hesitated, not in all that big a hurry to join him. That was the hardest part of her relationship with Wilkie, pretending to admire the creatures he collected, when she really wanted to cringe.

The table was mounded high with flour, potatoes, bags of seasonings and baking powders, jars of fruits and vegetables, and a large barrel of meat packed in lard. In the center of the floor sat several more packages.

Her mind whirled. How on earth had Wilkie managed to get so much food? But before she could even ask him how and where, tears sprang to her eyes. Sinking into a chair, she buried her face in her hands and cried.

Wilkie awkwardly patted her back. "Please don't cry. Morgan didn't mean to make you unhappy. He just wanted you to eat."

She blinked up at him through watery eyes. "Morgan? What has he got to do with—*Morgan?*"

Wilkie nodded warily.

She sniffed, wiping the tears from her cheeks. "How?"

Wilkie shuffled his feet. "He gave me the money he had in his boot. But he said not to tell anyone till

I got the food." He smiled, nervously watching her reaction. "I went all by myself, and I didn't have no trouble finding my way back, neither."

"That's wonderful. I'm proud of you," she automatically responded. But she was still in shock. Not only because Mr. Frazier had given Wilkie money for food, but because he still *had* money after being at the club the night her cousins took him. Her father and cousin never had. "Wilkie, would you put the groceries away in the buttery? I'd like to go thank Mr. Frazier for his kindness."

"You're not angry at him, are you?"

She smiled. "No." Leaving him to his chore, she gathered her skirts and headed for the stables.

Morgan was watching the door, apparently waiting for her, his eyes intent, his mouth in a frown. Sunlight glinted off his mass of silky black curls and brightened the deep tan of his skin.

Jade studied him silently for a moment, wondering how someone could be so kind to people he didn't even know. To people who'd made him their prisoner, for heaven's sake. No one else she knew would do such a thing. Well, *she* would, but that was different. "Thank you for the food, Mr. Frazier. And if there's anyway possible—"

"Morgan."

"—I'll repay you for it someday."

"My name is Morgan, damn it. And why aren't you angry? Where's that ill temper you're so famous for?"

Jade couldn't even smile at his remark. All she wanted to do was cry again. "Not long ago, I would have given you a fine example of my temper. But poverty has a way of humbling people. I'm not too proud to take charity anymore. I've progressed far beyond that stage." Gathering her composure, she managed to give him a stern look. "But don't use my cousin's innocence to do your bidding again."

"If there'd been any other way, I wouldn't have."

"I'm happy to hear that. Now, if you'll excuse me, I'll go see if I can't fix us something decent to eat for a change."

He gave her a little boy grin. "I'm partial to fruit and fluffy eggs if there are any."

"I think I saw some on the table."

"Good." He looked a bit uncomfortable. "I, er, was wondering if Sedgewick had gotten up yet."

"No, why?"

"I need to see him." He shifted from one hip to another. "Right away."

"I'm afraid you'll have to wait. He won't be up for hours yet."

"I need to see him now."

She shook her head. "It would have to be a matter of life or death before I'd wake Sedgewick when he hadn't had enough sleep. He's nasty enough when he's rested. You saw how he was yesterday."

"Jade, I'm trying to be a gentleman about this, but your cousin is the only one with the keys to these chains, and I've *got* to use the privy."

She thought she'd die of embarrassment right on the spot. Her cheeks flamed so hot, she was sure she'd set her hair on fire. "I . . . I'll get him." Whirling around, she ran from the stables.

As Morgan stepped out of the privy, he breathed a sigh of relief and glared at his captor, mindless of the gun pointed at his middle. "I need a shave, and a bath."

Sedgewick, his eyes still puffy from sleep, gave a

disgruntled snort. "We are not your bloody servants. Now get back to the stables. Keep your hands where I can see them."

Morgan would like to wrap them around Sedgewick's fat neck. Holding his arms out to the sides to relieve his stiff muscles, he took his time walking. "How about binding my hands in front for a while?"

"So you could strike out at whoever was near? Do not take me for a fool, Frazier."

Morgan didn't point out that the man *was* a fool.

"There is another solution, however," Sedgewick said with a sly grin.

"What's that?"

"You will see."

When they entered the stables, Morgan found out what it was. Sedgewick, holding the gun on him the whole time, chained Morgan's hands to two separate posts, stretching his arms out to the sides.

The position wasn't uncomfortable—not yet, anyway—but Morgan knew it would be much harder to loosen the posts, if not impossible, when he was ready to leave.

"Yes," Sedgewick mumbled to himself, "that is much better." He slipped the key in the pocket of his tailcoat. He'd just opened his mouth to say something else, when Jade walked in carrying a plate of fruit and eggs.

Sedgewick's eyes flared. "Where did that food come from?"

Jade glared right back. "Mr. Frazier."

"What? How?" His gaze pierced Morgan with the force of a speeding arrow.

"He gave Wilkie the money, and he took the wagon to town this morning."

Sedgewick's eyes widened as he stared at Morgan. "You have money? Where?"

"It was in my boot, but there's none left." Morgan couldn't stop the smug smile that curved his mouth.

"We will just see about that," Sedgewick hissed. He shoved the pistol into the front of his breeches and grabbed Morgan's foot. Angrily, he jerked off a boot and examined it closely, jabbing his fingers into the leather pocket, then he tossed it over his shoulder.

It landed with a thud in a stall across the way.

He checked the other boot and slung it toward its partner. Then he withdrew the gun, looking as if he had every intention of using it. "What else do you have?"

Morgan thought about his grandfather's pocket watch, the one he always carried, but it wasn't on him. Hoping he'd dropped it at the club instead of Sedgewick having pawned it for cash, he shrugged. "You've got everything I had."

"You bastard. How dare you hold out on me. And what in bloody hell makes you think we would take your charity?"

Jade set the plate on the crate near Morgan. "What choice do we have, Sedgewick? Starvation?"

Sedgewick slammed his hand against a stall gate. "Well, it will not be that way much longer. I posted a note to the sterling Viscount Ainshall last eve, demanding a ransom."

Morgan wasn't surprised, but some of the color left Jade's face.

"What did it say?" her voice trembled.

"That he must leave two hundred crown in Hyde Park between the Marble Arch and the Speaker's

Corner, or I would slit his son's throat. I plan to be there at dawn tomorrow to see the deed done."

She closed her eyes, but when she opened them again, there was a spark of disgust in those emerald depths. "Do you have any idea what you've done?"

"Found the means to free your father and get out of this hellhole."

"No, you haven't. You've just made certain that we spend the rest of our lives running from the relentless revenge of the Viscount Ainshall *and* the law."

"They will not follow us."

"You fool. They'll have us followed to the Orient if necessary." She massaged her temples. "There's no help for it, Sedgewick. You've got to let him go."

"No."

"If you don't then I will."

"Try it, missy, and I will make your father's beatings look like a child's game."

Morgan had taken all he could. "You lay a hand on her, you son-of-a-bitch, and I *will* track you to the ends of the earth." Morgan lowered his voice, to make sure the man got the point loud and clear. "And when I find you, I'll kill you."

The gun in Sedgewick's hand shook. "Do not threaten me, you whoreson."

"It's not a threat. It's a fact."

Sedgewick's face turned nearly purple with anger, and for a second, Morgan thought he would shoot. Then he regained himself. "In that case, Mr. Frazier, I will have to rethink the manner of your release." With a nasty smile, he brushed past Jade and walked out.

Morgan didn't have any doubt what he meant. If Morgan was "released" at all, it would be in a coffin.

Apparently Jade realized his intent, too. "I'll be back in a minute," she said quickly. "I've got to talk to him."

"Wait!"

"This can't wait." She whipped around and all but ran toward the manor.

Jade glared at Sedgewick. "What's the matter with you? Have you lost your senses? Blast it, Sedgewick, you can't possibly mean what you insinuated to Mr. Frazer."

"Of course, I can . . . and do."

"I'm going to free him whether you like it or not."

"Do not even try it."

"Give me the key," she demanded.

"It is time someone besides your father taught you about respect, missy." His hand shot out, and pain exploded in her jaw. She staggered and tried to grab for the table. Her fingers slipped off, and she landed hard on the floor. Another surge of pain stabbed through her hip.

Dazed, her hand cupping her jaw and feeling the burning imprint of his palm, she glared up at him, her eyes filling with tears. "You vicious cur!"

"Shut up! Or I will give you worse than that. I am the head of this family while your father is away, Jade, and you will do as I say." His stubby fingers curled into a fist. "You are not to go into the stables again."

"Why are you on the floor?" Wilkie asked as he walked into the room. He was frowning down at her, then his gaze flitted to Sedgewick. "Did she fall down?"

"Why else would she be sitting on the floor, idiot? Of course she fell."

Wilkie stared hard at her, as if he were trying to understand something that was beyond him. "Did you hit your jaw, too?"

"She hit it on the table when she fell," Sedgewick lied. "Help her up, so we can have our breakfast before it gets cold."

As Jade took her seat at the table, she began spooning eggs onto her plate, hating Sedgewick, and thinking about Morgan in the stables, sitting there with his plate beside him and unable to eat anything.

She fought the urge to run her knife through Sedgewick's black heart. He was so insensitive, and, although this wasn't the first time he'd struck her, he always did it when Wilkie was out of sight. Still, she knew she wouldn't obey him. Somehow, she would free Morgan. But, for now . . . "Wilkie, when you're finished, would you feed Mr. Frazier his meal?"

"Yes."

"Thank you."

Numbly, she listened to Wilkie talk about his trip to town and Sedgewick's monosyllable replies as she ate what little her upset, shrunken stomach would hold.

When her cousins had finished, and she couldn't force any more down, she rose and cleared the table.

Wilkie went to feed Mr. Frazier, while Sedgewick saddled the mare and headed for London.

Jade was glad to see Sedgewick go. Wishing he'd stay gone, she went to wash the dishes. She had just finished washing them when Wilkie came back to help.

"Jade?" he said in a quiet voice as she handed him a cup to dry. "I know I'm not very smart, but I don't think you fell down by yourself. I do that a lot, but you never do." He set the cup on the cupboard shelf. "Did Sedgewick hit you?"

Wilkie was such a compassionate person, and always her champion when he thought someone had wronged her. But she didn't want him in the middle of this. "I . . . tripped, Wilkie. That's all."

He didn't say anything while he finished drying the dishes, but when he'd placed the last saucer in the cupboard and started for the door, he stopped and turned back. "You know, Jade, you never lied to me before . . . and I don't think I like it." With that, he walked out and quietly closed the door behind him.

Morgan was angry enough to spit. Damn that Sedgewick, anyway. Why wouldn't he let Jade come to the stables? Wilkie had told Morgan when he fed him his cold breakfast. And why the hell hadn't Sedgewick let Morgan have his boots back?

Eyeing the Hessians in the stall across from him, he swore again.

His gaze shifted to the post on his right, and he wondered how long it would take him to uproot the thing. He'd had enough of this nonsense.

Footsteps sounded near the front doors, and Morgan glanced toward them.

Wilkie walked in, holding the draughts board and a box of disks. "Would you like to play some more?" he asked in the most serious tone Morgan had heard him use.

He wasn't in the mood for any kind of game, but a sixth sense told him something was bothering Wilkie. "Sure, but you'll still have to move for me."

"I know." He placed the board on its customary

crate, then sat cross-legged on the floor, his manner unusually somber as he set up the game.

Morgan studied him carefully. Something was different . . . "Wilkie? What's wrong?"

"Nothing." He made the first move. "Which do you want to move?"

"The second from your right."

A half a dozen moves later, Morgan tried again. "You're awfully quiet this morning. Is there something on your mind?"

Wilkie took one of Morgan's men and set the chip aside. "Why do people lie?"

Now there was an easy question to answer. "Has someone lied to you?"

"Yes."

"Who?"

"Jade."

It took Morgan a moment to grasp that one. Of all the things the dark-haired beauty might be, Morgan never figured her for a liar. "Are you sure?"

"I think so."

Morgan told Wilkie where to jump two of Wilkie's men, and the youngster took them off the board. "Want to tell me about it?"

"I don't know if I should."

"Will someone get hurt if you tell me?"

"Jade might."

That stopped Morgan in his tracks. "What?"

"If I tell you, and you say something, Jade might get hurt again."

"Again?"

Wilkie nodded. In his innocence, he had no idea how his words had affected Morgan.

Morgan didn't know what to think, but he had to get the truth out of him. He thought for a second, then fixed his features into a solemn expression. "I would never say or do anything that would hurt Jade. You must know that by now."

Wilkie's guileless eyes stared into his, then he dug his fingers into his hair. "Jade said she fell this morning and hurt her jaw on the table, but I don't think she did. I think Sedgewick hit her." Wilkie rubbed his nose with the back of his hand. "I saw him do it before, and he hits me sometimes and I fall."

The flash of rage that hit Morgan made his voice quiver. "Where is he?"

"In town, I think."

"Did you see him hit her?"

"Not this time. She was on the floor when I came in, and Sedgewick was beside her. He was angry. I could tell."

Morgan would have given anything he possessed to be free of his chains in that moment. Nothing would give him greater pleasure than shoving his fist into Sedgewick's face. Bloody hell, he couldn't wait for that bastard to come back. Then he remembered his promise to Wilkie, that he'd never do anything to hurt Jade, and he felt a jolt of impotent fury. Hell, he couldn't even *say* anything until she was out of that coward's reach.

"I win," Wilkie crowed as he captured the last of Morgan's men.

Morgan watched him gather the disks for a new game, but his thoughts were still on Sedgewick. When Morgan got loose, he was going to hurt that bastard.

Badly.

Chapter
6

Jade waited until she was sure Sedgewick was asleep before she crept silently from her room. The plank floors were chilly to her bare feet, but it didn't matter. Nothing did except seeing Morgan set free. She had seen the look in her cousin's eyes when he'd held the gun on his prisoner, and she knew what Sedgewick intended to do.

Kill Morgan.

Fear tightened her middle as she quietly crossed the hall to Sedgewick's room. She had to get the key from his pocket.

The boards in the hallway creaked beneath her feet, and she froze, holding her breath . . . praying.

When all remained silent, she slowly entered Sedgewick's room.

Moonlight filtered in from beyond the curtains, casting a pale light over her cousin's form in the rumpled bed. A heavy snore rattled through the silence.

Jade breathed a sigh of relief and tiptoed to where

he'd tossed his coat over a ladder-back chair. Ever so carefully, she slipped her fingers into the pocket and felt around until she touched metal.

Sedgewick's voice pierced the noiseless room.

Jade sucked in a sharp breath. Her gaze darted to the bed. Her hand trembled as it closed around the key. He was only mumbling in his sleep. She let out her breath, then hurrying back across the room, she pulled the door almost closed behind her.

Her nerves were in such a riotous state by the time she reached the lower level, her heart stamped like an angry horse. She'd never done anything so frightening in her life.

The night air was cool as she made her way through the overgrown yard to the stables, and it helped soothe her anxiousness. Pausing at the side of the door, she wondered if she was doing the right thing. What if Mr. Frazier brought the authorities back?

Now you think about that, her conscience chided.

Well, she had thought about it earlier. She just hadn't made a decision until now. But everything has gone terribly wrong with this wretched situation. She had to turn it around. She had to stop Sedgewick from hurting Morgan.

Trembling, and knowing what the consequences would be for her actions if Sedgewick caught her, she slipped inside the stables.

In the glow of the moon, she could see Morgan slumped against the stall, his arms stretched out to his sides, his head drooped forward. Sedgewick had done a good job making Morgan uncomfortable.

She watched Mr. Frazier as she silently walked toward him, not wanting to startle him.

"What are you doing here?" he asked in that rough velvet voice that did unspeakable things to her senses. He lifted his head to stare directly at her.

"I came to set you free."

"How'd you get the key?"

"I stole it."

"That was a foolish thing to do. If he'd caught you, there's no telling what he might have done. What he might *still* do."

Jade inserted the key in one of the locks and turned it. "You let me worry about my cousin."

Morgan's gaze fastened on her jaw.

Self-consciously, she turned away, knowing how awful she looked. "Sedgewick's asleep right now. As soon as I unlock these, I want you to leave."

"No."

"What?"

"I'm not going yet. But you can loosen the chains enough that I can escape when I'm ready."

"Morgan, you have to leave tonight. Your father's probably frantic over that ransom note. I can't handle any more problems. Our current situation, and my father's, are enough to bear for the moment. I certainly don't want to be hunted down by the law on top of that. I'll loosen your chains, but you have to leave, right now."

Morgan shook his head. "Jade, I give you my word, you don't have anything to worry about where my father's concerned. He's not going to believe that I've been abducted."

"But Sedgewick sent—"

"It doesn't matter. My father and I have been in a contest of *im*practical jokes and pranks since I was six years old. He's one up on me at the moment, and I'm sure he'll think I'm trying to get even with him."

Pranks? Jokes? The members of his family teased each other? Who was he kidding? "Lies don't become you, Morgan."

He stared at her for a moment, then he smiled. "I'm not lying. It's sort of a family tradition. My grandfather did it before my father, and so on."

"What will your father do once he knows you've really been abducted?"

"I don't know, but I'd rather not find out. I'll return before he becomes too worried."

"I wish you'd go tonight." She knelt at his other side and unlocked the opposite chain, loosening it enough for him to slip his hand free with little difficulty. Again she was overwhelmed by how small she felt next to his great size. No one had ever made her feel so dainty. So feminine. It was a wonderful feeling.

One she couldn't afford to explore.

As she rose, she thought of all the problems that had been piled on her shoulders; the loss of her mother, her servants and friends, her home, her father's incarceration, her cousin's high-handedness, and now Morgan Frazier . . . the prisoner who refused to escape.

Morgan hadn't seen Jade in two days, not since the night she'd loosened his chains. Since that day, Sedgewick had taken him to the privy twice a day, and Wilkie had brought—and fed him—all his meals. Morgan hadn't seen Jade, and he missed her. Several times, he'd considered sneaking into the house to find her, but his fear of what Sedgewick would do to her if he found out was enough to stop Morgan.

When Wilkie had arrived a few minutes ago for

their evening game, Morgan asked where she was. The younger man said Sedgewick still wouldn't let her come near the stables.

It was another mark against Sedgewick.

No sooner had the thought occurred, than the object of his anger walked in. "Wilkie, go back in the house," Sedgewick ordered. "Jade wants you to help her dust."

"But she never has—"

"Just go, idiot. Stop arguing."

Wilkie clamped his mouth together and rose, then hurried out.

Morgan stared at Sedgewick. "Do you always order him around like he's a servant?"

"What I do with my dull-witted brother is no concern of yours."

"He's a lot smarter than you give him credit for."

Sedgewick snapped the riding crop he held in his hand. "I am not here to discuss Wilkie." He picked up a bridle that had been left hanging on a nail. "I came to let you know I am returning to London to wait for the ransom money from your father." He sent him a knowing glance. "As soon as I get those funds, I will have no further need of you."

Morgan hadn't figured anything different, and he knew he'd better be prepared when the jackass returned. Sedgewick wasn't going to be civil when he came back without his money.

The minute Sedgewick left, Morgan wiggled his hands free and slipped them out, then massaging his cramped shoulders, he walked around, working the kinks out of his legs as he thought. He knew he was close to Stevenage, but he didn't know in which direction the village lay. Still, all he had to do was find a well-traveled road. Surely it would lead him to the town. Hell, for all he knew, the road could be right in front of the house.

But he wouldn't leave yet, nor would he ever go without talking to Jade. He couldn't explain that notion, nor did he try. All he knew was he couldn't leave without seeing her, and he just wasn't ready to go yet.

He started for his boots when he heard footsteps.

He froze. Had Sedgewick returned? A knot formed in his stomach as he watched the door.

Jade walked in carrying a plate of biscuits. Her step faltered when she saw him standing, and he knew she was shocked by his height. Most people were.

"So, you've finally decided to leave."

Was that a note of disappointment in her voice? "What are you doing out here? I thought Sedgewick ordered you to stay away—"

"He did. Do you want to eat before you go?"

"I'm not leaving, damn it. I'm just trying to get my boots on and some feeling back into my limbs. I want to be prepared when Sedgewick gets back. He's not going to be happy when my father doesn't leave him the money."

"You're sure he won't?"

"Absolutely certain."

She studied his hands. "Then you should leave before he returns."

She was awfully anxious to get rid of him. "I'm not going anywhere until I'm ready."

"Suit yourself." She set the plate down.

Morgan studied her lovely face and silky hair. He liked Jade. He liked her courage and daring, her levelheadedness. Hell, he even liked her sharp tongue.

And he liked her body. His gaze lowered to the low-cut neckline of the dress. She was bulging over the top of the tight material.

His body stirred, and he jolted in surprise. Then he grinned so wide he thought his face would crack. Thank Providence. He was back to normal.

"What are you smiling at?"

Don't say it. "I was smiling at the way you make me feel."

"And how is that?"

"Aroused."

She stared at him for a split second, then jammed her hands on her hips. "That was uncalled for."

"What's wrong, beautiful? Does it surprise you that I'm attracted to you?"

"I knew I shouldn't have unchained you."

He laughed. "That doesn't stop my thoughts." His gaze lowered again to her full breasts beneath the tight bodice. The tiny waist. The long, long legs. "It doesn't stop my body's response, either."

"I'm leaving." She lifted her skirt and started to go.

"If you do, I'll follow you."

She whirled back around. "What do you want from me?"

If he told her, she'd slap him. "How about a game of draughts. Wilkie said you knew how to play."

"Draughts? You insult me, and now you want to play draughts?"

"How the hell did I insult you?"

She didn't respond. All she did was stand there with her arms crossed, looking angry.

Morgan threw up his hands. "All right. I'm not attracted to you. I don't become aroused when

76

you're around, and you don't interest me in the least. There, does that make you happy?"

"Nothing about you makes me happy, *Mr. Frazier*. And I don't want to play draughts . . . or any of your *other* silly games." This time, she didn't hesitate to march out.

Morgan sighed and reached for one of his boots. What the hell had gone wrong?

Jade paced her bedroom floor, her arms crossed, her heart hammering. Why had Morgan said those things to her? Not that she believed for one minute that he was attracted to her. She wasn't stupid. She knew how she looked. The man was playing *more* games with her.

Games only he could understand.

Well, he could just play with someone else.

Unlacing her gown, she slipped it off, then undid the tabs on her petticoats, all the while thinking about how Morgan's words had made her feel in that first instant. No matter how hard she wanted to deny it, she couldn't. She'd felt a surge of heart-pounding excitement until her common sense had taken hold.

But now, she couldn't stop thinking about what would have happened, if she hadn't left. Would he have kissed her? Would he have taken her in his arms?

As she pulled on her nightdress and climbed into bed, she tried to push away images of them standing in the middle of the stables, wrapped in each other's arms, but the visions returned again and again.

She tried to tell herself she was a fool. She tried to remind herself what type of man he was, but nothing helped. Her mind had taken on a will of its own, and the images of Morgan and her together refused to leave. She grew so warm, she barely noticed the chill in the room, or when her eyelids started to droop. . . .

Jade was so tired the next morning, she felt as if she hadn't had any sleep at all. Her dreams had kept her awake most of the night. Dreams of the man in the stables, a man who was so wrong for her it was frightening.

Dragging on her clothes, she went to the cookhouse to put on a pot of tea and start breakfast. She wasn't anxious for this day to start, because she knew Sedgewick would be back that afternoon, and if Morgan had told her the truth, her cousin was going to be furious when he didn't get the money.

"What's for breakfast?" Wilkie asked as he walked in, his hair still rumpled, his eyes puffy from sleep.

"Flat cakes and sausage pie."

Wilkie wrinkled his nose. "Maybe I'll just have a biscuit." He filched one and ambled out.

Jade stared at the empty door for several seconds, trying to understand what was wrong with him. Wilkie loved flat cakes and sausage.

Sighing, she turned back to the sideboard and began preparing the meal.

When breakfast was ready, she found Wilkie lounging in the parlor, something he rarely did, and gave him a plate to take to Morgan.

She ate her own meal at the scarred dining room table, then gathered the dishes for washing. Wilkie brought Morgan's empty plate in and began drying the dishes she'd washed.

Oddly, she noticed his face appeared flushed. "Wilkie? Is something wrong?"

"No."

"Are you feeling all right?"

He sniffed and set a dry pan under the sideboard. "I don't think so. My head hurts." He picked up a plate.

Jade took it from him. "Why don't you lie down for a while? I'll finish these."

As if it took him a moment to grasp her words, he paused, then shook his head as if to dislodge something. "My ears are making music like chimes."

His ears were ringing? That wasn't a good sign. "Then you definitely need to lie down. Go on. I'll be up in a minute with a headache powder that will make you feel better."

With a listless nod, he sluggishly left the room.

By the time Jade finished and went upstairs with a glass of water and powders, Wilkie was in bed with the covers drawn up to his chin.

"I'm cold."

Concerned, she placed a hand on his forehead. His skin was much too hot. "Here, take this. It'll make you feel better."

When he'd downed the powders with water, he handed the half-full glass back to her. "I told Morgan I'd come back to play a game, but I'm too tired now. Will you tell him that?"

Jade would eat worms before she talked to Morgan again. "I'm sure he'll understand. You just rest now."

Sleepily, Wilkie snuggled further into the covers, not even noticing that she didn't answer his question. "I love you, Jade."

She smiled fondly. "I love you, too, Will."

Jade had just closed Wilkie's door and started downstairs when she heard Sedgewick's angry voice.

"Where the bloody hell is everyone?" he shouted.

She hurried to the parlor. "What is it?" she asked anxiously, knowing exactly what he was angry about.

Sedgewick, looking dirty and disheveled from his long ride into London, slammed his riding crop down onto the table, making a basket of flowers wobble as he did so. *"What is wrong?* Everything is wrong. This is how concerned the viscount is for his son." He withdrew a crumpled note from his pocket and tossed it in her direction.

The paper fluttered to the table, and she picked it up to read the words printed in bold letters.

Keep him.

So Morgan had told the truth. Still, she couldn't mention that to Sedgewick. "He can't possibly mean that."

"You are right," Sedgewick said. "The bastard thinks this is a jest. Perhaps if I sent him something of his son's, like a finger, he would think differently."

Jade fought the horrifying image of one of Morgan's long, slender hands missing a finger, but she couldn't stop a shudder. "Sedgewick, you can't!"

"Of course I can."

"But you mustn't! If you harm him, his father will never stop tracking us."

He relented like he usually did when he'd let his mouth run faster than his brain. He waved a hand. "All right. No fingers, for now. But I will send something."

Jade was afraid to ask what. But she knew she'd have to break the vow she'd made no more than a few hours ago. She had to speak to Morgan and warn him.

She had to make him leave.

Chapter
7

"What the hell do you mean you're going to cut my hair?" Morgan demanded, keeping his head back, a healthy distance from Sedgewick and his scissors.

"Not all of it, you fool. I simply need a few locks." Sedgewick's eyes narrowed. "Or would you prefer I sent your father one of your fingers?"

Morgan could feel the rage inside him building to explosive proportions. *Just try it, you son-of-a-bitch.* "Unchain me and hand me the scissors."

"No."

He arched a brow at Sedgewick. "If anyone's going to cut my hair, it'll be me." He hardened his gaze. "Anyone else who tries will find these chains around their neck." Morgan said a lot of things in jest, but this wasn't one of them. If that bastard came near him with those scissors, he'd strangle him.

Sedgewick must have sensed his sincerity. He removed the chain from Morgan's right wrist, fortunately not noticing it was loose, and handed him the scissors. "Make them good-sized locks, or I will not hesitate to knock you out and shave your bloody head."

If that was supposed to convince Morgan, it didn't work. His headful of curls had always been more of a hindrance than anything else. The damned mess never would tame into any kind of order. Still, he didn't want Sedgewick's hands anywhere near his head.

Unable to reach the back of his hair with one hand still bound, he leaned his head against the post and gripped a chunk of shoulder-length curls behind his ear, then cut the lock up to his collar. Hoping to at least keep balance, he turned and did the same to the other side.

He kept his hair long, because the weight helped straighten out some of the curls. Now, though, he could feel the hair behind his ears coiling into rings. Damn, he hated that.

"Hand them over."

Morgan pitched the scissors and hair at Sedgewick's feet. "This isn't going to work. My father won't be intimidated."

Sedgewick smirked. "If this does not work, next time I *will* send a finger."

Morgan wasn't worried in the least, because in order for Sedgewick to do that, he'd have to get within arm's reach of Morgan's hands. "I'll study them tonight and decide which one I can do without."

"You do that." Rechaining Morgan's hand much tighter, Sedgewick cast him a sarcastic smirk before stalking out.

Morgan waited until he was sure the man was gone before he tried to work his right hand free. It was no use. Sedgewick had done a good job of restraining him again.

Damn. Now what?

He slipped his left hand free and gave the post by his other arm a tentative shove. It was solid, but with a little work, he was sure he could loosen it enough to slip the chains off.

When he was ready.

Jade was exhausted from her day's work. Leaning back in the Queen Anne chair, she rested her head on the tall back and sighed. There was never an end to the chores.

Her gaze drifted to where pictures had once graced satin-draped walls. They'd been sold a year before the game, but the brocade settee that had once sat before the fireplace had been the last to go. Her mother had been adamant that guests needed something to sit on. She glanced at the striped settee that had been in her mother's sitting room. How disgusted she would have been to seat someone on that.

A tear slipped down her cheek as she thought of her mother. Consumption had been the cause of her death, but Jade wondered if her mother hadn't just given up. Father's gambling had taken everything her mother cherished.

She took a sip of steaming mint tea, and her thoughts turned to Morgan Frazier, knowing she had to feed him soon, even though she wasn't supposed to go to the stables. There was no one else.

She set her cup aside and leaned forward, lacing her fingers through her hair. Why wouldn't the man go. Just leave her and her cousins in peace?

She was certain it had to be for his amusement. Or perhaps he truly did want to get even with his father. Either way, he was making her life miserable.

Maybe if she refused to feed him? No, that wouldn't work. He'd come inside, and that was the last thing she wanted. If Sedgewick should ever find him here . . .

She really, *really* wished they'd never taken him.

Rising, she went up to check on Wilkie as she'd done several times that day, and found him still running a slight fever. It wasn't as bad as she'd feared it would be, but her heart ached for him, and she wished she could cradle him in her arms and protect him from all the bad things in the world. Sickness, men's treachery, games of chance . . .

She placed a kiss on his hot brow and drew the covers closer to his chin, then quietly left him to start supper.

As she gathered the ingredients for a kidney pie, she noticed how quiet the house was with Sedgewick gone and Wilkie ill. It was so quiet she was uncomfortable. Wilkie always brightened her days, and she missed that, no matter how temporary.

When the food was ready, she filled Morgan's plate and carried it to the stables, suddenly glad for his company. As she entered, she noticed he'd freed one of his hands, but not the other.

"You'll probably need both your hands to eat."

He turned, and those blue eyes collided with hers. His hair drooped over the bandage that was now in desperate need of changing—or removing altogether.

"I'd be happy to use them both if you have a spare key."

"I put it back. What happened?"

He explained about Sedgewick's last visit. "So, it appears I'm hindered once again."

"I'll try to get the key tonight."

"No. I've been loosening the post. I'll be mobile again soon." He glanced at the tray in her hand, then toward the door. "Where's Wilkie?"

She set the plate and utensils on the crate and moved it close to his free hand. "He's not feeling well. I sent him to bed after breakfast this morning."

"What's wrong with him?"

"A bout with the ague, I think. He's running a low temperature, and it's been so cold in the house."

"Maybe he should see a physician."

"Morgan, you know we don't have—"

"You can take him to my family physician."

Where was a man like this when her mother needed help? "Thank you. I will if it becomes necessary."

He nodded, then picked up his fork and speared a piece of kidney pie. "Are you any good with scissors?"

"I imagine that depends on what you want me to do with them."

"Cut my hair."

"Your hair looks fine. No damage." She studied his hair-roughened jaw. "Although, I do believe your chin could use some attention."

He gripped a ringlet of hair behind his ear that barely reached his collar. "I'm lopsided."

"The difference isn't even noticeable."

"It is to me."

"Fine. How short do you want it?"

"I don't want it short at all. My head will look like it's sprouted corkscrews. But I do want the length to halfway match. Would you fix it?"

She sighed. "I'll get the scissors."

"They're here." He nodded to a spot on the ground.

She saw her mother's scissors lying in the dirt. "He couldn't even put them away?"

"Apparently not."

Retrieving them, she glanced at the plate. "You'll have to finish eating first. I'll need the crate for you to sit on."

"As hungry as I am, it won't take a minute."

And it almost didn't. He practically inhaled his food, then handed her the empty plate.

As she set it aside, he maneuvered around until he could sit on the crate, leaving a couple feet between him and the railing, his chained arm outstretched. "You'll need a brush. My hair tends to wind around itself."

"There's one in my room." Handing him the scissors, she headed for the house.

As she reached for the brush, she paused, suddenly realizing the intimacy of sharing it with him. Not to mention how afraid she was to touch Morgan's hair. She would have to get close to him, and when that happened, funny things started going on inside her.

But what was she supposed to do? Tell him she couldn't cut his hair because she was afraid of being near him? Not likely.

Gripping the handle, she strode out the door, but stopped in the hall, figuring she might as well get everything over with at once. She went into Sedgewick's room and gathered his shaving implements.

When she entered the stables, Morgan was still sitting right where she left him. For just a second, she hesitated, unsure where to begin. She'd never been very good at this sort of thing. Deciding the back would be the safest, she stepped behind him. "Hold your head up and don't move."

She removed the bandage and checked his wound. Only a small pink scar remained. Running the bristles down the length of his hair, she marveled at the softness. The heavy thickness. She drew the brush back from his ear until she reached the end of the shorter strands, then braced two fingers against his head while she held the section of hair in place for cutting. She clipped the strands to the same length.

The hair sprang back, wrapping around her fingers, and her heart kicked into rapid beats. If the man's voice and eyes weren't enough, now even his hair was attacking her senses.

Morgan could feel the heat from her body against his back. Her lilac scent drifted around him, and it was all he could do to sit still. The touch of her fingers in his hair made his scalp tingle.

"Did Wilkie tell you about the haircut he gave me when I was six?" she asked in that husky voice.

Morgan smiled, remembering the boy's tale. "He told me your mother cried."

"She did more than that." Snip. Snip. "She broke every pair of shears and scissors in the house and ordered our clothes sent out for mending. She didn't buy another pair for years."

"Where are your cousins' parents?"

"They were killed in a fire when Sedgewick was eleven and Wilkie five."

"Have they lived with you ever since?"

"Eighteen years now." Snip. Snip. "Bend your head forward."

Morgan stared at the ground. "You must have been young when they came."

"I wasn't born until two months after they arrived. They're more like my brothers than my cousins."

Snip. Snip.

The sound of the scissors was getting on his nerves. He'd hated haircuts since he was a child. "Did you have any brothers or sisters?"

"I had a sister. But she died right after she was born, and Mother couldn't have any more children after that." She moved to the side, and he felt her fingers brush his ear.

His pulse jumped, then broke into a gallop. Out of the corner of his eye, he saw that her breast was very close to his cheek. He swallowed. Talk, damn it. Talk. "Where's your mother now?"

There was a moment's hesitation. "She's buried on the hill behind the house."

"I'm sorry."

"So am I." Her voice sounded brittle. Then she sighed. "I guess I still can't talk about her without getting upset."

She stepped around in front of him. "Do you have any brothers or sisters?"

Morgan could hardly speak. Her breasts were even with his mouth. His gaze was fixed on the flesh rising above the too-small bodice. He could see her pulse beating rapidly at the base of her throat. Jesus, he wanted to press his lips to that spot.

"Morgan?"

He started. "Umm, yes. I have a brother. He married last year and moved to the Colonies."

"Older or younger?" Snip. Snip.

"He's three years older." Morgan couldn't drag

his eyes away from the tattered rim of lace that trimmed her bodice, or the way her flesh moved when she raised her arms. The way it quivered with each breath she took. He'd never seen breasts so milky white. So smooth. His gaze followed the edge of the material again, and he could make out the darker skin surrounding her nipples.

His sex expanded.

"I always wanted a sister. I had a cousin who was the closest thing I ever had to one, but she went to live in the Colonies, too."

Morgan was staring at the smooth tip of her breast covered by peach-colored muslin. He wanted to close his mouth over her and feel her nipple harden against his tongue. He wanted to suckle her until she moaned with pleasure.

His sex throbbed.

"Morgan? Is something wrong?" Snip. Snip. "You're awfully quiet." Her hands were at the crown of his head, her arms near his ears, her nipples a breath away.

He couldn't speak. Hell, he couldn't even let out his breath, lest he did something she'd probably slap him for. He had to get away from her.

Lifting his hand, he placed it on the side of her waist and eased her back a couple steps. The warmth of her skin through the gown tingled across the tips of his fingers. He leaned away, trying to put more distance between them.

"If you don't hold still, you're going to end up looking like Wilkie's draughts board." She snipped again. Then again. "All done." She smiled down at him.

It was a mistake. She was too close. He was too full of wanting her. He heard her small gasp an instant before he pulled her to him and took her mouth.

Her lips trembled, and her fingers tightened in his hair, but she didn't make any move to resist. Then he felt her soften and move closer. Her breasts touched his upper chest.

Desire exploded through him like a cannon blast. He eased his tongue between her lips.

She gave a start of surprise, but he didn't stop. He sank into her sweet mouth, reveling in the warmth. The incredible softness.

More than anything, he wanted to wrap his arms around her and pull her against him. He wanted to slide his hands over the curve of her waist . . . her breasts.

He slid his arm around her waist and urged her down, until she was on her knees between his legs, his mouth over hers now, need so strong it hurt.

He deepened the kiss, wanting desperately to make love to her right there, right that minute.

Suddenly, as if she'd read his thoughts, she wrenched away and sprang to her feet, the scissors gripped in her hand, her eyes flashing green fire. "Don't you *ever* do that again." She pointed the scissors threateningly at his groin. "Or so help me, I'll unman you."

That sparked his own anger. "I didn't *make* you respond, woman. You did that all by yourself."

"You bastard." Slinging the scissors to the side, she kicked the shaving mug as she stormed out.

Morgan jerked against the chain, angry enough to break the post in two with his bare hands. Damn the woman. She was making him crazy!

Chapter
8

That bloody whoreson! I should send his son back to him in pieces!"

"Sedgewick, calm down and tell me what happened," Jade said in the most soothing voice she could muster. "Did Mr. Frazier's father refuse to pay the money when you sent the locks of hair?"

"Refuse!" Sedgewick roared, his hefty jowls wobbling with anger. "He did a bloody sight more than that." He shoved an envelope in her hand. "This is what he did."

Jade watched her red-faced cousin as she opened the envelope and read the missive.

Inside, you will find the amount of money I feel my son is worth.

Morgan was wrong. His father had paid. She looked in the envelope, but nothing was inside. "How much was in it?"

Sedgewick clenched his fist. "I gave the envelope to you in exactly the same manner in which I received it. There *was* no money. The bloody coxswain still thinks this is a jest!"

"What are you going to do now?"

"Prove to the bastard this is not a game."

A nervous skitter tripped up her spine. "How?"

"As much as I would like to do what I first wanted, I cannot. In that respect, you are right about them hounding us. But I will think of something. You will see." Slamming out of the room, he pounded up the stairs to his bedchamber.

Jade retrieved the pile of cloths she'd been taking up to Wilkie's room when Sedgewick came in. Her cousin was becoming irrational. If Morgan didn't leave soon, there's no telling what Sedgewick might do.

She glanced toward the door, knowing she'd have to get the key again soon, and this time, she'd force Morgan to go if she had to do it at gunpoint.

Just the thought of facing him again after her behavior the day before yesterday, sent chills up her spine. Since then, she hadn't spoken a word to him. She'd simply set his food on the crate that day, retrieved Sedgewick's shaving gear, and left. She continued to ignore him yesterday and this morning, collecting his dirty dishes as she brought new ones so she didn't have to see him more than absolutely necessary.

He'd tried to talk to her, but she'd refused to even look at him. He'd gotten angry again. But it didn't matter. Between caring for Wilkie and listening to Sedgewick's tirades, she had enough to do without battling her own emotions, too.

Wishing that card game five months ago had never happened, she headed back upstairs to sit with Wilkie.

* * *

Morgan was beginning to feel like a caged animal. Even though he could move around somewhat, and the post was nearly loose enough to slip the chains off, he was sick of the smell of the stables. He was sick of dust.

And he was damned sick of being ignored by Jade.

Fleetingly, he thought about leaving that night, but something inside him held him back. Jade. If he left, he might never see her again. She and her cousins would probably run.

He closed his eyes and leaned against the post, remembering the kiss they'd shared. Hell, he hadn't been able to stop thinking about it.

Even now, he could feel the softness of her lips, smell her warm lilac scent, hear the throaty sound of her voice.

For the hundredth time that day, his body stirred to life, and he didn't know whether to damn or bless the reaction.

Forcing his thoughts away from Jade, he focused on his father. It had been five days since Morgan was taken, and his father would soon come to realize the abduction was real by his continued absence. Morgan didn't know what he would do, but his father had a ruthless side, a *vengeful* side that was frightening at best.

"Do you have jewelry? A ring, perhaps?"

Startled, he turned to see Sedgewick standing in the center of the stables. He hadn't even heard him come in. "What? My grandfather's pocket watch wasn't enough for you?"

"Pocket watch?"

"The one you stole from me in the alley."

Sedgewick moved closer. "We took nothing from you."

"I had it on me when I left the club." Morgan was beginning to feel ill. Had it fallen out in the alley? Had someone taken it? He thought Sedgewick had, and Morgan knew he could retrieve it from whoever bought it. But if Morgan didn't know . . .

Sedgewick frowned and studied him for a moment, then he spun around and walked out.

Curiously, Morgan watched the door.

A few minutes later, he came back in, carrying Morgan's timepiece. "Is this it?"

"I thought you didn't take it."

Sedgewick's nostrils flared. "It was in the bed of the bloody wagon. Now, would your father recognize this?"

"Probably, why?"

"It is either that or a finger."

"We're back to that again, are we?"

"So it would seem." He stuffed the watch into his fob pocket. "You had better hope this works." His gaze lowered to Morgan's fingers. "Otherwise the niceties are over."

Morgan's hands drew into fists as he watched Sedgewick leave. The man's time was coming, and very, very soon.

Jade sat beside Wilkie, holding a damp cloth to his brow. He wasn't getting any better. His fever had risen, and his coherent moments had grown farther and farther apart. But the worse part was the awful rattle in his chest.

Her own chest constricted just listening to him.

Brushing back a lock of dark hair from his brow, she studied his sweet face. He was such a handsome young man. So kind and genuine. That's what she liked most about him. He never put on airs like

Sedgewick did, never tried to be something he wasn't. He simply went about his days in a world that was full of adventure, with innocent enthusiasm, and a child's blunt honesty.

It hurt her to see him like this, and more and more over the last couple days, she'd considered Morgan's offer of taking Wilkie to the Frazier physician.

Dampening the cloth again, she wrung the water out and placed it again on Wilkie's brow. She had to feed Morgan soon, something Sedgewick had finally consented to because Wilkie couldn't do it, and Sedgewick was rarely here. But he'd warned her not to talk to Morgan. Just give him his food and leave. Not that she would have done any differently, anyway. She was still too upset over that kiss.

Her first kiss.

Not wanting to start thinking about *that* again, she glanced at the clock on the mantel, knowing Sedgewick would be back at any time, and he wasn't going to be happy when he returned. She had neglected the chores to care for Wilkie, and Sedgewick had complained about her spending so much time with him already. To Sedgewick's way of thinking, Wilkie would be better off dead.

For the hundredth time, she tried to understand why Sedgewick was so hateful. The only thing she could imagine was his size.

He hated being short, and he was always trying to prove himself to her father. To everyone. She knew Sedgewick had nearly convinced her father to leave him Wentworth Hall before her father had given it as a marker.

Maybe that was another reason for Sedgewick's behavior. He was losing everything he'd worked for so diligently over the years. Even if he wasn't entitled to it, he'd always seen himself as master of Wentworth. Always did anything possible to impress her father to see that end.

Sickened by his greed, she tucked the covers closer to Wilkie's chin and headed for the cookhouse.

Morgan apparently didn't hear her walk in carrying his tray an hour later, because he didn't stop shoving and yanking on the post that was almost loose enough to pull out. One of the notched rails attached to the post's side had already fallen from its groove.

"Sedgewick's due back any time. You might want to hold off until this evening."

Startled, he swung toward her. "Are you speaking to me?"

"Aside from the fact that Sedgewick has forbidden it, I wouldn't if it weren't necessary."

"That figures." He righted the post and shoved the rail back in place. "Why is it necessary?"

"Wilkie's getting worse." She set the tray down, then stepped away.

"Take him to Samuel Verde, on Pentonville Road, near London, when Sedgewick returns. Tell Sam I sent you." His eyes had softened at the mention of Wilkie, but now grew bright as they consumed every inch of her, as if he'd been starved for the sight.

Jade felt herself growing warm again. "I'll repay you some—"

Dust rose in billowing clouds as a horse rumbled to a stop just outside the doors.

Morgan's gaze shot to hers. "Get out of here. Go out the back, quick."

Jade didn't hesitate. She hiked up her skirts and ran.

Morgan breathed a sigh of relief as he watched her

disappear around the back side of the stables, then he turned to wait for Sedgewick.

A few seconds later, Sedgewick strolled in, his face alight with triumph. "Your bloody father is not fooling me anymore. I am on to his game now."

"What are you talking about?"

A smirk twisted Sedgewick's thick lips. "Both letters I have received from the viscount led me to believe he was not taking my threats seriously. I now know that was a lie."

Morgan had trouble following him. "How?"

"If your father thought my ransom demands were a jest, then why did he hire Harrod Sawyer to track us down?"

Morgan didn't know whether to be pleased his father had finally been convinced, or very, very concerned that his father had hired the most ruthless, determined, *vicious* son-of-a-bitch who ever walked the earth.

But in that instant, Morgan knew what he had to do. Tonight.

Jade stepped from the tub and dried, then tossed the towel aside and pulled on the only chemise she had that wasn't worn through in several spots. This chemise only had one hole—near her left breast—still it was as thin as gauze.

Wishing she'd been taught how to sew clothing instead of merely the art of fine stitchery, she took a brush to her damp hair and drew the bristles down the full length.

Her hand stopped as images of those same bristles sliding through Morgan's thick hair swarmed her. She remembered how shiny his hair was. How soft. As soft as his lips.

Don't start that again.

Giving herself a mental shake, she set the brush on her tiny dressing table, then went in to check on Wilkie again. Sedgewick had refused to let her use the horse to take Wilkie to a physician, but she would take the animal in the morning anyway, while Sedgewick was asleep.

It didn't matter how angry he got afterward.

Returning to her room, and with a long stretch and yawn, she climbed into bed and snuggled down into her pillow, knowing she'd have to get up early.

Unfortunately, her visit with Morgan that afternoon had rekindled memories of the other day. Of how his lips had felt on hers, the strength of his arm.

She determinedly willed the image away—for all the good it did. His handsome face danced through her thoughts again and again.

There has to be some way to get rid of him. She closed her eyes tight and covered them with her hand, as if force alone could keep the thoughts at bay.

It didn't work.

Finally, in desperation, she got up and walked to the window overlooking the front of the manor. She pressed her palms to her temples. "Go away, Morgan," she whispered. "Leave me alone."

"If only I could," a rough voice said from close behind her.

Jade spun sharply.

Morgan had one shoulder braced against the foot of her four-poster, his muscular arms crossed over his chest. The opposite window stood open behind him, and a slight breeze fluttered the sleeve of his loose white shirt. He looked so attractive, she had to remind herself to breathe.

"What are you doing here?"

"Returning the favor you bestowed upon me."

"And what favor was that?"

"You took me out of that cellar before I went completely insane. In fact, I think you probably saved my life. I really couldn't breathe down there." He came toward her, his movements graceful for such a big man. "So, I'm going to return the favor by saving your life."

"I wasn't aware it was in jeopardy."

"You're in *danger*. The man my father hired to find you and your cousins won't stop at simply capturing you. He'll kill you."

"What man?"

"Harrod Sawyer." He glanced around the room. "Gather some clothes. We're getting out of here."

"I've never heard of this Sawyer person, and I'm certainly not going anywhere with you."

Those blue eyes narrowed dangerously. "I'm not giving you a choice. Now gather your things or we'll leave without them."

Even though Morgan was a large man, she wasn't afraid of him. She set her hands on her hips and glared at him. "Get out of my room."

In a move so swift she barely saw it, he gripped her shoulders. "Damn it, Jade. This is real. Harrod's a madman."

She shoved at his broad chest. "I'm not going anywhere with you. Leave me alone!" Twisting to the side, she slipped out of his hold.

He reached for her, but she dodged again. Her leg hit the edge of the bed, and she lost her balance.

Morgan grabbed for her just as she fell; he landed on the bed—on top of her. Before she could move, he caught her hands above her head and held them pinned to the bed. "Don't fight me, damn it. It won't do any good."

She was too stunned to respond. He was such a big man, she'd been sure his weight would crush her. But it hadn't. He was solid and firm, but not heavy.

Suddenly, she became aware of the way his body covered hers from knee to chest. Through the thin material of her chemise, she could feel the beat of his heart against her breasts. She could feel something firm and warm nestled at the juncture of her thighs.

Heat rushed to her cheeks, and she squirmed, trying to get free. The sensations that streaked through her lower body caused her to gasp—then blush even more. "Get off me," she hissed.

For several seconds, he didn't move, then finally, he rose and pulled her up with him. "Get your things. And put on a cloak."

"I'm not leaving Wilkie."

"I didn't ask you to."

That shocked her. "Where do you think you're taking me—us?"

"We're taking Wilkie to the doctor, then someplace where you'll both be safe." He pulled a portmanteau from the bottom of her wardrobe. "This is all we have time for." He glanced toward the hall. "Where's Wilkie's room?"

"Two doors down. On the right."

"You finish packing what you can." He opened the door and quietly moved down the hall.

If this hadn't been her chance to get Wilkie to the physician, she'd have told Morgan Frazier to jump out the window. But it was her chance. Wilkie's chance.

Morgan came back in a moment later, carrying

Wilkie bundled in his blankets. His gaze skimmed over the cloak she had put on. "Ready?"

"Is he awake?" She tried to see Wilkie's face.

"He's sound asleep. Now, hand me your bag." He extended a hand, still holding her cousin securely.

She looped the handle of the portmanteau over his palm. "Where are we going?"

"I'm not sure yet. But getting Wilkie to a doctor is the first priority." As they walked silently down the hall, Morgan leaned close to her, his voice barely above a whisper. "Can you ride?"

"Yes, why?"

He shook his head, not saying any more until they were outside. "Which way to Stevenage?"

"I thought the doctor was in London."

"He is, but we're going to need more than one horse, and ones that are faster than the old mare."

"You still have money?"

"No."

"Then how are we going to get the horses?"

He gave her a cheeky grin. "I'm going to steal them."

Chapter
9

Morgan left Jade and Wilkie at the edge of Stevenage under an oak tree as he darted behind a row of buildings to reach the livery he'd seen not far down. His gaze scanned the church, the old school, and the marketplace that had been granted in 1281. No one was about.

The entire town had closed up for the night. Only coaching inns and a pub at the other end spilled light onto the boardwalk.

He had told Jade he was going to steal horses, but that hadn't been entirely true. He would leave a note for the proprietor, telling him where to send the bill. Providing Morgan didn't get caught in the act.

It was a sobering thought. One he kept with him as he made his way to the livery and pried open the rear door with a twisted horseshoe he'd found in the alley behind the building.

Moonlight illuminated the interior of the livery through the open doors, and Morgan saw that only one stall was occupied by a mare that didn't look to be in much better shape that Jade's. He released a sigh. It was going to take them all night to get to Samuel's.

The horse nickered as Morgan looked for a bridle and saddle. He found the bridle hanging on a peg by the front doors and a saddle draped over a stall rail.

He'd just slipped the bit into the mare's mouth and secured the head gear when he heard a sound.

His muscles tensed, and he stepped into the shadows, his gaze fixed on the open door. Damn, that's all he'd need, to be arrested as a horse thief.

"Morgan? Are you in there?" Jade's voice whispered into the silence.

He relaxed just long enough to become angry. "What the hell are you doing here? I told you to wait at the edge of town."

"I wouldn't follow your orders if they were engraved in silver. I only came in the first place because of Wilkie, and I only followed *you* because I'm getting worried. He's starting to shake."

"Ah, damn. Lead the horse out. I'll get the saddle."

"I thought you were going to bring two."

"I would have if there'd *been* two."

Jade released a frustrated breath, then led the mare out.

Morgan looked around for something to write on to leave a note. There wasn't even a scrap of paper, or even a nail to scatch a few words on wood. Damn, he'd have to send the money straightaway.

Hoisting the saddle over his shoulder, he walked quickly down the alley.

Something moved off to the side, and he turned his head just in time to see a window curtain fall closed.

A spark of uneasiness went through him. Someone had been watching . . .

What else could go wrong?

He picked up his pace, and when he reached Jade and Wilkie, he wasted no time seeing Jade into the saddle, then gathering Wilkie into his arms and mounting himself.

The ride into London was long and tiring, and like Jade, Morgan was becoming concerned about the way Wilkie was shaking. During the entire ride, he'd held the boy close to his chest, hoping his body heat would warm him.

Jade had ridden alongside in silence, but her gaze had never left her cousin for more than a few seconds.

When they finally reached Sam's cottage, it was more than an hour after dawn, and the tenseness in Morgan's stomach had formed a thick knot. What if Sam couldn't help the boy?

Morgan leapt from the horse, his arms tightly around the youngster as he hurried up the steps and gave the door a swift kick.

Jade was right behind him.

Sam answered immediately, his gray hair rumpled, his nightgown half tucked into his breeches. "Morgan? What is it?" He glanced at Wilkie, then bellowed for his wife. "Norah! Put water on to boil! Take him into the examining room, Morgan." He glanced at Jade. "You, come with me, miss. Tell me what's wrong."

The next few minutes were chaos, with Norah bustling around clanking pans and pumping water, Jade talking rapidly, and Sam pulling at Wilkie's clothes to examine him.

"Put some camphor in a bowl of steaming water, Norah, and bring a towel."

"What's that for?" Jade asked anxiously, watching her cousin.

"To help him breathe easier."

"Is it bad?"

"I've seen much worse. Norah! Bring the laudanum, too." He smiled at Jade. "That will ease the fever and let him rest. He'll be fine in a couple days. Now why don't you and Morgan wait in the drawing room. Have some tea while I tend the young man."

When Morgan saw Jade hesitate, he stepped away from the window in the examining room and took her arm. "Come on. It's this way." Without giving her a chance to protest, he led her down the wide entry to the shelf-lined drawing room, where he motioned her to Sam's chair, then took a seat by the window. The scent of liniment and some medicine he couldn't name lingered heavy in the air.

"Have you known the physician long?" Jade asked.

"My entire life. He brought me into this world— and saw me through a score of injuries and a few bouts with sickness."

"The ague?"

"Once. When I was ten."

"I can't imagine you being that young."

Morgan chuckled. "Well, hold onto your petticoats, beautiful, there were times when I was even younger. I lost my front teeth when I was six, I got muddy on rainy days when I was seven, frightened my nanny with insects when I was eight, and I received my share of punishments like any other child from the time I could walk."

"That makes you sound so . . . normal."

"What the hell did you think? I was born fully grown?"

She laughed. "I guess I did."

"You've had a lot of misconceptions about me, so I imagine one more won't hurt."

"What misconceptions?"

He arched a brow. She really didn't know? "Well, for one, I was going to give the damned beans back when Wilkie and I were using them in the card game."

She rose and walked to the door, glancing down the hall before she turned back to him. "You shouldn't have been gambling at all—at least, not with my cousin."

"It was just for enjoyment."

"That's what my father used to say."

"Damn it, Jade—"

"Here's your tea, Morgan. Miss." Norah walked in behind Jade, smiling in welcome and carrying a tray laden with tea and biscuits.

Morgan bit back an angry retort at Jade and returned Norah's smile. She was a small, thin woman with gray hair pulled into a bun at the crown of her head beneath her mobcap, and she was one of the kindest people Morgan knew. Even after all these years, he couldn't remember a time when she hadn't had a kind word and smile for him.

"I imagine you could use some refreshments after riding all night the way you did." Norah set the tray on a table and sent Jade a warm smile. "There's a chamber across the hall, if you'd like to change, or even lie down for a while."

Jade gathered the front of her cloak closer to her, trying to conceal her nightclothes beneath. "Thank you, Mrs. Verde. I may do that."

Morgan rose. "I'll bring in your bag."

Jade ignored him and reached for a cup of tea.

Norah sent him a curious glance, then returned her attention to Jade. The old woman's eyes twinkled as she tried to contain a grin. "I'm going to see if Samuel wants my help. If either of you need anything at all, let me know."

"Thank you, Mrs. Verde," Jade said with genuine gratitude. "You've been more than kind."

An aged hand closed over the much younger one. "That's what the good Lord put us here for, child."

Morgan couldn't help wondering what the good Lord had in mind when he made Sedgewick.

After retrieving the portmanteau and seeing Jade to the chamber Norah mentioned, Morgan jotted a quick note to the livery in Stevenage for Sam to post, then he looked in on Wilkie. The youngster was resting comfortably, and his fever was almost gone.

With a relieved smile, Morgan sought the privacy of the parlor. He was so tired, he could hardly keep his eyes open. And the thought of lying on Sam's comfortable-looking sofa was too inviting to pass up.

Sighing, he stretched out on the cushiony sofa below an open window and yawned. Lord, it had been almost a week since he'd slept on anything so soft.

As he fought to keep his eyes open, he thought about where to take Jade and Wilkie. He couldn't chance taking them to his apartments or Ainshall until Sawyer was called off. The man was sure to watch those places.

Snuggling deeper into the comfortable sofa, he gave into the need to close his eyes and tried to think where else they could go.

Christian's, he thought sleepily. He'd take the cousins to Royal Oak. . . .

Jade woke to the sound of hens cackling. She blinked and stared around in confusion. Where was she? Then she remembered Wilkie and the physician.

Shoving the hair out of her eyes, she sat up abruptly and glanced out the window. It was still morning? She could have sworn she'd been asleep for hours.

As she stood, she noticed the green frock she'd put on just before she'd lain down. She hadn't intended to go to sleep, only rest for a few minutes. Well, she had slept, but fortunately not for long. It didn't look as if an hour had passed.

Brushing out the wrinkles in her skirt and finger combing her hair, she went to see how Wilkie was doing.

He was sitting up, nibbling on a jam-filled scone.

She stared in disbelief. Good heavens, he'd certainly recovered quickly. "Well, I'm glad to see you're feeling better."

Wilkie frowned. "The doctor said you were sleeping, but I didn't think you'd sleep *that* long." His mouth drew into a pout. "I've been awake for hours."

She smiled at the way he exaggerated. "Well, I'm here, now. And I'm glad to see you're doing better. Whatever Mr. Verde gave you must have worked wonders."

"He made me drink some stuff that smelled like lemon and Uncle Fredrick."

Uncle Fredrick? What did her father smell like to Wilkie? Then she knew. "You mean brandy?"

"Mmm-hmm."

The doctor had given him *alcohol?* That wasn't something she approved of, but remembering how her grandfather had often done the same, and considering how quickly it worked, she wasn't going to complain. "Where is Mr. Verde?"

"Mrs. Verde said he had to go get a babe."

"Deliver."

"What?"

"He went to *deliver* a baby."

"Uh-huh." He sent her a doleful pout. "How come you slept so long? Morgan, too? No one here knows how to play draughts. I spent the whole night staring at books—and they didn't have no pictures. And why didn't you get up for supper? We had potatoes and beef with sauce and—"

"Supper?" Her gaze drifted to the window, and by the sun, it looked to be about seven in the morning. Seven? Wasn't that when they arrived? "Um, Will, I'll be back in a minute." She hurried out, anxious to find Mrs. Verde.

Jade found her in the small cookhouse out back.

"Well, good morning, child. Did you sleep well?"

Apparently so. "Mrs. Verde? How long have we been here?"

The elder woman turned a slab of pork with a fork. "What an odd question. Don't you remember?"

"I think I do. What I mean is, I remember coming here, and lying down, but when I got up, I assumed I'd slept for only an hour or so."

A smile caused deep creases in Norah's cheeks. "Oh, child. You and Morgan both slept round the clock."

Jade could only stare. She'd slept a *whole* day?

"I . . . er, I'm sorry. We didn't mean to imposition you."

"Oh, pooh. You were no imposition at all." She opened a metal door on the brick oven and checked the contents. "Neither was that sweet cousin of yours. He's such a joy."

The aroma of warm bread caused her stomach to groan, and Jade quickly placed a hand over her middle, but she couldn't help feeling a surge of pride on Wilkie's behalf. "Thank you."

She glanced again at the position of the sun. She still couldn't believe she'd slept a whole day. "Where's Mr. Frazier?"

"In the parlor across from the drawing room the last I saw him."

"If you don't mind, I'd like to speak with him for a moment, then I'll help you with breakfast."

"Go, child. There's nothing to do here." Her eyes creased at the corners. "But I do expect you and those young men to do my meal justice with some exemplary appetites."

"I'm sure we will." Feeling a comfortable warmth, Jade returned to the house to find Morgan. She needed to talk to him.

But, when she stepped into the parlor, she halted midstride. Morgan was lying on the sofa . . . sound asleep. Her heart softened when she realized how tired he must be.

He looked so young in sleep, so vulnerable. So devastatingly handsome. Her gaze roamed his stockinged feet that were crossed at the ankles and jutting beyond the arm of the sofa. He was much longer than his bed. His buff breeches weren't as snug as they had been before, and she knew he'd lost weight during his time with them.

Uncomfortable with the thought, and how desperately his shirt needed laundering, she shifted her gaze to his hands folded over his stomach. His fingers were long, the nails short and clean, and she remembered seeing him use a sliver from one of the posts to tend them.

She explored the smooth line of his brow where she could see a faint trace of the pink scar near his temple. Another of Sedgewick's reminders.

Morgan's hair curled around his head in a silken black halo, and his lashes rested on those high, tanned cheekbones. He hadn't shaved, and the dark shadow along his jaw gave him a rugged, masculine appearance that sparked something inside her she couldn't define.

She didn't have to wonder why he slept so soundly. In the week he'd been at Wentworth Hall, he'd slept sitting up every night. He was probably exhausted.

Feeling a rush of guilt for what her cousin had put him through, she backed out of the room and quietly closed the door. There'd be time enough later to tell him she wanted to take Wilkie home. She and her cousins would defend themselves against that Sawyer person.

The noon meal was on the table, when Morgan finally roused himself enough to climb from the sofa and wash up. He couldn't believe he'd slept so soundly. He hadn't done that for years.

Feeling more relaxed than he had in a very long time, he took a seat near a window and smiled at his companions. "Good morning."

"It's past noon, Mr. Frazier," Jade pointed out,

but there was a gentleness in her tone he hadn't heard before.

His gaze met hers, and there was a warmth in her eyes that made his heart kick. "Er . . . good afternoon, everyone," he corrected. "I see Wilkie's awake."

"How did you know that?" Jade asked with a note of surprise.

"I stopped to check on him. He looks a lot better."

"Much better," Samuel said. "His fever broke around two yesterday, and he's been improving since."

Morgan swung to Sam. "Yesterday?"

Jade chuckled. "I know how you feel, Morgan. I felt the same way. It appears that we both slept round the clock."

"Good God. I can't believe it."

"Neither could I." She smiled at Norah. "But it's true."

"Speaking of a day, Morgan," Sam said around a mouthful of hot buttered bread. "I didn't get your note posted yet. I've been on the run since first thing yesterday. Mrs. Franklin had her babe, a boy, and little Walton Daniels fell out of a tree and broke his ankle. Martha Brookhold came down with a bout of dysentery, then—" He waved a hand. "It's been a busy couple days, but I'll try to see your note posted today."

An uneasiness slipped through Morgan when he thought of the person who saw him through the window in the alley. If that person recognized him, or could describe him well enough . . . He shook away his fears. "Thank you, Sam. I'm sure there's no problem. Just post it as soon as possible." He bit into a piece of fried pork. "Is Wilkie well enough to travel yet?"

Sam shrugged. "How far do you want to take him?"

"To the Stanfields."

The physician studied on that for a moment. "That's quite a ways, but as long as you keep him wrapped warm, there shouldn't be a problem. But it might be good if you stop and rest a few times during the journey."

"I will." Morgan shifted his gaze to Jade. "After we eat, you'll need to gather your things. It's going to take us at least five hours, without stops, so I'd like to be on our way soon."

"I'd just as soon take Wilkie home."

Morgan clenched his teeth. What was the matter with her? She knew they were in danger there. "Royal Oak is closer."

"Mr. Frazier . . ."

Ah, hell. He wasn't going to argue the matter in front of Sam and Norah. He couldn't let them know about the abduction. "Fine. If that's what you want, I'll take you home."

The look of surprise on her face nearly made him laugh. He knew she was shocked at his easy acceptance. Of course, she didn't know he was lying, either. He had no intention of taking her back to that run-down manor.

Jade's hand fluttered to the high collar of the green gown she wore, but her confused gaze hadn't left his.

Morgan smiled to himself. So that was how to stop her from arguing. The mere act of agreeing with her left her speechless. He'd have to remember that in the future.

When dinner was over, and the bag tied to the saddle, Morgan and Jade said their farewells, then Morgan bundled Wilkie up to his eyebrows and carried him to the horse.

"Where are we going?" Wilkie asked as Morgan kneed the mare into a slow trot down the winding road.

"To Royal Oak."

Jade jerked her horse around. "What?"

"You heard me."

"But you said—"

He shook his head. "I'd have said *anything* to keep you from arguing in front of the Verdes. Sam is a good friend, Jade, and he wouldn't have taken kindly to knowing I'd been abducted, held at gunpoint, and shackled in chains. But there is no argument about where we're going. Until Sawyer is dismissed, you're staying with me. Do I make myself clear?"

Those eyes of hers flashed green fire. "We took care of ourselves long before you came, Morgan Frazier, and we're quite capable of continuing to do so. *No one* is going to tell me what to do."

Morgan took a chance. A big one. "Fine. If you want to risk your life needlessly, then go ahead. Leave. But Wilkie stays with me."

"I don't want Jade to go," Wilkie blurted nervously.

Morgan gave him a helpless shrug. "Neither do I, but I can't make her stay."

Wilkie turned his head to peek over the edge of the blanket at his cousin. "Jade? You won't leave me, will you?" There was such an anxiousness in his voice, Morgan's heart twisted.

Jade's gaze softened on her cousin, then she

narrowed her eyes on Morgan, and he knew she'd like to kick a hole in him. Still, he couldn't stop a satisfied smile. She was outmaneuvered, and they both knew it.

Loosing a long breath, she shook her head. "I would never leave you, Will. You know that."

Morgan tried to stop smiling, but he just couldn't, and his grin earned him another scalding look, before Jade reined her horse around and nudged it into a trot.

It was dark when they rode up in front of Royal Oak, which was located several miles northwest of London, and Morgan knew he'd never been so glad to see the place. Every muscle in his body ached from guiding the mare while holding onto Wilkie, and Morgan made short work of dismounting and climbing the wide steps.

Jade stopped to stare at the towering columns that supported the upper balcony and the long veranda that ran around the perimeter of the huge brick mansion. Her eyes still filled with wonder, she joined him, then reached for the brass knocker.

One of the doors swung open before she even touched it.

Morgan smiled at the thin, wiry butler dressed in black. "Rawlins, are you related to my father's butler, Liberty?"

"No, Master Frazier. Why do you ask?"

Morgan carried Wilkie over the threshold. "He has a penchant for opening doors before a person has a chance to knock, too."

Rawlins sniffed. "Then, apparently, the man takes his duties quite seriously."

A chuckle climbed Morgan's throat. "It's good to see you, Rawlins."

"It is good to see you, too, sir. But I am afraid you have come at a rather inopportune time. Master Christian is not home."

"I know, but I need a place to stay for a few days."

"Has something happened at Ainshall?"

"No."

The butler sniffed again, then eyed Jade. "I see. Very well, Master Frazier, follow me, and I will take you to your . . . ?" He glanced at Morgan for direction.

"Rooms," Morgan supplied. Even the thought of sharing a chamber with Jade made him squirm.

Still, Rawlins did manage to put them upstairs, in adjoining rooms. Morgan in Christian's old room, and Jade in Christian's sister's room—and much too close for Morgan's comfort. Wilkie, they put in a downstairs bedchamber so Rawlins's motherly wife could look after him. Jade tried to object, but Martha had just clicked her tongue and told Jade she needed rest tonight.

As soon as he saw Jade settled, and Wilkie situated, Morgan went in search of Rawlins and found him in the cookhouse, brewing a pot of tea.

The elder man turned as Morgan entered. "I thought the lady might be in need of refreshments."

"Thank you, Rawlins. I'm sure she'll appreciate your thoughtfulness. Where's Martha?"

The butler checked the water on the stove and spoke without turning. "With the youngster." He gave Morgan a curious glance. "Do I detect something afoot?"

Morgan knew Rawlins wasn't just being nosey. He had known Morgan most of his life, and he was concerned. "I'm afraid so." As clearly as possible, Morgan explained about everything that had happened, exonerating Jade and Wilkie of any wrong-doing.

The butler's face remained expressionless as he poured two cups of tea and carried one to Morgan. "Perhaps you should leave them here while you go talk to your father."

"I had planned on that. I just wanted you to know what was happening before I left. Their lives are in danger, and until I can see the threat removed, someone has to watch after them while I'm away. As much as I hate to, Rawlins, I'm leaving the task to you and Martha."

Rawlins set the remaining cup on a tray and placed a bowl of sugar and a spoon next to the cup before he walked to the door. "You may rest assured, Master Frazier, they will be cared for quite competently." He pushed through the swinging door and turned back. "Do you mind if I summon my grandsons to help tend the guests?"

"Of course I wouldn't mind. How are they, anyway?"

Rawlins smiled a little sadly. "Nearly grown now."

As the butler departed, Morgan drank the last of his tea, then rose and headed for his bedchamber upstairs. It had been several days since he'd had a bath, and he was looking forward to a long, soothing soak. But, more than that, he desperately needed a shave.

Chapter
10

Jade paced the feminine room she'd been given, furious over Morgan's high-handedness. How dare he use Wilkie against her! How dare he *force* her to do his bidding!

She kicked a towel she'd dropped after her bath and sent it tumbling across the Aubusson carpet. Who did Morgan Frazier think he was? He had no control over her. She'd blasted well show him that. The moment the house retired, she and Wilkie would leave—and that should happen soon.

Leaving on the nightdress the butler's wife had insisted on helping her into earlier, she slipped her chemise and cloak on over the soft batiste and pulled on her shoes, her movements quick and angry. Curse the man to Hades!

She thought about sneaking down the hall, but she'd have to pass Morgan's room, and she was afraid he might hear her. Moving to the window, she looked out to see if there was a way down.

A rose trellis climbed the side of the building a

couple feet from the window, and it was near the window to Wilkie's room below.

Still . . . her flesh would probably be in ribbons by the time she reached the bottom—if she didn't fall and kill herself first.

Then she again saw Morgan's satisfied smirk, and her temper rose another notch. A few cuts and scrapes would be worth seeing that grin wiped off his arrogant face.

Deciding to make the trip as hazard-free as possible, she caught the bottom of her nightclothes and cloak and drew them up between her legs, holding them to her stomach as she pulled one of the curtain ties free. Wrapping the drapery cord around her waist, she tied it tight, making certain her clothing was secure and her legs unhampered by yards of material.

Satisfied with her handiwork, she gently eased the window up and climbed onto the ledge, stretching her foot toward the trellis.

The wood creaked as her weight settled on the thin support. Thorns scraped her bare legs, then her hands as she pulled herself fully onto the lattice.

Slowly, gently, she eased down to the next rung.

The trellis moaned. A thorn tore a gouge in her left thigh.

Wincing against the pain, she tightened her hold on the fragile wood and took another downward step.

Her foot had almost reached the next level when she heard an ominous crack. Then the trellis shifted beneath her hands.

Panic gripped her, and she frantically grabbed for the window ledge.

Her fingers caught the edge—and slipped off. Then she was falling . . .

Morgan heard a soft scraping sound and turned his head toward the window. The noise had come from outside.

Tossing the covers off, he strolled naked across the room and opened the window. There wasn't anything out of place that he could tell.

He'd just started to pull back in when something moved to his right.

In stunned disbelief, he watched Jade climb onto the window ledge and stretch her foot toward the rose trellis tacked to the wall.

She was going to get herself killed! Unmindful of his nakedness, he bolted downstairs and tore open the rear door.

He'd just about reached the lawn below Jade when he heard the sound of cracking wood.

His gaze flew upward.

Jade toppled down from the second story.

"No!" he bellowed. He lunged frantically, his arms outstretched.

Her body slammed into his forearms, pitching him forward, and they both crumpled to the ground.

"Ow!" Jade cried as he landed on top of her. "You big oaf, get off me!"

Morgan sprang to his feet and pulled her up. "Are you all right?"

"I was until you fell on me." She jerked free and tore something from around her waist, then brushed her skirts down. "What are you doing out here this time of night?" she hissed.

"Shouldn't that be my question?"

"I was going to get Wilkie and leave."

"And I was stopping you."

"Why?"

"My question, again."

Jade glared up at him. "You know very well why—" Her eyes sprang open in shock. *"My God! You're naked!"*

Until that moment, Morgan had forgotten, but it was too late to do anything now, especially with the way she was staring at his loins.

Heat raced to that spot, and against all his control, he felt himself harden.

Jade's eyes grew wide with what he was sure was horror. It wasn't the first time a woman had stared at him with such shock. Shock that would turn to gut-wrenching fear at the thought of intimacy with him. He'd seen that look more times than he cared to count.

Gripping her arm, he marched her toward the house. "If you hadn't been jumping out of windows in the middle of the night, I wouldn't be standing here in the buff, shocking your tender sensibilities."

When they reached her room, he gently shoved her inside. "If you try to leave again, so help me, I'll tie you to my bed." With a warning glare, he closed the door and stalked toward his own room. Damned woman. She was going to be the death of him. He rubbed his naked chest. If not from catching her falling from two-story windows, then undoubtedly from the ague.

The next morning, Jade awoke to the sound of splashing water and turned over to see two young servants filling a large brass tub from buckets.

When the tub was filled, one of them uncorked a small bottle and dribbled liquid into the steaming water.

Instantly, the scent of roses filled the air.

She closed her eyes and inhaled deeply. She loved roses. They reminded her of her grandmother.

When the servants left, she got out of bed and raced to the door to make sure they were gone. Convinced they were, she made short work of her garment and quickly submerged herself in the heavenly aroma.

Sweet heavens that felt wonderful.

Running a cloth over her bare arms, her thoughts drifted to Morgan . . . and how he'd looked without his clothes last night. For years, she'd sketched pictures of men in the fields without their shirts, but she'd never seen a man without his breeches.

She'd been so amazed by the huge size of his—

Someone turned the latch, and Jade whipped around to watch the door, praying it wasn't Morgan.

Sinking low in the tub to shield herself, she listened warily to the door slowly opening.

Martha, the housekeeper she'd met last night, stepped in carrying a clean bundle of towels. She set them on a trunk at the foot of the bed, then took a lovely pale blue gown out of the armoire. "Master Frazier thought you might like to wear one of Lady Fiona's gowns."

Jade's breath slid out in a relieved whoosh. "Who's she?"

"The Stanfields' daughter. The young miss left a few of her gowns behind when she married and moved to France."

"Is Mr. or Mrs. Stanfield here?" Maybe one of them would loan her a carriage. It would certainly

JADE

make the trip to Wentworth Hall much more comfortable for Wilkie.

"No, mum. Lord Stanfield has been dead for years now, and Lady Stanfield lives in France near Miss Fiona."

Just her luck. Jade eyed the gown Martha spread out on the bed. It looked as if it would fit Jade much better than any of her own, but it was much too short. "Martha? Do you have an extra piece of material I could use for a ruffle?"

"Why, miss?"

As if she didn't know. "I'm sure you noticed my extraordinary height last night. I'm too tall for the dress."

The servant didn't bat an eye. She simply studied the matter, then picked up the gown. "You finish your bath, dear. I will take care of this." In a whirl of gray wool, she was out the door.

Jade's chest swelled with warmth. Since leaving with Morgan, she'd met such wonderful people. People who were nothing like the men in her family.

Leaning her head on the rim, she closed her eyes, thinking about her mother. Even she hadn't had the warmth and kindness Jade had seen in the last few days. Her mother had always cowed around her father. For goodness sakes she'd even submitted to Sedgewick's demands, and Jade couldn't help wondering if fear hadn't made her mother bitter. Her smiles and warm looks in the last years could be counted on one hand.

It saddened Jade to think that her mother was so unhappy, but it hardened her resolve, too. Jade would never marry a man like her father.

The door opened again, and Martha came in carrying the blue gown, now with a lacy blue ruffle dripping from the bottom hem. "Here you go, miss."

Jade was shocked to realize how long she'd been in the tub thinking about her family. "Thank you, Martha. I'll be finished in a few minutes."

"Just give the bellpull a tug when you are ready for my help."

She watched the woman leave, then her gaze again slid to the gown, and she felt a thread of excitement at wearing the lovely dress.

It had been so long since she'd worn anything beautiful. So very, very long.

Morgan stared at himself in the oval mirror above the oak bureau. He still couldn't believe how short Jade had cut his hair. The damn curls sprang up in every direction. It was barely long enough to pull back into a queue.

He couldn't blame her, though. If he hadn't chopped off the sides so short, she wouldn't have had to cut the rest to match.

Cursing himself—and Sedgewick—Morgan gathered the thick mass at the back of his neck and tied it with a leather strip, then he pulled on Christian's shirt, tucking it into his pants as he walked to the door. Damn, it felt good to be clean again.

Morgan emerged from his room at the same instant Jade did hers.

She blinked in surprise as she explored his cleanly shaven face.

He could only stare. Fiona's frock fit Jade like it had been made for her. With stunning accuracy, it molded snugly to each and every one of her lush curves. Until that moment, he hadn't realized how truly full her breasts were, how shapely her hips . . .

She was absolutely stunning.

He was annoyed. She had no right to look that good in someone else's clothes. Hell, she didn't have the right to look that good *period*. Frustrated by the way just looking at her turned him inside out, he sought to distance himself from her. "Well, I see Fiona's castoff fits."

She started at the sound of his voice and tore her gaze from his jaw, but she showed no signs that his barb had struck. In fact, she now looked perturbed at him. "How thoughtful of you to worry about my clothing. After all, it's not as if *you're* responsible for taking me from my home and *trunks.*"

Morgan sighed. The woman was really single-minded. "Jade, listen to me. Contrary to what you think, I didn't take you because I wanted to make you miserable. Damn it, why can't I make you understand that you're in danger? I swear to you, I have no other reason for bringing you here than to keep you safe."

"How gallant."

"I know, I'm a paragon." Wanting to shake some sense into her, he forced himself to be civil. "The gown never looked that good on Fiona."

"Is that a compliment, Morgan? Or a feeble attempt to pacify me?"

"It's a compliment. Damn it, stop looking at me like that."

"Like what?"

"Like you'd never seen a man who'd shaved before—or were you remembering how I looked last night?" Damn, that hadn't occurred to him until now. *Was* that why she'd been staring?

She crossed her arms and glared dead into his eyes. "Your nakedness last night didn't affect me one way or the other, and I was staring at your face, because I had just noted how blasted arrogant you look."

He wasn't sure whether to be angry or amazed at her lack of embarrassment. "Just how many men have you seen without their clothes?"

"Including you? One."

He shook his head. He just didn't know what to think about her. "That's one too many. Come on, they're waiting breakfast on us downstairs." He took her arm and led her toward the stairs, but he was surprised that she didn't make some cheeky remark. What happened? Had he left her speechless again?

The meal passed much too quietly for Morgan, with Wilkie still abed and Jade unusually silent, but at least some of her anger seemed to have lessened. Picking up his cup, he sat back in his chair, sipping tea and watching her over the rim. As he did so, a thought hit him that made him more uncomfortable than it should have. Once Sawyer was no longer a threat, Morgan would have no reason to keep her with him. No reason to listen to her snippy comments, or argue with her, or . . . look into those beautiful green eyes.

"Why are you staring at me, Morgan?"

"You mean like you were watching me last night?" The barb slipped out before he could stop it.

She clamped her lips together.

Wanting to forestall the argument he could feel brewing, he set his cup aside. "I apologize. I didn't realize I was staring. I was thinking of something else."

"And was that 'something else' about returning us to our home?"

"Yes." *More or less.* "I'm going to see my father today. Once Sawyer's dismissed, I'll take you and Wilkie back." Something inside him really rejected that idea.

Jade apparently had no such qualms. "I can't wait to put all this behind me. But a thought just occurred to me, that's frightening at best."

"What's that?"

"Suppose your father seeks recourse."

Morgan knew where that statement came from. The Viscount Ainshall wasn't noted for his compassion when wronged. If she'd lived near London for any length of time, she'd have heard stories about his father. For all his prankish gaiety, Robert Frazier's swift, sometimes fierce, punishments were noted by all.

He wanted to reassure her, but he wasn't entirely certain that he could. His father's anger was as unpredictable as Morgan's own. "My father's a reasonable man for the most part. I don't imagine he'd go against my wishes in this matter." He'd like to give her more reassurance than that, but in all honesty, he couldn't.

Rising, he started for Wilkie's room to tell him he was leaving.

"When will you return?"

He stopped and glanced back. "Why? So you'll know how much time you have to attempt another escape?"

"No. I won't try that again. I'm still sore from the last time. But I would like to know how long it will be before I have to put up with your insufferable presence again."

Any sympathy he'd started to feel for her mishap

last night was crushed under the weight of that remark. "I imagine you won't have to *suffer* my presence again until supper time." With a curt nod, he walked out, controlling the urge to slam his fist into the doorjamb as he passed.

He was still fuming when he arrived at Ainshall several hours later, but the dark mood quickly dissipated when the aging butler, Liberty, didn't beat him to the door. Never recalling that happening before, he curiously ambled through the multitude of rooms in the manor.

Not a single one was occupied.

Where was everyone? Then he remembered it was the Sabbath. They were probably at the small chapel down the road.

Deciding to wait for his father's return, Morgan made for the room he used when he stayed here to change into his own clothes. Christian's were a little too tight—and short, since Morgan, at six feet six, had three inches on him.

When Morgan entered his room, he was shocked to see his father sitting on the bed, his head bent, his hands clutching Morgan's pocket watch, his thumb lovingly stroking the gold surface. There was a haggard, dismal look about him that tore at Morgan's heart.

"Father?"

Robert's head snapped up, and for a heartbeat, he just stared, then with an anguished "Oh, God!" he sprang from the bed and caught Morgan in a hug that nearly crushed his ribs.

Suddenly, he shoved away. "It was a prank, wasn't it? I've been through hell over a *goddamn prank!*"

"No," Morgan assured him. "I didn't plan my own abduction to get even with you." He gave him a tilted smile. "Although, I might have if it had occurred to me."

His father searched his face, apparently trying to ascertain whether Morgan was telling the truth or not, then, obviously coming to a conclusion, he reddened with anger. "Who did it? I'll see the bloody bastard hang!"

The image of Jade's beautiful neck encircled by a hangman's noose didn't set well with Morgan. In fact, it gave him a queasy feeling. "They didn't harm me. Actually, they were quite inept. How else could I have escaped so soon?"

"So soon? It's been over a week."

"I didn't think you'd believe it. And I only stayed because I wanted you to see the need to end these foolish games. I'm tired of pranks. Damn it, I'm tired period."

"You could have just told me."

"Would it have done any good?"

A smile lit his father's blue eyes. "No."

Morgan laughed. "You really did believe I'd been abducted, didn't you?"

"After they delivered your grandfather's pocket watch, I did. I didn't think you would have given that up easily."

Morgan shrugged. "It was either that or a finger."

"I thought you said they didn't harm you."

He held up his hands and wiggled all ten digits. "They didn't."

"But they would have."

He could feel his father's anger starting to build. "No, they wouldn't. They weren't criminals. They were just in desperate need of money. Hell, they didn't even have enough food for a decent meal."

"Are you defending them?"

"I'm not defending what they did, but I do understand their motives. You or I would have done the same in their circumstances, I imagine."

"You, perhaps." Then Robert smiled. "It's good to have you home, son."

"It's good to be here. But I want you to dismiss Sawyer. Why on earth did you hire that maniac, anyway?"

"When you need a job done, you hire the best."

"Even if they're mad?"

"He's not mad. Just single-minded."

"He kills people."

"So do we, through the magistrate and gallows."

"That's different."

Robert arched a brow. "Really? It's all in the name of justice, isn't it?"

Morgan knew there was no arguing with the man. "Well, regardless, I want you to call him off."

"It's not as easy as it sounds. I had to go through several acquaintances before I could contact him. It may take a while."

That didn't disappoint Morgan like it should have. In fact, all he could think about was that Jade would have to stay with him for a while longer. "Well, do it as quickly as possible. And there's another matter I want you to attend."

"What's that?"

"I want you to send a healthy sum to the owner of the livery in Stevenage."

"Why?"

Morgan explained about the excursion with the "borrowed" horse.

His father's eyes widened with surprise. "You actually *stole* the horse?"

Morgan knew how unlike him that behavior was,

but he'd done a lot of uncharacteristic things since he met Jade. "I was desperate, and I'll leave a note with Liberty to post to my solicitor. You'll be reimbursed in a few days."

His father smiled, and Morgan could have sworn he saw a flicker of something in the man's eyes. Praying he was wrong, Morgan headed for the liquor-stocked sideboard in the parlor, suddenly needing a strong shot of brandy.

Following at a leisurely pace, his father joined him, his mood considerably brighter.

After catching up on the latest news, which amounted to next to nothing, Morgan started for Royal Oak, then changed his mind. There were a couple of things he wanted to pick up in London.

Besides, his absence until tomorrow afternoon would make Jade deliriously happy.

When he reached London, he headed for Miss Bovier's dressmaking shop even though it was closed for the night. He wanted a decent riding habit for Jade, something that might curb that waspish tongue for a while, then he would pick up his hellish horse, Midnight Flame.

Since Morgan planned to be at Royal Oak for a few days, he might as well work with the beast, if the animal hadn't forgotten everything Morgan had taught him so far.

With a horse like Flame, one never knew.

Jade gripped the window curtain in the parlor as she stared down the long drive leading to Royal Oak. It was after midnight, and Morgan still hadn't returned.

Slapping the curtain back into place, she crossed to the fireplace and sat on the hearth. Why was she driving herself to insanity with worry? Curse it all, she *knew* where he was. Like her father, Morgan had gone to the clubs at the first opportunity. It was a compulsion men just couldn't seem to control.

What had she expected? That Morgan would be different? Not likely.

Checking on Wilkie and finding him sleeping soundly, Jade figured he must be exhausted after the score of games she'd played with him. He was improving rapidly, and for that, she would be eternally grateful to Morgan.

Not wanting to feel charitable toward him, she went to her room and changed into her nightclothes. Fleetingly she thought about leaving, but she'd told Morgan she wouldn't try again, and she would keep her word. *Hers* meant something.

She blew out the candle and climbed into bed, then drew up the covers. Blankly, she stared into the darkness, trying not to let Morgan's actions bother her. But only one thought kept darting into her head.

Why couldn't he have been different?

Morgan reined his horse to a halt in front of Royal Oak around one the next afternoon. He was tired and damned sick of battling Flame's lead rope all the way from London. When he took the beast out later today, he was going to run some sense into him. Stuffing one of Miss Bovier's packages under his arm, he tied the reins to a hitching post, then sprinted up the steps.

Jade met him at the door, her mouth set in a grim line, her eyes heavy with disappointment. "Was your excursion profitable?"

He was so filled with the sight of her, he didn't hear what she said. "What?"

She gave him a disgusted look. "Never mind. What did your father say about Sawyer?"

Morgan shifted the parcel, then closed the door and walked beside her toward the parlor. "It'll take time before he can contact the man."

"How long?" she demanded, her gaze trying to stay focused on him instead of the paper-wrapped bundle.

Morgan smiled to himself. "I'm not sure. Apparently, it's a complicated task to reach Sawyer. How's Wilkie?"

"Better than I am. He's playing draughts with Rawlins's grandson." She massaged the back of her neck, causing her dark hair to ripple over her arm. "When is this going to end?" Her gaze drifted again to the package. "And what *is* that?"

He smiled at the curiosity she wasn't able to hide. "It's a gift for you."

She eyed him warily. "What, a gag and chains?"

"I was tempted, but I bought something more practical." He handed her the parcel.

Her expressive face revealed the battle that was going on inside her. She was torn between excitement and reservation as she untied the string and shook out the royal blue riding habit and trio of petticoats.

"Morgan! Where—"

"I got them in London. Now, perhaps I won't have to listen to any more remarks about your lack of clothing."

"You didn't have to do this—not that I don't appreciate it. But—"

"Don't carry on too much, or I'll start thinking you like me."

"There's no chance of that."

He laughed at her impish tone and decided to wait until later to tell her about the other clothes. "Listen, why don't we see what Christian's stable has to offer for you? Maybe a ride would help your disposition."

"Nothing's going to do that." She ran a slender hand over the garment. "And I'd have to change."

"I'll wait."

She offered a small smile as she started to her bedchamber, then she stopped and turned. "Which one is Christian, by the way? I saw portraits of several men on the wall of the stairwell. But I didn't know which one was our absent host."

"He's the youngest."

"The handsome one with the gray eyes and black hair?"

"You're very observant."

"Well, he is remarkably attractive. I'd have to be dead not to notice that."

There was a twisting feeling in his gut, and he had a strong suspicion that it was jealousy. Yet, since he'd never truly experienced that particular emotion, he couldn't be certain. But he knew he didn't like it. "Don't worry about my *remarkably attractive* friend. Just get changed."

Jade loved the way the riding habit fit, but she knew that Morgan had only purchased the garment because he felt guilty about his jaunt to the clubs. Her father had often brought her mother gifts to make himself feel better.

Forcing the disturbing thoughts aside, she glanced at the row of stalls, amazed at the horses in the Stanfield stables. Not even when her mother inherited Grandfather's money had they owned such magnificent animals. Her Arabian gelding was an excellent breed, but nothing compared to these. The Stanfields had to be one of the richest families in England.

Her gaze drifted to a particularly beautiful thoroughbred stallion in the center stall. He was a shimmering black with a russet mane and a stance that proclaimed a heritage of nobility. His lines were perfect, his muscle tone flawless.

"Is that Mr. Stanfield's horse?"

"Midnight Flame belongs to me. I picked him up from my stables in London. I figured while I was here, I could work with him."

Considering the animal, and the expensive riding habit he'd bought her, maybe the Stanfields weren't one of the richest families in England after all. "May I ride him."

"If it was any horse but this one, yes. But he's more animal than even I can handle most of the time. My father gave him to me as a prank, and the horse has the disposition of a crazed bear. I've been working with him for over a year, and I'm only now to the point where I can sit in the saddle without being thrown."

"I have a way with animals. Maybe I can help." At least she had with the Arabian before her father sold him.

Morgan shook his head, causing a curl to topple onto his brow. "Flame isn't a normal animal."

Jade didn't argue the point, but she knew she could ride the horse. In fact, she might, if she changed her mind and attempted another escape.

No, she decided. She wouldn't steal from Morgan. Not because of any misplaced honor, but because she was quite sure he could find his way to Wentworth Hall again.

Chapter

11

Jade sat atop the horse Morgan had saddled, her legs at a comfortable position in the stirrup that he'd lengthened to fit her long leg, the sidesaddle reasonably comfortable, the blue linen habit soft against her skin. But what gave her pause was Morgan's stallion. She couldn't believe the animal was so volatile. The horse snorted and stomped and tossed its head, refusing to let Morgan command him.

Still, she couldn't help but admire Morgan's ability and patience. It made her wonder again why the horse behaved that way, since she was sure that Morgan had never been cruel to him. "How old was Midnight Flame when you got him?"

Morgan pulled back on the reins as Flame tried to ram the stall gate. "A yearling."

"Who had him before that?"

Tightening his thighs as the animal reared up, Morgan shook his head. "I wish I knew."

"It might be wise if you found out. If you knew who had him and how he was treated, you might learn the reason behind his poor obedience."

Morgan glanced at her, his eyes alight with humor. "Been studying animal behavior long?"

"No. My cousins. I know Wilkie's behavior is a matter of birth, but I can only attribute Sedgewick's to the fact that he worships my father and wants to be just like him."

"Is that bad?"

She shrugged. "My father has his faults like any other man, but he's not truly a bad sort. Still, he's not one I'd think others should wish to emulate, either." Unless, of course, they had a penchant for gambling, she added silently. Which Sedgewick most certainly did.

At the thought of her father's games, and all they had cost them, her mood turned black. Once her father was out of prison, she would make sure he never laid hands on a deck of cards again. She didn't know how, but she would.

"Was your father the only male influence in Sedgewick and Wilkie's life?"

"Most of it, yes."

"Then it's only natural for one or both of them to want to be like him."

That thought didn't relieve her. "You're probably right." Wanting to change the subject, she did so by nodding toward the door. "Are we going for a ride?"

Morgan glanced down at the big beast under him and sighed. "Might as well." Tightening his legs, he gripped the reins and turned the animal toward the opening. Flame balked several times before relenting to Morgan's firm rein.

Still the stallion sidestepped and pranced anxiously, then even more so as they wove their way into the woods behind the house.

"I've never seen a woods like this around here," Jade said, scanning the shadows.

"Christian's great-grandfather wanted his own forest for hunts, so he had the trees planted."

"It's beautiful."

He smiled as he kneed the stallion into a canter.

As they rode, she focused on the wonderful feel of the young mare beneath her. But it brought back memories of her Arabian and the Equestrian Competition she'd planned to enter. Unfortunately, by the time the date for the event was set, there were no longer funds for the entry.

Not wanting to dwell on her unhappiness, she peeked at Morgan, and in that instant she knew why she hadn't been able to blame him for what happened. If it hadn't been Morgan that night, it would have been someone else another night. Regardless of the day or time or opponent, destitution would have overtaken them sooner or later.

"Have I grown fangs?" Morgan asked suddenly.

Jerked from her thoughts, she realized she'd been staring at him. A little embarrassed and trying to make light of the situation, she pretended to study his mouth. "Hum, yes. I believe I do see short ones."

He burst into laughter, a deep, vibrating sound that made her feel good all over. In fact, she'd be quite content to sit for hours and just listen to him. It was an unsettling thought, at best. She didn't want to feel anything—good or otherwise—about Morgan Frazier.

He was still grinning as he wrestled his mount into an open field. "Come on, woman. Let me show you one of Flame's finer points. I'll race you to the other side." Without waiting for her answer, he nudged the stallion, and it broke into a gallop, then a dead run. By the way the animal obeyed so easily, it was obvious that Flame loved to race.

Jade didn't move for several seconds as she watched Morgan become one with the horse. The unleashed power radiating from both man and beast was exhilarating.

With a smile of her own, she urged the mare into a brisk canter, then a full gallop.

Wind whipped at her clothes and tousled her hair, but she didn't mind. For the first time in years, she felt alive and free. Her troubles drifted away on the warm afternoon air.

Morgan was waiting for her when she finally reached the other line of trees, his hand still firm on the reins. "It's about time," he teased. "What took you so long?"

"I was watching you—I mean—the stallion run. He seems to enjoy speed."

Morgan ran an appreciative hand along the sleek neck. "That's the one thing about him I find acceptable. If only he excelled as well in other areas—like behavior."

"He's behaved fairly well so far. He's allowed you to ride him. At least that's a start."

Morgan snorted. "Only because he's come to realize that I'm too damned big to throw."

Sensing a note of disgust in his voice when he spoke about his size, she couldn't help wondering if it bothered him like it did her. Apparently, it did. She eased her leg off the pommel and slid to the ground. "What's that?" She pointed to a row of white fencing she'd noticed in another section of trees.

Morgan dismounted and tied the stallion's reins

to a branch, then walked up next to her, his gaze fixed on the trees. "The family graveyard. Several generations of Stanfields are buried there."

Jade shivered and rubbed her upper arms. She really didn't like graveyards. "I think we should go back now."

"Not yet. There's something I want to show you."

"What?" Surely not one of the graves . . .

"It's a surprise. Come on, woman. Mount up." Closing his hands around her waist, he lifted her and set her atop the mare's saddle as if she were a child, and again she experienced that dainty feeling. It was a unique sensation, and something warmed inside her. Something she shouldn't be feeling for Morgan Frazier.

They rode through the forest for quite a while before they finally came to another clearing.

"There's my surprise," Morgan announced, gesturing to a small pond lined with rocks and thick foliage. Not far from the water sat a white gazebo nestled in the trees at the edge of a grassy glen.

"It's beautiful."

He dismounted and tied the stallion to a branch, then reached up and caught her by the waist. "You won't believe how warm the water is."

She placed her hands on his shoulders as he lifted her down, and their bodies touched. Streaks of heat raced through her, and she drew in a sharp breath.

Morgan set her gently on her feet. "Did I hurt you?"

Lie. "Um, just a bit. I guess I'm still tender from that fall."

Real concern shadowed his heart-stopping blue eyes. "Maybe you should see Sam."

140

"No. No, I'm fine. I'm just tender is all." She avoided his eyes as she stepped away from him. "Did you say something about warm water?"

He hesitated for a moment, then turned toward the pond. "Right there."

The horses whinnied behind them as she and Morgan crossed the cushiony grass to the pool's edge.

Jade inhaled the pungent scent of damp foliage, then gaped in surprise when she saw a small waterfall nearly concealed by thick ferns and overgrown ivy. "How wonderful." She knelt and swirled her fingers through the water. "What makes it so warm?"

"It's fed by a hot spring on top of that hill." He nodded toward a heavily wooded knoll behind the pond. "Christian and I found it when we were still in knee britches."

"May I see it?"

"Are you sure you're not too sore to make the climb?"

Jade felt a blush steal into her cheeks. "I'll be fine."

"Come on, then." He took her hand. "The view alone is worth the effort." He led her around the pond and through the trees. The grass muffled their footsteps, and she could feel the warm mist from the falls as they climbed higher, then came to the small pool that led into a stream running down the hill.

She marveled at the steaming water bubbling out of the ground.

Morgan placed his hands on her shoulders and turned her to see the view. "Look down to the right, and you can see the glen from here."

She could. A small emerald dale surrounded for miles by a thick, dark forest. "It's magnificent. How far are we from Royal Oak?"

"Several miles."

Her gaze fixed on a spot in the glen, and she frowned. "Morgan?"

"Hmm?" He had turned back to look at the spring.

"Where are the horses?"

He raised his arm to gesture to their location. "They're right . . ." His eyes widened. "Ah, damn it. I'm going to turn that miserable stallion into glue!" He grabbed her hand, and all but ran down the hill.

When they reached the glen again, their fears were confirmed. The horses were gone.

Morgan swore roundly and slapped a tree branch. "I knew I shouldn't have taken that hellion horse. I *knew* it!"

"Why is the mare gone, too?"

"She pulled free and followed the stallion, I imagine."

"What are we going to do?"

"We don't have a whole lot of choices, Jade. We can stay here or walk. And if we start walking now, we might reach the manor by dark. Barring any unforeseen setbacks."

Jade hadn't known what Morgan meant by "unforeseen setbacks" until a few minutes later. That's when Morgan turned to say something to her and stepped in a chuckhole.

She knew she'd never heard such language as when he dropped to the ground and grabbed his right ankle, cursing everything from horses to insects.

"Help me get my boot off," he growled, then broke into another string of curses.

Jade could tell by his eyes he was in severe pain, so she overlooked his spicy language and carefully knelt at his feet. "Do you think it's broken?"

"It damn well feels like it." Then softer, "But I think it's only sprained. Pull, will you?"

She was a little nervous about touching him for fear of hurting him worse, but she closed her hands around the heel and toe of the boot and tugged gently.

Morgan's sharp curse startled her, and she immediately let go.

"Jesus, that hurts," he hissed through clenched teeth. Moisture beaded on his brow, and he closed his eyes for several long seconds before he finally nodded. "All right. Try it again."

"Maybe we should cut it off?"

"My leg?"

"Very funny. You know I meant the boot."

"I don't carry a blade. Do you?"

"No."

"Then what are we going to cut it off with?"

"All right, Morgan. Take a deep breath and grit your teeth." Placing her hands in the same positions she had before, she gave a swift tug.

Morgan flinched and his face paled, but he didn't utter a sound. She was sure his silence was for her benefit.

That didn't make her feel any better. His quiet suffering was worse than his cursing. She gave another gentle pull and his heel slipped some. "Almost there." When he didn't respond, she glanced up to see that he'd closed his eyes again, and his lips were pressed together so tightly that a pale ring had formed around his mouth.

Empathy moved through her in waves, and she loosened her hold.

"Don't stop," he said on a ragged breath. "Just get the damned thing off."

There was so much pain in his voice, she had to bite her lip to keep from cursing for him. Wishing she didn't have to cause him more pain, she slowly inched the boot off his foot.

Through his white stocking, she could see how nicely his foot was shaped, long and slender, his leg blending perfectly into his ankle, but the unnatural swelling looked very, very painful. "I wish we had something cold to put on that."

"Try my hands, they're pretty cold and clammy about now."

"I'm serious."

"So am I." He placed his palms against her cheeks.

They were damp, and cold from sweat, but so very gentle. Her belly fluttered at the sensations that simple gesture caused. "That's the only thing I know to do for a sprain."

"Take off your petticoat."

"What?"

"I need some strips of cloth to bind my foot so we can go on."

"You can't walk on that ankle."

"Do you plan to carry me?"

"As if I could . . ."

"Then how else are we going to get home?"

"I'll go for help. I have to. Wilkie—"

"You don't know the way—and don't worry

about your cousin. Martha and Rawlins will take care of him."

She really hated it when he was logical. And there really wasn't much else they could do. Stepping behind a stand of trees, she removed one of the new petticoats and reluctantly tore it into strips. Joining him again, she began looping strips around his injured leg. "After I finish this, we'll rest for a while."

"The more I sit, the more it's going to swell."

"And it won't swell if you walk on it?"

"Of course it will."

"Then we have no choice but to elevate your foot and wait for someone to rescue us."

"More of your grandfather's teachings?"

"As a matter of fact, yes."

"And you think we'll be rescued?"

"Of course." She sounded much more certain than she felt.

"By whom?"

"Rawlins, most likely."

Morgan shook his head. "He'll think we've gone to Ainshall. We have to try to make it back."

That didn't sound like such a good idea to her. "How far do you think you can walk before you can't bear the pain any longer?"

"I have no idea."

"Well, I'll wager it won't be far, so if we're going to walk any distance, it might as well be toward the pond. At least that way, when you collapse, we may die from the elements or hunger, but we won't die of thirst."

Morgan stared at her in disbelief. Any other woman would be in hysterics by now, not thinking along reasonable lines. But he was quickly finding out Jade was far different than any woman he'd ever known. The longer he knew her, the more she surprised him. The more he liked her.

"All right, beautiful. The pond, it is."

Chapter
12

When it became too painful for Morgan to walk with a stick, he leaned on Jade, and she was assailed by the firmness of his muscles, his clean leathery scent. Who would think just a smell or touch could make a person go mushy inside?

Another unique experience.

When they reached the glen, she left him on the lower step of the gazebo, then raced into the trees to find a log or stump she could use for a footstool. The benches in the gazebo were narrow for his big body, but he would have to sit on one to brace his foot, and he certainly couldn't relax for long without something comfortable to lean against, even if it was the back of a bench.

As she walked, she glanced down at her skirt. She was already missing one petticoat, and she would soon take off another one. When she found a log, she needed to use the material to cushion Morgan's foot. Besides, who was there to see? Morgan was in too much pain to notice.

She searched for nearly a half hour before she

finally found one suitable for a footstool and small enough for her to carry.

Satisfied with her booty, she braced the log under one arm and turned to go back, but something occurred to her that caused her step to falter. If no one came to look for them, she and Morgan would have to spend the night in the glen together.

Alone.

Morgan checked his pocket watch for the third time and glanced again at the line of trees Jade had disappeared into more than a half hour ago. What the hell was taking her so long? She'd only gone to find a lousy piece of wood, for bloody sakes.

Cursing against another stab of pain, he massaged his ankle and glared at the trees. He had to do something.

Hoisting himself up onto his good foot, he grabbed a gazebo post for balance and winced against another jolt. He swallowed and glanced around for the crutch he'd used.

It leaned against the railing within arm's reach.

Recalling how it dug into his underarm, he peeled off his shirt and rolled it into a ball to use as padding.

Whether the padding worked or not was of no consequence. Even if he had to discard the crutch altogether, he was going after Jade.

"What are you doing?" Jade hissed when she saw Morgan coming toward her, his hand gripping the crutch, his shirt tucked under his arm, his bare chest gleaming with perspiration.

He stopped in his tracks. "Where the hell have you

been? I thought something had happened to you—or *would*. Damn it, what took you so long?"

The ungrateful blackguard. "Stop growling at me. I was trying to find what I *thought* would make you comfortable!"

"Did you have to go clear to London to find it?"

"If I had, I wouldn't have come back." She tossed the log on the ground. "Here's your footstool, Mr. Frazier."

"Damn it, Jade, I'm sorry. I was worried. You don't know these woods, and I was afraid—Ah, hell. Never mind." He hobbled toward the log.

He was worried about her. Truly worried. The knowledge made her heart beat a little faster, and she suddenly realized how easy it would be to fall in love with this man. Horrified by the thought, she quickly reached for the log. "I'll get that."

He covered her hand with his. "I'll carry it." He grinned, showing those boyish creases. "You can carry me."

Her hand tingled beneath the warmth of his, and she fought for control. "I think you're getting the better end of the deal." Reluctantly, she wedged her shoulder under his arm, trying not to notice the leathery scent about him. Which was absolutely futile.

When they finally reached the glen, she helped Morgan up the steps and onto one of the benches. He'd grown pale, and moisture dotted his forehead.

Still her erratic heartbeat hadn't calmed. Her senses were filled with him.

Busying herself by bracing his foot on the log and using her petticoat as a cushion, she straightened. "I'm going to look for something to eat."

"Where?"

She pulled her gaze from his handsome face and nodded toward the mountain they'd climbed earlier. "Up there. I think I remember seeing some wild radishes."

"I'd rather go hungry."

"That's a likely possibility." Ignoring his frown, she headed up the hill, willing her heart to behave and firmly telling herself to stop thinking about him.

Focusing on the task ahead, she carefully made it to the small hot spring. Just as she'd remembered, there was a clump of radishes not far from the edge of the water, and she knelt to gather them. They weren't much, but as she'd learned over the last few months, just about anything would do when you're hungry.

Another of many reasons to stop the foolish thoughts about Morgan.

Using the front of her skirt as a tote, she collected the early vegetables and made for the gazebo.

Morgan was still sitting right where she left him, tightening the cloth around his ankle. "Find any?"

Her heart did an odd little flip at the way he looked with a lock of dark hair curling over his brow and his tanned shoulders gleaming in the late afternoon sun.

"Jade? Did you find the radishes?"

She flushed when she realized she'd been staring at him so intently she'd forgotten to answer him. "Yes. Some good-sized ones, too."

"Wonderful." His tone was less than appreciative.

"If you don't want any, I imagine I could pick some of those green berries I saw."

"Sure. Then I could have a stomachache to go with the rest of my pains."

"This just isn't your day, is it?"

"Apparently not."

Holding onto a smile, she went to the small pool and washed the radishes, then placed them on a piece of bark and carried them to him. "Your dinner, sir."

"Where's yours?"

"I'm not very hungry yet. I'll have some later."

He watched her for a moment, then the corner of his mouth quirked. "Not your favorites, either, eh?"

"Not until I'm starving." Her gaze drifted to the darkening sky. "Since we're apparently going to spend the night here, I'm going to fix us something to sleep on."

"Out of what?" He bit into a radish, and it crunched between his strong teeth.

"Pine needles and petticoats."

He chewed quickly and swallowed. Then he glared. "Don't even think about taking anything else off. I'm not a damned saint."

"What's that supposed to mean?"

"It means, Miss whoever-the-hell-you-are, that my urge to make love to you is barely controllable as it is. I can't handle any more temptation."

Jade's whole body tingled, but her mouth refused to work. He wanted to make love to her? Good Lord. What was she supposed to say to that?

Ignore it, an inner voice warned. He's just irritated and looking for an argument. He didn't mean it. Swallowing against a tightness in her throat, she turned away. "If you don't want a pallet to sleep on, that's up to you. But *I'm* going to make me one." Not daring to look at him, she began gathering pine needles and limber ivy vines. But her heart was going crazy inside her chest. The mere thought of being held in those strong arms again, feeling his mouth on hers, was enough to make her tremble.

As she worked, she peeked at Morgan out of the corner of her eye and saw that he was watching her as he munched on the radishes.

Her heart skipped another beat, and she quickly jerked her attention back to her task. Once she had the makeshift bed made, she straightened, not looking at him again. "Turn the other way so I can remove my underskirt."

"No."

What was he doing to her? She didn't want to find out. Clenching her teeth, she marched down the steps and into the trees, where she removed her undergarments and draped them over her arm.

Keeping her eyes averted, she returned and spread the taffeta and satin over the pine bed, then immediately climbed between the coverings, turning her back to him as she pulled one up to her chin.

"You don't listen well, Jade—and we both might be sorry because of it."

She didn't want to know what that meant. *She didn't want to know!*

Closing her eyes, she pressed her lips tightly together. Go away, Morgan, she silently pleaded. Just go away.

His movement startled her, and she had to stop herself from turning toward him. She listened to his harsh expulsion of breath as he rose, then his uneven gait when he hobbled down the steps. Only a couple of minutes passed before she heard the distant splash of water and knew he'd gone to wash up or bathe.

She tried not to envision how he'd look dripping

with water. For all the good it did. Again and again she could picture the smooth, hard muscles of his arms and chest, and she could imagine what they'd look like coated with glistening droplets.

The mere vision caused her stomach to tighten, and the thought she'd tried so hard to avoid crept back in.

He wants to make love to you.

Morgan was still damning himself for that remark to Jade, but it was the truth. Since he'd set eyes on her, he'd wanted to make love to her, and the urge had become so strong tonight, he hadn't been able to take any more.

Even now, he could still see the outline of her firm little rear end after she'd removed her underclothes and made the bed. His body had reacted just as he'd feared it would, and he'd needed to go to the pond, just to get away from her. Just to ease some of the fierce desire.

Splashing water on his face, he tried to wash the sensation away. It didn't help. All he could think about was kissing that soft mouth, sliding his hands over her firm breasts and tight rear end.

She'd be terrified if she could read his mind, he thought morosely. He remembered her expression when she'd seen him without his clothes. He remembered the look of horror. She'd swoon if she could see his body now, with the way he'd hardened.

Damn it, he had to stop thinking about making love.

Swiping the water off his face and chest, he climbed to his feet, ignoring the stab of pain that shot up his leg. He limped to the gazebo and eased onto the bench, wishing there was somewhere else to go. Being this close to her wasn't healthy for either of them.

He leaned his head back and closed his eyes, but in the darkness, he could hear her soft breathing and the swish of satin as she shifted.

Trying to focus on something else, he listened to the rustle of leaves, the trickle of the falls, and the scampering of a small animal. It didn't do any good. Jade still dominated his thoughts, and her misconceptions about him were starting to grate. Maybe that's what he needed to take his mind off sex.

"Jade, I'm not a gambler like your father." There, he'd said it, and it felt good to get that aggravating misunderstanding off his chest.

She sat up, and in the moonlit darkness, he could see her looking in his direction. "Aren't you?"

"No."

"You mean you don't play cards?"

"I do, but—"

"You don't wager money?"

The breath hissed out of him. "Yes, but—"

"You don't wager more than you should?"

"Damn it, Jade—"

"Wait, I know. You don't ever stay out late or not come home at all, right?"

The woman was deliberately misunderstanding him, and doing her best to make him angry. "I have."

She brushed the hair out of her eyes. "Then how can you say you're not like my father?"

"I wouldn't let the people I love suffer because of something I did." He smiled to himself. Get around that one, beautiful.

"Not yet, you wouldn't. My father didn't either, in the beginning."

She really was starting to irritate him. "Maybe we should talk about you for a minute."

"What about me? I don't gamble."

"Who are you?"

There was a long silence, then he saw her straighten a fold in the petticoat in a nervous gesture. "You don't want to know."

"I wouldn't have asked if I didn't."

She lay back down, and for several moments, he thought she wasn't going to answer, then he heard her nearly inaudible sigh. "You'll find out anyway, so I guess it won't matter. My name is Lenora Jade Wentworth."

Wentworth? Morgan frowned. He knew that name. He tried to think from where . . . then it hit him. He held the deed to *Wentworth Hall* as a marker. "Son-of-a-bitch!"

"I told you you didn't want to know."

"Bloody hell. So *that's* why you abducted me!"

"I had nothing to do with that."

Morgan wanted to pace, and rage, and slam his fists into posts, but his foot hurt too much to do any of those. Still, he managed to smack his palm down on the bench. "Hell and damnation! I wasn't to blame for Wentworth's incarceration. I gave him until May not only to pay the marker for his home, but his other ones as well."

"He had other debts besides yours. And Sedgewick didn't care whether you were to blame or not. He merely wanted to pay for Father's release."

That gave Morgan pause. "Where's he going to get the money now?"

"I don't know."

Morgan was afraid he did. Sedgewick would steal the money from someone . . . but who? He leaned back again and tried to calm his riotous emotions. Lenora Jade Wentworth. Fredrick Wentworth's daughter. Who would have thought? Morgan certainly wouldn't have.

"Morgan?"

"What?"

"Since we're clearing the air, so to speak, I'd like to know what happened to you in the cellar."

Now there was an appealing subject. "You saw what happened."

"Yes. But why?"

"I react that way because of an accident I had when I was four. I fell into an abandoned well, and half of it caved in on me." Morgan could feel himself starting to sweat, just thinking about it. "I was covered up to my face in dirt, with only a small space to breathe out of. I stayed like that for two days while my father and his men worked round the clock trying to dig me out."

He glanced out over the moonlit glen, trying not to let the horror of that day overwhelm him, but he could already feel his chest growing tight. "Now, whenever I'm surrounded by walls, I can't breathe, I can't—Damn. I don't want to talk about this."

"I can understand why. You must have been frightened to death."

"Something like that." What he'd actually been was paralyzed. He hadn't even been able to help dig his way out.

"I imagine your father was very upset."

"He nearly fired every field hand on the place because they hadn't filled the well in—even though none of them were aware it was there. Then, when I showed the first signs of my phobia about enclosed spaces, he had extra windows added to every room in the manor."

"He must have loved you very much."

Morgan smiled. "He still does. Though, by the rotten pranks he pulls on me, no one would guess." Jade Wentworth. Jesus, he still couldn't believe it.

"What started the pranks?"

"I told you, tradition. Surely your family has some kind of tradition, too. A way of celebrating holidays, or special occasions?"

"Not that I'm aware of. My mother never wanted to entertain much, because she always ended up embarrassed when Father disappeared to the nearest game."

"What was your mother like?"

"Mother?" He saw her smile. "Beautiful and quiet. Never in anyone's way. And she was very, very small. Nothing like me."

"Oh, I don't know. You're beautiful." He chuckled. "Of course, *petite* and *quiet* aren't words I'd use to describe you."

"*Tact* isn't one to describe you, either."

He couldn't stop another chuckle. That's one of the things he liked about her. She had a quick, sharp wit. But that wasn't *all* he liked, and his body was making him very aware of the fact. In the moonlight, he could see the swell of her breasts over the bodice of the riding habit, the way the material made her skin appear milky white, the way her dark hair tumbled around her shoulders.

He needed to get away again.

"Listen. Why don't you try to get some sleep. I'm going to soak my foot in the pond for a while."

"I hope it doesn't do more damage." She lay down and turned her back to him. "Good night, Morgan."

That was easy for her to say. There wasn't going to be anything good about it as far as he could tell. Not when the only thought in his head was about lying down beside her and making slow, sweet love to Lenora Jade Wentworth.

Pulling himself to his feet, Morgan hobbled down the steps toward the pond. He had to get hold of himself.

If he could.

Chapter

13

Jade came awake to the feel of something warm on her stomach and between her legs. She blinked and tried to focus in the semidarkness, then Morgan's leathery scent drifted over her, and she slowly turned her head to see him lying next to her, his arm draped over her stomach, his uninjured leg nestled between hers, his breathing deep and solid.

He was sound asleep.

She lowered her gaze to the shadow of his mouth. Although she was unable to see the entire outline in the dim light, she remembered its beautiful shape. Its softness.

Tiny wings beat against her middle. She shouldn't be staring at him like this. She shouldn't be remembering things about his mouth. *Especially* not how incredibly soft his tongue had been that day in the stables at Wentworth Hall.

The fluttering grew to frightening proportions.

Turn over, her mind shouted. *Turn your back to him and keep it there! Right now. Don't wait another second!*

SUE RICH

She had just started to turn when Morgan's arm moved upward from her stomach. She froze, hoping he'd withdraw. Suddenly, the heat of his palm covered her breast.

An explosion of desire slammed into her most private place, and she caught her breath at the force of the sensation. She'd never felt anything so frightening—or exciting—in her entire life.

Morgan moaned and closed his fingers around her breast, and she thought she'd melt into a puddle of flesh and pine needles.

She tried to take a slow, deep breath to calm herself, but the air caught in her throat when she felt her nipple grow hard and pebble against his palm. And it was so sensitive, she could swear she could feel the veins in his hand pulsate against the tip.

She didn't know what to do. She certainly didn't want to move and wake him. That's all she'd need, for him to find them in such an intimate position. Heaven only knew what would happen if he did— and she didn't want to find out.

Do something, her conscience screamed.

Do what?

Push him away.

I'll wake him.

Chance it.

She turned her face toward the circular roof, where slivers of silver light seeped in through the cracks. She studied them for several moments, then hit on an idea. What if she pretended to be asleep and rolled over—away from him? That might work.

Closing her eyes, and praying for strength, she slowly rolled to one side.

Morgan's hand slipped from her breast, only to

cover the other one. Another rush of desire surged through her, and she bit her lip to silence a gasp.

That was a brilliant move, her conscience chided.

Jade chewed her lower lip, trying to decide what to do. If she rolled over any farther, she'd be on her stomach and his hand would be on her back.

Well, as much as she liked the feel of his hand where it was, her back would be a much safer place. Cautiously, she rolled again and felt his palm slide to her spine.

She breathed a sigh of relief. The position she was in was disconcerting to say the least, but not quite as intimate.

His hand moved, and her eyes flew wide. Was it really less intimate?

His palm traveled down over her bottom to the back of her thigh.

In all her eighteen years, she'd never swooned, but she was certain she was about to. The warmth of his fingers on her inner thigh was mind-numbing. She moaned—it was either that or faint dead away.

His response—instinctive even in sleep—was instantaneous. He molded his hand around her flesh and kneaded gently, his fingers coming dangerously close to an overly warm place between her legs.

Jade knew she had to stop this, even if she didn't want to. And to her utter horror, she realized she didn't. She wanted him to touch her. She wanted to feel his hands caress every single inch of her flesh, especially the place very near his fingers. It was insanity. It had to cease. "Morgan," she breathed into the darkness. "Don't do this to me."

"I haven't done anything yet, beautiful."

That was it. She was going to die now, if not from pleasure then from embarrassment.

"But I'm going to," Morgan continued as his hand began to move up her thigh. "I tried to warn you."

Not hard enough. She wanted to say the words, but she couldn't speak. She couldn't even move. His fingers were between her legs, sliding gently back and forth over her woman's place. Flashes of heat raced through her body and settled in that one pulsating spot.

She had to stop him! She rolled away, onto her back. "Morgan—"

His mouth was on hers, hot and hungry, his hand reclaiming her, his fingers moving with sensual expertise.

Oh, God. She couldn't bear it. She arched upward, and he increased the erotic rhythm. His tongue, so warm and moist, moved against hers in the same stimulating motion.

The feelings took her breath away, and she felt as if she were about to shatter into a million pieces. She arched higher, her stomach growing tight and quivering.

He groaned against her mouth and thrust his finger against her woman's core, his penetration stopped only by the material of her skirt.

But that delicious pressure hurled her into an explosion so intense, so incredible, she thought she'd finally succumbed to death. It was only when she felt her skirt being lifted that she knew she hadn't. Not yet, anyway.

"It only gets better from here, beautiful."

Better? "Morgan, I don't think—"

"That's right. Don't think. Not now." His mouth was a breath away from hers as he gently slid his bare palm over her curls, his thumb softly stroking her lower belly. "Just feel." Lightly, oh so lightly, he brushed his tongue over her lips.

Sensations she'd never felt raced through her at alarming speed, then crashed into the spot beneath his fingers. Her thighs tightened around his hand, holding him there.

His lips touched hers, then covered them completely, his tongue sinfully smooth as it eased into her mouth to mate with hers. His fingers parted her and slowly caressed the most sensitive area on her body.

She didn't know which sensation was more intoxicating.

"I want to taste you, beautiful," he breathed against her lips. "All of you."

She wasn't sure what he meant, but it sounded wonderful.

His mouth slid to her ear, and tingles rushed over her. He nibbled the lobe and stroked it with his tongue.

It was a marvelous feeling, the heat of his breath against her moist ear. She raised her hands to his hair to hold him there, her fingers loving the silkiness of his curls.

Morgan pressed his finger gently into her as he nibbled his way down her throat to the tops of her breasts.

Tremors shook her to the teeth when he slowly moved his hand, easing in and out of her as his mouth traced her low bodice.

Stop him! her conscience screamed. *You can't allow this to happen.*

Ignoring the inner voice, Jade drew Morgan's head closer to her chest. She loved what he was doing to her and didn't want him to stop, conscience or no conscience. She'd probably never have another chance to experience something like this.

Morgan buried his face in the roundness of her breast, nipping at the tender flesh, then nudging aside the material to move lower.

When his mouth closed over her nipple, Jade nearly choked on a gasp. She never would have imagined how incredible something like that could feel. She arched closer, wanting to absorb the exquisite sensation into her very soul. Every delicious feeling, every slow seductive sweep of his tongue, every intoxicating movement of his mouth as he suckled her.

Suddenly his hand and mouth were gone.

She reached for him, confused.

"Easy, beautiful. I'm only going to remove the obstacles between us." He unbuttoned the front of her bodice and slipped the material off her shoulders. Then he moved to the ties at her waist.

She knew she should be embarrassed, and if it was light, she might have been. But in the darkness, she didn't feel big or awkward. She felt beautiful.

"Oh, Jesus," Morgan groaned in an awed whisper. "You take my breath away."

Surprised, she glanced down and saw that the spears of moonlight illuminated her body like hazy sunlight. He could see every inch of her. Flames of humiliation burned her cheeks, and she moved her hands to cover herself.

"No. Don't. I want to look at you." His voice was thick with desire. "I want to taste you."

Remembering how he'd just *tasted* her, the way his mouth had felt on her breast, caused a new round of tingle to course through her. But before she could form a response, he'd lowered his mouth to her belly.

Oh my God! She held her breath, then a moan escaped, and she closed her eyes to savor this new sensation. She never knew a man's mouth could do such wonderful things to a woman. She squirmed beneath the gentle torture.

Morgan caught her hips in his big hands and lifted her. Then his mouth was there, in that secret place, covering her, his tongue moving in slow, fluid strokes.

Her world spun out of control. Her body began to tighten and shake. Her hips surged upward of their own volition, and she felt him increase the pressure, the stimulating rhythm. His hair-roughened cheeks brushed the insides of her thighs as he moved his head back and forth, taking her closer and closer to the edge of a steep precipice.

Then it happened. She toppled over and burst into a million pieces. A scream of pleasure ripped from her throat as her body arched and twisted with the force of the impact. Then he was gone and something firm and hot pressed against her opening.

Before she could understand, he thrust sharply, yet held himself back.

Blinding pain streaked through her middle, but it only lasted a moment before it was replaced by the astonishing feel of him inside her, of the overwhelming fullness, the hardness.

He caught her head between his hands and ground his mouth down on hers in fierce possession as he began to ease deeper inside her, slowly, as if he expected to hurt her again. At last, he filled her completely, and with a hoarse groan, began to rotate his hips in slow, deep thrusts.

To her astonishment, she responded like a demon had possessed her. She bucked, trying to get more of him, clawed his back, bit his shoulder and neck, clamped her legs around his to pull him closer yet. Her hips thrust upward and ground against him, harder, faster.

She was coming near it again, that wonderful precipice, and she held onto him, waiting for the pleasure so intense it bordered on pain.

His body tightened, and he plunged wildly, driving into her, then retreating, and plunging again.

She tumbled over the edge, fierce and hard, her body convulsing with wave after wave of pulsating gratification. Somewhere in the midst, she felt him stiffen and heard his deep rumbling groan. A moment later, he collapsed on top of her.

She lay motionless for several seconds, listening to their labored breathing, and feeling the joint heavy beating of their hearts. Warm moisture melded their chests and legs, and the scent of him filled her. He was still inside her, and it felt so right.

Her mother had told her about the marriage bed, and the horrible pain. And that had been true.

But her mama had never said a word about the way it made a woman feel so warm and completely content. So wonderfully satisfied. So whole.

Jade wished she could experience this feeling for the rest of her life. Every day. Every hour. Every beautiful moment.

But she couldn't.

No matter how much Morgan denied the fact, he was a gambler, and she could never, ever, allow herself to love a man who held nothing sacred but a deck of cards.

Chapter
14

Morgan pulled up his breeches and dragged himself up onto the bench, the pain in his ankle mild compared to the churning knot in his stomach. How could he have been so stupid? Damn it, what was wrong with him? He'd known this would happen when he lay down beside her, even if he had tried to convince himself he'd only done it because he was so tired.

Tired? That was a laugh, he'd been anything but that when he'd brushed up against Jade and felt the heat of her body next to his. Oh, sure, he'd tried to be honorable, turning away and determindly closing his eyes. But what good had it done? Even in sleep he hadn't been able to stop wanting her. And when he'd awakened and found his hand filled with her breast, his control had snapped.

Now, no matter how much he wished otherwise, he would have to take a step he hadn't thought he'd ever be prepared for. For the sake of her reputation, and the fact that there could be a child, he had to marry her.

That didn't make him as unhappy as he thought it would.

"Morgan?"

Damn, he wasn't ready for conversation. "Why don't you try to get some sleep?"

"I *did* try."

"Make another attempt."

"I'd rather talk."

That's the last thing he wanted. "We should have both done more of that, earlier, instead of—Never mind. Just give me a few minutes to get over being angry before we attempt conversation."

She sat up, holding her gown in front of her to hide her nakedness, but she couldn't quite conceal all of her breasts. Her hair tumbled over her shoulders in silken chocolate waves. "Don't you dare try to blame this on me."

"I'm angry at myself. Not you. I should have had more control. Why the hell didn't you try to stop me?"

"Apparently, I have even less control than you do."

Against his will, his body stirred again, and he inwardly cursed his lust. It had already caused enough trouble. "The ramifications of our 'uncontrollable' actions are going to cost us both."

"How's that?"

"You know we'll have to marry."

She rose, wrapping the gown around her as she walked down the steps to the grass. "I'm not going to marry you, Morgan. Not for any reason."

He should have known she'd be difficult. "Neither one of us has a choice. Your reputation—"

"I've never had a reputation to taint."

"That's not the only thing to be concerned about. Even now, you could be carrying my child." Morgan didn't realize the impact of his own words until he said them. A warmth filled him at the vision of Jade's belly swollen with his baby. At the image of a tiny daughter with her mother's dark hair and flashing green eyes.

"I'll worry about that when—*if*—the time comes."

And their daughter would definitely have *his* common sense. "We'll talk about this in the morning, when we're both thinking more clearly."

"My thoughts are as clear as they'll ever be on this matter." She stepped away from him. "Why don't you lie on the pallet and get some sleep? It'll be a long time before I'm tired enough to sleep again." Ignoring the scalding look he gave her, she whirled around and walked to the pond.

Morgan watched her for several minutes as she knelt at the water's edge and splashed water on her face and arms, then she disappeared behind a large bush, to answer nature's call most likely.

Smiling he turned to go back up the steps.

A sudden splash stopped him, and he glanced again at the pool.

Jade was swiming across the pond to the waterfall, and in the moonlight, he caught brief glimpses of bare white flesh.

Ah, damn. His body surged to life, and no power on earth could have stopped him from going to the pond, where he shed his breeches and sank silently into the warm water.

Jade wanted to hit something. After what happened tonight, there was no doubt in her mind that she loved Morgan Frazier. But just as solid, was the fact that she'd never marry him.

She closed her eyes and dipped her head under the trickle of water from the falls, remembering how she'd felt when he said they'd have to marry. For one brief moment, she'd been elated. She'd even allowed herself to imagine what it would be like to share Morgan's bed every night, to revel in the wonderful things he made her feel, to hear his laughter, to bear his children.

Then images of her mother's torturred eyes rose, and Jade knew, no matter how much she loved Morgan, she'd never be able to live like her mother had. Jade had borne enough of that kind of pain to last a lifetime.

But, dear God in heaven, how she *wanted* to marry him.

Raising her hands to her head, she arched farther back into the fall and massaged the water into her hair.

Arms slid around her waist and pulled her against a hard naked body.

Shocked, her eyes sprang open, and she saw Morgan in front of her, holding her against him, his eyes bright with need, his manhood pulsing with desire against her belly.

Her flesh tightened, and the tips of her breasts pebbled against his wet chest. "W-what are you doing?"

"Condeming myself to hell." His hands slid up her back, then down over the curve of her bottom. His lips brushed the sensitive area where her neck and shoulder joined.

"Morgan, we shouldn't . . ."

"We both want this, beautiful, and the damage is done. Just enjoy the feelings."

He was right, and she also knew this would probably be the last time they'd make love.

Lifting her hands to his chest, she slid her palms over the hard muscles and smooth planes. There was so much strength and power emanating from him it heightened her senses to a fevered pitch.

He took her hand and placed it on his bare stomach, just above the line where his breeches buttoned.

Her fingers trembled against his skin. His flesh was so firm, and the narrow trail of hair that arrowed downward was silken to the touch. Heat rushed into her midsection when she thought of where that trail led.

He covered her hand with his and slid her fingers back and forth across his abdomen.

Tingles raced up her arm, and she stared at the pulse beating rapidly at the base of his throat.

A sensual smile touched his lips, and he released her hand, then lowered his mouth close to hers. "When you look at me like that, I burn." Slowly, lazily, he kissed her.

Her body exploded with need, and she gripped his shoulders. Hungrily, she opened her mouth for him and welcomed the gentle thrust of his tongue. She knew she'd remember the way he kissed for the rest of her life. And the way he touched her, the way he made love to her so completely.

She slipped her arms around his neck and raised up onto her toes, pressing into him, wishing she could absorb him inside her.

A tremor moved through him, and he deepened

the kiss, his hands sliding up to cover her breasts, to gently stroke the tight tips.

She met his tongue with her own, and lovingly assaulted his mouth the way his hands did her breasts. Stroking, nipping, caressing.

Suddenly, he swooped her up into his arms, barely limping in the water as he carried her to the edge of the pool, where he lowered her to the grass, then came down on top of her.

Earlier, his lovemaking had been slow and deliberate, but now he was as hungry for her as she was for him. He slid his hand down and caressed her inner thigh, moving higher and higher with each delicious stroke.

Then he slid his palm over her curls, his fingers alive as they stroked her, his mouth almost savage in its possession of her lips.

Jade barely had time to take a breath before that splendid feeling was on her again. She cried out and bucked, her fulfillment so great, she never wanted it to end.

Then he was there, filling her. Driving and plunging. Grinding. Taking her deeper and deeper into an inferno. The heat was so great, she was burning alive.

When Morgan felt her stiffen and heard her cry, he drove his full length into her. That was all it took. His body erupted with the force of a volcano. His hot lava poured into her.

When he'd nearly reached the end, she surged up and tightened around him, pumping him for more than he thought he had to give. The hot waves went on and on, never ending, draining the very life from him.

She at last relaxed her hold, and he collapsed in complete exhaustion. Never in his life had he experienced anything so volatile, so *earth-shaking*. He'd be content to spend the rest of his life right here in this glen, making love to Jade.

Food and sleep be damned.

"Morgan?"

"Hmm?"

"Do you always take advantage of sleeping women?"

He smiled against her neck and caressed her hip. "You weren't asleep this time." He moved his chest, enjoying the feel of her hard little nipples.

"I was daydreaming. It's almost the same."

He chuckled and raised up to look into her face, their bodies still joined. She was so lovely he ached just looking at her. "What about?"

"Nothing in particular. I was just enjoying the waterfall and letting my thoughts wander."

"Like to spend a little more time here, would you?"

"I wouldn't mind."

He kissed her shoulder, then her long neck. "I think my ankle needs another day to mend before we start back. What do you think?"

She rubbed her palms up and down his back. "That might be wise."

He moved his hips against hers, already starting to feel himself grow. "All right, but if there's anymore daydreaming, I want to be a part of them."

She brushed the hair away from his ears, then slid her fingers into the thick strands and pulled his mouth down to hers. "There's one I want to share with you right now. It's about a woman and a man lying naked in a glen. . . ."

He chuckled and lowered his mouth to her breast. "Not a bad scenario for a start. But I can think of a few things to spice up this little dream of yours." And he proceeded to show her how very well he could do that.

Chapter
15

Jade stretched against the grass, the warm sunlight a gentle caress to her naked body. She and Morgan had made love two more times, and she was so pleasurably tired, she wanted to sleep the afternoon away. But she didn't want to miss one single moment with Morgan. Not one.

But she did want a bath.

Rolling her head to the side, she saw that Morgan didn't have the same inclination about being with her. He was sound asleep. A little affronted, she decided to bathe before he woke up. Easing to her feet, she stretched again and strolled to the water's edge. It would be nicer if she had soap, she thought longingly. But the waterfall would feel heavenly.

As she started into the water, she glanced back at Morgan. For several seconds, she studied his naked form. Then suddenly, an idea struck her. One that wouldn't wait until after she bathed.

Scampering over to the fire pit, she picked up a piece of charred wood, then hurried to silently retrieve one of her petticoats from under the gazebo.

Moving away from Morgan so as not to awaken him, she tore off a square of cloth, then searched for a flat piece of bark.

When she found a suitable piece, she stretched the material over the wood and tied it securely in the back. Inspecting her handiwork, she smiled. It would make a good drawing pad.

Taking a seat on a rock near the grass where Morgan lay, she studied his relaxed form. He was a beautiful subject. Lying flat on his back, he had one arm folded under his head and the other bent with a hand resting on his stomach. One leg, the one farthest from her, was bent upward, while the injured one was stretched out straight. His head was turned, facing her, and those gorgeous black curls spilled onto the grass.

The charcoal in her hand flew across the makeshift easel, capturing his strong jaw, and long, long lashes. The straight, almost arrogant jut of his nose, that chiseled mouth and corded neck.

With his arm bent, the muscles bunched beneath smooth, tight flesh, his forearms corded and lined with strong veins. It was time-consuming capturing the whorls of hair on his chest, but she enjoyed every moment of it. She could watch him forever and never get tired of looking at him.

There was no change in the color of his skin between his flat stomach and narrow hip, which made her wonder if he didn't spend time swimming without his clothes, too. He was the same golden bronze all over.

She felt her cheeks warm as she sketched the length of his manhood draping his hip. Even relaxed, he appeared very large. Her stomach tightened at the memory of their lovemaking, and she quickly sketched his powerful thighs, and long, muscled legs.

His feet, like the rest of him, were long and slender, and very nicely shaped. The problem was, she'd never been good with feet, and when she finished, to her the toes looked too long. The ankle too swollen.

Never fully content with her work, but as satisfied as she was going to get for now, she carried the drawing into the gazebo and set it on the bench. Not wanting Morgan to see it until she was ready to show him, she dropped his shirt on top of it.

A little nervous about what his reaction might be, she headed back to the pond.

She waded into the pool until water covered her shoulders, enjoying the soothing warmth, before swimming to the falls. She stood up and tilted her head back, letting the water run through her hair and down her spine.

Wanting more of the flow to pour over her, she stepped back, but her foot hit a rock, and she tumbled backward—right into an open cave— where she landed hard on her backside on a sandy surface. In stunned amazement, she saw a short path through the foliage leading to where she sat.

She stared at the cavern behind her. It appeared to be very big, the ceiling high, and it looked as if it went a long ways into the hillside. Curious, she went inside. The thick sandy floor shifted beneath her feet as she walked.

The walls narrowed and turned, but she could see light at the other end, so she kept going. After what seemed like several yards, she at last came to the end. It was a giant cavern with a towering ceiling that rose up a good twenty feet. Water ran down one of the walls into another, smaller pool, and in the center of the ceiling a shaft of sunlight pushed through to illuminate walls that sparkled like diamonds. It was such a beautiful place, it brought tears to her eyes. "Curse you, Morgan. Why didn't you tell me about this?"

The answer came to her immediately. Morgan would never have gone inside the cave. He couldn't.

On that thought followed another. If he woke up and found her gone, he'd go traipsing into the woods after her. She had to get back.

When she stepped from beneath the waterfall again, she saw him standing near the edge of the trees, his naked body a golden bronze in the sunlight, his gaze searching the trees. In one hand he held his shirt, in the other her sketch.

A groan slid past her lips. But at least she'd gotten back before he went looking for her. "Hey, mister? Care to join me?" she teased.

He swung around, but he wasn't smiling. "When did you do this?" he asked in a hard voice, holding up the sketch.

She sank lower in the water, feeling at a terrible disadvantage without her clothes. "While you were sleeping, maybe thirty minutes ago."

He limped to the edge of the pool. "Why didn't you tell me you could draw like this?"

The way he was looking at her made her feel giddy inside. "Do you think it's good?"

"I don't think it, I *know* it, and all I've seen is one drawing." His gaze drifted down to the sketch in his hand, and an expression of awe softened his features. "It's a little intimidating, seeing me the way you do, but I think that's what makes it so powerful."

He was staring at the picture so hard it was making her uneasy. She cleared her throat and tried to lighten the moment. "You didn't answer my question. Care to join me?"

Tearing his gaze from the sketch, he stared at her for a moment, then sent her a dazzling smile. "Well, I don't know, miss. Do you think it's proper?"

"There are no laws of propriety in this mystical glen." She lowered her gaze to his bare middle.

His gaze raked her neck and shoulders with such sensual heat, she shivered. "I'm glad to hear that. Because, at this moment, I don't feel very proper." He set the sketch aside and walked toward her, wincing as he put pressure on his ankle.

She glanced at the swollen area. "Is it still as painful?"

"Not as much." As he stepped into the pond and sank deeper, she saw his features relax as the buoyancy eased the weight on his foot.

Enjoying himself now, he turned his back to her, then spread his arms and pushed off the bottom, allowing the water to take his full weight as he floated toward her.

It was an intriguing, very stimulating sight, and she had the strongest urge to kiss his body the way he had hers. Warmth moved through her at the mere thought, but she wasn't entirely sure such a thing was acceptable.

Morgan rolled over and swam to her, slipping his hands around her waist as he stood up. "I think this water has healing properties, like those in Bath. I feel much better today."

She toyed with the hairs on his chest. "Perhaps

you should have spent more time in the water, instead of—"

"Making love to you?"

"Instead of standing on it so much."

A devilish smile tilted the corners of his mouth and he slid his hands up to cover her breasts, his palms cradling her weight. "I'll stay off my feet all day if you'll stay with me."

It was extremely difficult to talk with her heart pounding in her throat. The man's hands were wonderful. "If I must."

He rewarded her with that soothing chuckle again. "Minx."

She slid her hands over his chest, marveling in the silken feel of him. "I think I want to kiss you all over, the way you did me."

He went deathly still.

She stared at the rapid beat of his pulse in the hollow of his throat.

He didn't speak for several seconds, then he let out a slow, heavy breath. "You may kiss me anytime, *anywhere* you like."

"Right now?"

That eased some of his tension, and he smiled. "You'd drown."

"I can hold my breath a long time."

He choked on a laugh, then gave a mock sigh and spread his arms out to the sides. "I'm yours to do with as you will."

Now there was an intriguing thought. She smiled to herself as she ran her palms over his hard chest, stopping to tease his nipples in the same manner he had hers.

He leaned his head back and closed his eyes,

telling her without words, just how much he enjoyed her touch.

It was the most powerful feeling she'd ever known. She lowered her mouth to his nipple.

His stomach tightened at her touch, and he grew hot and hard against her.

"I'll check the gazebo," a man's voice rang out. "You check the hot spring."

Jade tensed. "Did you hear that?"

He had already turned for shore—and his clothes. "It's my friend Christian, and it seems that we're rescued whether we want to be or not." He glanced back at her. "It sounds like they're not far, so it might be a good idea if you got dressed."

She'd been so shocked, she hadn't moved. But at his words, she bolted for the bank. Unfortunately, just as she'd stepped up onto the grass, a tall man on horseback rode into the glen. There was no way she could shield herself before he saw her. In stunned horror, she watched him turn toward her.

At any other time, she might have thought about his striking features, the thick black hair, firm jaw, and cool gray eyes. But not now. Not when she was about to perish from embarrassment.

Christian glanced at her briefly, then turned away. If he was surprised to find a strange woman standing in the glen with his friend, without a stitch on, he certainly didn't show it, and it made her wonder just how many times he'd come upon Morgan in a similar situation.

Christian's gaze fixed on Morgan. "You might want to give the lady her clothes before Rawlins gets here."

Morgan yanked up his breeches, then swooped up

her clothes and tossed them next to the water, giving her an apologetic look as he did so. Then he hobbled over to his friend, and both turned away from her.

"What happened to your foot?" Christian asked.

"It's sprained," Morgan said. "I thought you weren't going to return until Friday."

As Jade scrambled into her garments, she kept an eye on Christian.

The man dutifully kept his gaze averted as he spoke. "So I was."

Morgan limped over to his shirt and pulled it on, carefully turning her sketch over so Christian wouldn't see. "So what happened?" He surreptitiously stuffed the drawing inside his shirt as he laced it.

"The restoration of mother's castle was completed ahead of schedule." Christian glanced briefly at the lump in Morgan's shirt. "There wasn't any reason for me to stick around after that."

"How is she and your sister?" Morgan picked up his boots. "Did you bring another horse?"

Christian arched a brow. "The women in my life are fine, and, no, I didn't think to bring another mount. When I saw Flame and my mare grazing in the field, I thought you were both dead. Otherwise, I figured you would have walked back." His gaze lowered to Morgan's foot. "I figured even if one of you was hurt, the other would have returned for help."

"Providing," Morgan inserted testily, "the *uninjured* person knew the way to Royal Oak."

His friend smiled, showing beautiful straight white teeth. "I hadn't considered that." His features softened. "But I'm damned glad you're alive."

Jade finished dressing and straightened her skirt.

She didn't really want to face Morgan's friend, but it was either that or spend the rest of her life in the glen. With no real choice at all, she joined Morgan and glanced up at the man who looked to be about Morgan's age. "It's a pleasure to meet you, Lord Stanfield."

Christian's mouth quirked. "The pleasure's mine, madam. I assure you."

Jade blushed to the roots of her hair.

"Give way, Christian," Morgan grated. "She's embarrassed enough."

"Sorry," the other man mumbled, but he didn't really sound like he meant it.

"Master Christian?" Rawlins's voice rang out. "Any success?"

Christian turned toward the sound. "They're over here, Rawlins. And no worse for the wear."

"Thank heavens," the older gentleman said as he rode into the glen. "I was afraid . . . well, I am certainly glad everyone is all right."

"So are we," Morgan agreed. "And, Rawlins?"

"Yes, Master Frazier?"

"I do hope you have something besides radishes to eat at the manor."

"Radishes?" A smile pulled at the corners of the servant's mouth as he spied the leafy tops littering the glen. "I am quite sure we do."

Chapter
16

Morgan pushed away his empty plate, unable to eat another bite—and not because he was full. But if he had to sit at the table much longer and listen to Christian banter with Jade, he was going to be ill. The man had seen Jade without her clothes, and Morgan knew, now that he had, Christian would do just about anything to see her that way again—in his bed. If there was anything one could say about Christian, it was that he had a sex drive that made normal men feel wholly inadequate.

The only thing that would stop Christian was if he believed that Jade was Morgan's woman—and Morgan would see that he did—even if he had to move Jade into his bedchamber with him. Which, come to think of it, wasn't a bad idea. He glanced at the butler, who stood next to the dining room door. "Rawlins, will you have Jade's things taken to my room?"

Jade made a choked sound.

The butler coughed.

Christian arched a brow, and for the first time since they sat down to supper, he shut up.

Morgan pretended not to have seen or heard anyone's reaction. He simply smiled at his friend. "Have you decided when we're leaving for the Colonies?"

Christian looked uncomfortable as hell, which lightened Morgan's mood considerably. "Saturday. That's the day of the arrangement."

"Good." Morgan tried his best not to look smug. "That'll give my ankle a chance to heal." *And give me more time with Jade.* Morgan hadn't expected that thought, but he knew in his heart it was true. He did want to spend more time with Jade. A great deal more time.

Christian's gaze drifted to her, then back again, and Morgan saw a spark of understanding as if Christian had read his thoughts. "Yes, perhaps things have worked out for the best after all." He rose. "Now, if you'll excuse me, I'd like to take a bath. I've been on a ship for days, and I went looking for you the moment I hit the door."

As he started to leave, Morgan stopped him. "Christian?"

"Yes?"

"Thank you."

Christian shook his dark head. "Seeing that silly grin of yours is thanks enough." With a wink at Jade, he sauntered out of the room.

Morgan didn't know whether to smile or grit his teeth. But when he saw Jade watching Christian, her cheeks flushed pink, he knew. Morgan clamped his teeth together and ground them against each other. Damn Christian. And Jade.

* * *

Jade was going to murder Morgan. How dare he embarrass her like that in front of his friend. And for what purpose? During their time at the glen, she thought they'd come to be friends as well as lovers.

As she rose, she decided she was going to have a serious talk with him as soon as possible. After she checked on Wilkie again—and *after* she calmed down enough not to physically harm the man who'd taught her such wonderful things about her body.

But, truly, she couldn't complain about the arrangement. Her days with Morgan were numbered, and she wanted to spend time with him. Private time.

She just didn't want the whole world to know.

Wilkie was still playing draughts with Martha's youngest grandson, so Jade left him to it and followed Martha upstairs. Fleetingly, Jade wondered what her family would think if they knew about her deplorable behavior with Morgan. Behavior she couldn't seem to control, no matter how hard she tried. Nothing was of any importance anymore— except being with him.

It was a frightening feeling. He was becoming much too important to her, and for the life of her, she couldn't stop thinking about his proposal.

She tried to think about how it was going to be once they parted, but she couldn't. She didn't want to.

"The boys have already brought up your bathwater, mum," Martha said, tucking a strand of silver hair back under her mobcap before opening the door to the room Jade had been using. "I've laid out one of the gowns Master Frazier brought you."

Morgan had gotten her more clothes? She didn't know how to feel. Thankful, surely. But she wouldn't take them. Nor the riding habit. She couldn't bear to return home with them, only to watch Sedgewick sell them to stake another game.

"And, contrary to Master Frazier's wish," Martha continued, "you will remain in Miss Fiona's room. That boy doesn't have a lick of sense, it seems. The very idea of him wanting to share a chamber with you. Why, your reputation would be ruined beyond repair."

Jade smiled at the woman's concern—although, at this point, it was rather misplaced. "Thank you, Martha. I appreciate your thoughtfulness."

"That's perfectly all right." She patted Jade's hand. "Sometimes young men just don't think before they speak. But there's no harm done. None at all." With a brief squeeze to her fingers, Martha left.

Jade turned from the door to see the gown she'd mentioned lying on the bed. It was a lovely gold silk, with a ruffled, white satin underskirt showing between the wide part in the skirt's front. Beside that lay a lacy satin corset and several more petticoats. Morgan's taste in women's clothing was impeccable.

A pinch of an emotion she figured was jealousy skipped through her middle when she wondered how he'd become such an expert.

It wasn't any of her business. By Saturday, they would both go their separate ways.

Turning to the huge steaming brass tub in the center of the room, she took off her clothes and climbed in.

As she sat in the scented water, she thought about the pond and gazebo, and the things she'd felt for Morgan. She knew she had fallen in love with him, and now, she doubted if she'd ever think about ponds and waterfalls again without envisioning him.

She sighed. In three days, Morgan would go away, and she'd never see him again. She'd go home and spend the rest of her life remembering those two glorious days.

A tear slipped down her cheek, but she brushed it back. No. She wouldn't cry. There would be plenty of time for that later. For now, she would enjoy every wonderful second she had left with him. She'd store up enough memories to last her throughout eternity.

She smiled when she thought of her cousins and how they'd abducted him for ransom. Had that ever been a mistake. But not to her. She wouldn't give up these last days for any amount of money. Knowing Morgan for this brief time was the best thing that ever happened to her.

Still, her father would have to stay in prison, at least for a while. She was fairly sure Sedgewick would never consider ransom again. Things would return to the way they were before Morgan came into her life. Except now, he'd given her a knowledge about herself she'd never had before. A confidence.

Sedgewick wasn't going to like that. As far as he was concerned, she was already cheeky enough. Well, Sedgewick could jump off a cliff for all she cared. In fact, she'd been thinking seriously about not going back at all. She and Wilkie could make it on their own, probably better than they had with Sedgewick. At least Wilkie wouldn't take any of their paltry earnings to the gaming tables.

Lifting a washcloth from the side of the tub, she rubbed it with scented soap and began to wash, her thoughts delving deeper into the possibility of going her own way.

She heard uneven footsteps in the hall, then a door

opened and closed. A second later, another opened again, and Morgan's voice rumbled down the corridor.

"Jade? Where are you?"

She smiled but didn't answer.

"Damn it, woman. I know you can hear me. And I know this was Martha's doing. Now, where are you?" Doors opened and closed down the hall, then drew nearer. "You're trying my patience," he warned. "I told you before, I'm getting too damned old for games."

"Oh, for goodness sakes, Morgan. I'm in the same room."

Her door swung open, and he filled the opening with his powerful frame. "Why the hell didn't you tell Martha . . ." His gaze slid over her naked shoulders. ". . . to show you to my room."

"She was concerned about my reputation."

His eyes sank into hers. "Then you'd better hope she doesn't come back for a while, or she's going to become a whole lot more than *concerned.*"

Her heart leapt to her throat. The man could set her on fire without even touching her. "Morgan, you wouldn't!"

"Yes, I would." He locked the door, then pulled off his shirt and started undoing his breeches as he limped toward her. "I'm going to make love to you."

A rush of heat spread through her. "You've already done that."

"Not nearly enough." He lowered his breeches and stepped out of them. His bronze body looked sinfully inviting as sun from the open draperies touched him. He was intimidating in his size, but he was beautiful, too.

"I don't think I could ever get enough of making love to you," he said slowly.

If he said one more word to her, she was going to melt all over him.

He stepped into the tub and sank down in front of her. His feet and calves stroked her thighs as he slid them around her, then he stretched his arms out on the rim of the tub and leaned his head back. "Come here."

That was the word.

He opened those heart-stopping blue eyes and stared into her very soul. "Let's touch heaven, beautiful."

And they did. Several times.

When Jade dressed for breakfast the next morning and headed for Wilkie's room, she ran smack into Christian at the end of the hall.

He smiled in greeting. "Well, you look rosy this morning."

Jade imagined she did. After the shocking things Morgan had done to her body last night—and she had done to his—she should be permanently flushed from her hair to her toenails. "It's nice to see you again, Lord Stanfield."

"None of that. Call me Christian. Or Chris, if you prefer. But never *Lord* anyone. I refuse to be on such stiff terms with a woman as lovely as you."

"Well said, Christian," Morgan's voice grated from behind them.

Jade swung around to see Morgan had changed in his room into snug black breeches and a white shirt that he hadn't bothered to lace. "I thought you'd already gone downstairs."

He grinned boyishly. "What? And miss escorting

my favorite lady? Not a chance." He looped her arm through his and winked at Christian as they passed him.

Christian's laughter could be heard all over the house.

Jade was happier than she'd ever been in her life. But her mind refused to stop thinking about the time she had left with Morgan. Two days . . . only two. *And two nights.*

Morgan and Christian headed for Ainshall after breakfast because Morgan needed to know if his father had been able to reach Harrod Sawyer yet. There was no way he could leave Saturday with Sawyer still looking for Jade and her cousins.

"Morgan, tell me something," Christian said as they rode up the drive to Ainshall several hours later.

"What?"

"How serious are you about Jade?"

That surprised Morgan. He and Christian never discussed their relationships with women. In that, they were both extremely private people. "That's an unusual question, coming from you."

Christian merely shrugged. "Just curious."

"Why?"

His cool eyes met Morgan's steadily. "She's a lovely woman."

That wasn't what Morgan wanted to hear. He had enough trouble worrying about his own feelings for her without worrying about Christian's. "I plan to marry her if that's what you're asking."

"You do?"

"When I can convince her." Morgan didn't elaborate on the reason. Not even to himself.

"You're a lucky man."

He certainly didn't feel lucky as he reined his horse in at the railing in front of Ainshall and dismounted.

As usual, Liberty opened the door before they reached it, and, after a cheerful greeting with Christian, Morgan and his friend joined Robert Frazier in his study.

His father turned as they entered, and without preamble, he gave Morgan his answer. "I paid Harrod Sawyer off and sent him on his way."

Christian swung his gaze to Morgan. "Sawyer? What the hell is this about?"

Since Morgan hadn't yet told Christian the whole story, he did so now.

"She abducted you?"

"Her cousin did. That's why Father hired Sawyer."

"Ah, damn, Morgan. That man's insane. And I can't imagine why you'd want to marry the woman who abducted you."

Morgan felt heat creep up his neck.

"Marry?" his father asked in a stunned voice. "You're going to *marry* this woman?"

What could he say now? "If she'll have me."

"This is another prank, isn't it?"

Christian chuckled and sent Morgan a conspiratorial wink. "I don't think so, Robert. He hasn't been able to keep his hands off the girl."

"Shut up, Christian."

"Sure." His eyes were filled with laughter, his shoulders shaking lightly.

Morgan's father sank into the chair behind his desk, looking more than just a little stunned. "Well, I'll be blessed. I would never have thought . . ."

"You both seem to forget that there's a very likely possibility she'll turn me down."

"She wouldn't dare," his father said indignantly.

Christian took a seat in one of the two wing-backed chairs. "She'll accept. I've seen the way she looks at him."

Morgan clenched his teeth. *"Christian."*

His friend waved a hand. "I know, I know—shut up."

"When do I get to meet her?" his father asked.

Morgan was getting in deeper and deeper. "I'll arrange it. *Providing* she says yes."

"She will," he said with all the confidence and biased pride a parent could offer.

Morgan desperately wanted to change the subject. "If she does, I'll need to book passage for her and Wilkie on the ship."

"Wilkie?" His father looked puzzled.

"Her cousin." He wasn't going to try to explain Wilkie to his father just yet.

"Travel space is at a premium this time of year, Morgan. We may not be able to find a suitable cabin on the *Sea Skimmer,"* Christian pointed out.

"Wilkie can share your cabin then."

"Not a chance." Christian arched a brow. "Of course, I *would* consider sharing with Jade."

Morgan gave him the sour look he deserved.

Robert rose and looped an arm around both men. "Why don't we discuss this over dinner. I'm sure you'll find an amicable solution."

Morgan wasn't sure there was a need for one.

It was late afternoon when they left Ainshall, and Morgan had decided to go into London to get the deed to Wentworth Hall. He was going to give it and the markers to Jade.

He reined up as they came to the road that turned toward Royal Oak and told Christian his plans. "Tell Jade I *will* be home tonight—or by noon at the very least." He'd be there if he had to walk. Because if he didn't, she'd think he'd gone to the clubs again.

"You sure you're willing to leave me alone with her?"

"Don't start."

His friend laughed. "I wouldn't dream of it. And I'll give her the message, but I imagine she'll want to know the reason for your trip to London."

"I'd rather not say right now." He wanted to surprise her.

"See you tomorrow, then."

Morgan watched him ride away, not in the least worried about Christian being alone with Jade. Morgan had drawn the line. Christian wouldn't cross it.

Jade on the other hand was going to be very suspicious until he returned.

Somehow, he was going to have to convince the woman he wasn't like her father.

He just wished he knew how. Reining his horse toward town, he nudged him into a gallop.

It was after dark when he reached his apartments, and he only went inside long enough to retrieve the deed and markers from his safe before he turned for the door again.

Two men were standing in the opening. Two of the king's men.

An uneasy feeling swept through Morgan. "Did you need something?"

The elder of the two men stepped forward, his palm resting on his sword. "We've come to arrest you in the name of the king."

"What? Why?"

"Stealing a horse, Mr. Frazier."

"But my father sent the mon—" Morgan clamped his mouth shut as a sinking sensation weighted his middle. Ah, damn.

His father had done it again.

Chapter
17

Jade pulled her dressing robe closer over her chest as she stared at Christian across the parlor. It was well after midnight, and she was having trouble clearing her head. When Christian had banged on her door a few minutes ago, she'd thought it was Morgan . . . until she'd heard Christian ordering her to meet him in the parlor.

"What's this about, Mr. Stanfield? What is so important it can't wait until a decent hour?"

Christian poured himself a brandy and sank down into a chair. "Just following orders."

"Whose?"

"Morgan's. He went to London, and he wanted me to tell you he'd return by noon tomorrow." Christian tossed his drink back. "I imagine he was afraid you'd worry—or become angry—if you awoke and found he wasn't here."

Jade could feel the disappointment rising. "Did he say specifically why he went?"

"No."

"It doesn't matter. Whatever the reason, I'm sure it had something to do with a game."

"What game?"

"I wouldn't know."

"You're not making sense."

It made perfect sense to her. Morgan had gone to London for whatever reason, and he planned to go to one of the clubs. That's why he'd wanted Christian to tell her he'd be late. The truth be known, Christian probably knew exactly where Morgan went. "Never mind. It isn't important. Now, if you'll excuse me, I'm going back to bed."

Christian wasn't easily put off. "What game?"

Jade really didn't want to talk about this. In her heart, she'd hoped Morgan was telling the truth when he said he wasn't like her father. Yes, she had hoped . . . "I'm speaking of games of chance, Mr. Stanfield."

"You think Morgan's at a card game?"

"Yes."

"What on earth would give you that notion?"

"I'd rather not have this conversation in the middle of the night." She placed her hand on the door latch. "But, in answer to your question; Morgan's priorities of late have centered on games of chance."

Christian sprang from the chair. "Who the hell told you that?"

"No one had to tell me."

"It bloody well isn't true."

Jade tightened her fingers around the latch. What was it about men like Morgan, who instilled such dedication? Friends who would lie for him as her father's acquaintances had done for him. "Mr. Stanfield. It's nearly one in the morning, and I'm just not up to arguing over Morgan's virtue." She opened the door. "If you wish, we can continue this conversation tomorrow."

"I think you need to talk to Morgan."

"I already have." With a dip of her head, she stepped through the door and closed it quietly behind her, but inside, she felt like slamming it.

Curse Morgan Frazier to hell.

Morgan watched the sunrise through the two side-by-side windows in his cell at the Tower of London, in the Bloody Tower, his anger at his father growing by the second. He knew Robert was to blame for this. Why else would the guards have escorted him to one of the cells with large windows? Where he wouldn't feel enclosed? And why else would they have rushed him through the narrow halls at a breakneck pace and opened a barred window the moment they were inside the cell? He rubbed his sore ankle on the opposite leg to ease the discomfort he still felt.

Oh, yes. His father had done this.

Bracing his hand on the top ledge of the window, he stared out at the White Tower, centering the walled-in compound that was surrounded by thirteen smaller towers. Again, he reaffirmed the need for these blasted games to stop. This one would cost Morgan more than he was willing to pay.

Jade's trust.

Loosing a heavy sigh, he leaned a shoulder against the thick stone wall and thought about her. In his mind, he saw her for the first time. He remembered how entranced he'd been by her earthy beauty and tall, willowy stance. But that's not what had drawn him to her. He liked her sharp wit, her saucy mouth, and husky laugh that he hadn't heard often enough. But most of all, he was impressed by her strength. There weren't a handful of women in England who would work so hard to keep their family together under such devastating circumstances. But Jade had.

Because she cared.

His thoughts drifted to the time they spent in the glen, and he closed his eyes. Making love to Jade had been a breathtaking experience, but being close to her as a person had been even more exhilarating. Everything about her made him feel a completeness he'd never known.

When he'd proposed to her, he told himself he'd done it out of honor, but that was a lie. He *wanted* to marry her. He wanted to share her dreams, see her eyes light with pleasure when she was happy, and wrap her in his arms when she was sad.

He wanted to hear her voice when he woke in the mornings and feel her softness next to him at night. He wanted her to be a part of his life. He wanted . . . ah, hell. He just wanted *her*.

But for that to happen, he had to convince her he wasn't like Fredrick Wentworth.

Jade watched the sun slowly creep across the floor in her bedchamber as it spilled in from the open curtains. She hadn't been able to go back to sleep for thinking about Morgan, but she'd forced herself to stay abed until daylight.

Tossing back the covers, she rose and walked to the window. Her gaze drifted over the immaculate lawns surrounding Royal Oak, but her thoughts were still on Morgan, on how he made her feel when they were together. On how he made her feel when they weren't.

Like now.

She turned for the armoire and withdrew a yellow frock that had been among the clothes Morgan had given her. Clothes Martha said had kept a seamstress and her staff up all night while they completed Morgan's urgent order.

She'd forgotten to thank him for them, but she would when he returned—whenever that might be—but she wouldn't take them when she left.

Jade was lifting out a trio of petticoats from the drawers beneath the armoire when she heard the door open and turned to see Martha peek in.

"Oh, good. You are awake. I was hoping you would be." She came in and closed the door, then took the petticoats and draped them over the foot of the bed. She began helping Jade out of her night-clothes. "I wanted to tell you that Rawlins and I and the boys are going into London for supplies, and I have left yours and Wilkie's breakfast—and Master Christian's—warming on the stove. Since we won't be back until tomorrow, I have also left a plate of boiled chicken and roasted beef in the cooling compartment beneath the kitchen floor. Master Christian knows where it is. Anyway"—she waved her hand—"there are several plates of fruits, sweetmeats, and biscuits on the table and a crock of lemonade in the larder." She fastened the last tab on the petticoats. "I imagine that will do until we return."

Jade figured that amount of food should do for a week. "Thank you, Martha. That was very thoughtful."

"Oh, poo, dear. I could not leave you and your sweet cousin without anything to eat." She pulled the frock over Jade's head and buttoned the back.

JADE

"If there is anything else you require while I am away, ask Master Christian. He is familiar with everything's place." Picking up a brush, she began styling Jade's hair.

When Martha and Rawlins left, Jade checked on Wilkie and found him still asleep.

Christian hadn't risen either.

Not really hungry yet, she went to the kitchen and brewed a pot of tea, then took a steaming cup out to the front portico, where she relaxed on a wooden swing and tried not to think about Morgan.

Of course, that was impossible, so she merely sat back and closed her eyes, envisioning him again as he'd been in the glen . . .

"I'm hungry."

Startled, she opened her eyes to see Wilkie standing beside her, his brown hair rumpled, his cherubic face softened by sleep.

"Good morning. How are you feeling?"

"Hungry."

She smiled. He was much better. "Come on then, let's go to the kitchen."

While Wilkie ate, Jade nibbled on a fig and watched a bluebird peck at the ground outside the open door. "Martha's grandsons went to town with her, so I guess I'll have to be your draughts partner today."

Wilkie grinned around a mouthful of jam-filled scone. "You're more fun."

Her heart swelled with love as she ruffled his hair, then headed for the house to set up the draughts board in the parlor.

They played several games, only pausing for dinner, then continued.

Jade had stopped waiting for Christian's footsteps

telling her he'd awakened, and she'd ceased watching the clock. She'd known Morgan wouldn't be home by noon, and she'd been right. Focusing again on the board, she wished just this once she could have been wrong.

"Morgan home yet?" Christian strolled into the room, his hair neatly combed and pulled into a queue, his clothes immaculate.

"No, he isn't."

"What time is it?"

"After one."

"Hellfire. I haven't slept that late in years. And why isn't Morgan here?" Then, answering his own question, "Something must have happened to him. He would have been here."

A spark of concern flickered, but she quickly doused it. "A card game is what happened."

"Bloody hell, we're back to that again." He picked up her teacup and drained it, not even bothering to ask. "I don't know where you get your ideas, woman, but Morgan isn't at some game."

"Spoken like a true friend."

"God's eyes, you're single-min—"

"Maybe he's sick," Wilkie inserted. "Like me."

"You're not sick anymore, and maybe Morgan is just having too much fun to come home yet." Jade really wished she wasn't so waspish. But she hurt. *Morgan* was hurting her.

"I'm going to find him," Christian said, then abruptly whirled around and stalked out the door.

Wilkie jumped two of her disks and removed them. "Morgan wouldn't stay away unless he had to. He must be sick."

Jade sighed and slid one of her remaining disks to another square. She wasn't going to argue the matter with her cousin. In fact, she wasn't going to think about Morgan at all. "Your move, Will."

The rest of the day passed at a snail's pace, and Jade, against her will, kept darting glances at the door. What if Christian was right? What if something has happened to Morgan?

No, she told herself firmly, she wasn't going to drive herself crazy with worry the way her mother had. She wasn't going to turn gray before her time over a man's foolishness.

When Wilkie retired for the night, Jade changed into her dressing gown and robe then retrieved the book she'd started yesterday and went into the parlor. She had just settled into a chair when she heard soft footsteps in the hallway.

If it was Morgan or Christian, she hadn't heard them ride up or open the door.

A rush of uneasiness swept her, and she rose to her feet, her eyes never leaving the open parlor door.

A shadow appeared on the tile floor.

Jade took a nervous step back.

Then she saw him.

"Sedgewick! What are you doing here?"

He darted a glance around the room, then relaxed. "Do not be obtuse. You know exactly why I am here. I have come to take you back where you belong—something you had better have a bloody good explanation for—and free Uncle Fredrick." He peered at the staircase. "Which room is Frazier's?"

"How did you know I was here, and where did you get the money for Father's release?"

"Unlike you, missy, I used my head. I learned the location of Frazier's apartments, and when I found he was not home, I talked to his valet—pretending to be a visiting friend, of course. He told me Frazier planned to go to the Colonies with Christian Stan-field. It was simply a matter of finding this place and watching."

She was stunned that he'd gone to so much trouble. "But how did you get to town? You didn't have a horse."

"Our neighbor down the lane had an acceptable animal." He headed up the stairs toward the bed-chambers. "As for the money . . . I am about to collect that now."

He was going to steal from Morgan or Christian. "Sedgewick, you can't."

"Certainly I can." He opened doors up and down the corridor, checking each for clothing or a trunk before going on to the next.

Jade didn't know what to do. She couldn't stop him. Even though he was shorter than she, he was stronger. Her only option was to try to reason with him. "Sedgewick, don't do this. For *all* our sakes, don't cause us more problems than we already have. Morgan has—"

"Morgan?" Her cousin snorted. "So the bastard has turned your head, has he? How quickly you forget that he put your father in prison."

Jade could have bitten off her tongue. She knew better than to make a slip around Sedgewick. "Fa-ther put himself there."

Sedgewick gave her a disgusted look as he opened Morgan's door and spied the trunk at the foot of the bed. Lifting the heavy lid, he rifled through the stacks of neatly folded clothing. A moment later, he withdrew a drawstring bag and poured the contents on the bed.

A card and a waterfall of gold trickled onto the coverlet.

Jade had never seen that much money in her entire life.

"There is a bloody fortune here," Sedgewick crowed.

"Put it back."

"Shut up!" He gathered the coins and put them back into the purse, then stuffed it into his belt. "Get my witless brother, then we will check the stables for another horse and be on our way."

"No. I'm not going with you and neither is Wilkie. You've got the money, that's all you really want anyway, so just go."

Before she realized he'd moved, he'd grabbed her by the hair. "Do you wish to argue? I would not recommend it." He shoved her hard toward the door. She stumbled, and her shoulder slammed into the frame.

Fighting tears caused by the pains shooting through her scalp and shoulder, she cursed Sedgewick with every step toward Wilkie's room. She hated him. But even as she obeyed him, she knew it wouldn't be for long. She would go back to Wentworth Hall just long enough to gather her and Wilkie's belongings and leave.

Wilkie roused sleepily at Sedgewick's command, but when he recognized him, the disappointment in Wilkie's eyes was so strong, Jade felt it herself.

If Sedgewick noticed, he didn't mention it as he ordered Wilkie to dress, then paced impatiently while his brother complied.

Jade wanted to change, too, but she would wear this dressing robe for the rest of her life before she'd let Sedgewick know about the clothes Morgan had purchased.

When Wilkie was at last ready, they went out to the stables, where Jade hoped Sedgewick would only take Patience and not one of Christian's horses. But the moment her cousin laid eyes on Morgan's stallion, she knew it wasn't Christian's geldings she had to worry about.

"I wouldn't take the stallion," she warned. "He's uncontrollable."

"I can get a fortune for that beast. Now mount up on the horse I borrowed from our neighbor. Wilkie, you ride that gelding over there." Sedgewick nodded toward one of Christian's sorrels.

"What about Patience?" Jade demanded.

"Leave that bloody nag. She is as worthless as you are."

Jade opened her mouth to argue, but the hard look Sedgewick turned on her was enough to still her tongue—for now. Hoping Flame tossed her tyrannical cousin in the dirt, she mounted the mare he'd stolen, then watched as Wilkie saddled the gelding.

Sedgewick had trouble getting the stallion to stand still long enough to fasten the cinch on the saddle, but he managed, then determinedly climbed on the animal's back.

Jade bit back a satisfied smile when Flame rammed the stall gate, then sidestepped, pinning Sedgewick's leg between the horse and a railing.

Sedgewick swore roundly, then cuffed Flame on the side of the head.

"Sedgewick! Don't!"

"Shut up!" He cuffed the horse again.

Flame's eyes rolled wildly, and he snorted, but he settled down, allowing Sedgewick to open the gate and ride him out.

Jade wished she was big enough to strike Sedgewick the way he had Flame. She watched Morgan's horse, knowing the animal was much too docile. She was sure that boded ill for her cousin.

As they rode into the trees, she saw Flame's nostrils flare and she reined her horse closer to Wilkie. The stallion was on the verge of something disastrous. She could feel it.

Suddenly, the big stallion reared up, his powerful hooves pawing the air.

Taken by surprise, Sedgewick tumbled off.

Flame lunged toward Wilkie's horse as if to ram it headfirst.

Jade grabbed for her cousin. She jerked Wilkie toward her—just as the stallion struck.

She and Wilkie toppled backward off her horse, and she fell hard on the dirt. Pain exploded in her head.

Wilkie landed backfirst on top of her, and the breath whooshed out of her lungs. Pain tore through her chest, and she fought for breath.

Immediately her cousin sprang to his feet, his eyes wide with concern. "Jade? Are you all right? Did I hurt you?"

She tried to answer, but she couldn't. Although she wasn't badly injured, having the wind knocked out of her made it hard to talk. Several seconds passed before she finally dragged in enough air to force out a raspy "I'm all right."

Sedgewick's voice exploded in a vicious tirade of cursing.

Jade turned to see Flame race off into the trees, her angry cousin flailing his arms in anger as he chased after him.

In spite of her discomfort, she smiled. Sedgewick had gotten just what he deserved.

Wilkie knelt down in front of her. "Do you want me to help you up?"

She nodded, then eased into a sitting position and took Wilkie's hand. As she came to her feet, Sedgewick's voice erupted from the trees.

"The bloody bastard is gone!" He stomped toward them in quick, jerky strides. "You and the idiot take that horse. I will ride the gelding."

Jade would rather rest for a few minutes, but to mention that to Sedgewick would only make him angrier. Holding her side, she raised her foot to the stirrup and grabbed the pommel, then carefully lifted herself to the saddle.

Wilkie hesitated to mount behind her for fear he might hurt her more, but Sedgewick's angry order to hurry forced him to move.

Warmed by her cousin's concern, Jade leaned back against him and whispered over her shoulder. "I'm fine, Wilkie. Don't worry."

"You sure?"

"Positive."

"All right."

Jade urged their neighbor's horse into a trot.

The ride to Wentworth Hall was long and trying, and all she wanted to do was get off the horse and lie down. Soreness from the fall was increasing by the second.

Wilkie, sensing her discomfort, dismounted immediately, when they rode into the yard, then helped her up to her bedroom.

Jade collapsed on the feather tick and closed her eyes.

"I'll get you a headache powder," she heard her cousin say just before he darted from the room.

Jade smiled at Wilkie's thoughtfulness. She was

going to be sore for a few days, that was for sure, but that wouldn't stop her from carrying on with her plans.

When Sedgewick left for London to pay for her father's release, she'd have two days to pack . . . then she and Wilkie would leave Wentworth Hall forever.

Chapter 18

Morgan glared at the man in the long white wig and black robe seated on the other side of a towering desk. George Coffland, the stipendiary magistrate. "How much did my father pay you?" Morgan asked without preamble, his knowing look daring the man to deny Robert Frazier was responsible for the arrest.

Coffland's eyes crinkled with laughter. "Enough. Although it was a bother to have to be so careful about windowless rooms." He gestured to where Morgan now stood by a long, slender window.

"Did it ever occur to you that I might seek recourse?"

"You wouldn't be that foolish."

"You arrested me falsely."

Coffland's countenance became stiff, and he was suddenly all business. "Did I? I think not. You did steal a horse, after all. Whether you meant to pay for it or not is of no consequence. You *stole* it." He dipped his bewigged head toward the door. "Now, before I reconsider, you might want to leave."

Morgan decided not to press his luck. He'd gotten his remark in, that would have to be enough. With a condescending nod, he limped toward the door.

When he stepped through the outer gate and started across the bridge, he saw Christian on the other side of the moat, sitting atop his horse.

"What are you doing here?" Morgan asked as he hobbled toward him.

"Deciding whether to go in after you or not. It was a difficult choice. One I'm glad I didn't have to make." He studied the twelve-foot wall. "I know as well as I'm sitting, if I *had* gone after you, I would have became a hunted man, myself, for breaking you out."

Morgan smiled. "You wouldn't have done it."

"Yes, I would."

Christian's tone had turned deadly serious, and Morgan was glad his friend wouldn't be put to the test. "Is Jade with you?"

"I wouldn't take that minx anywhere. She defamed your character—and she had the idiotic notion that you were playing cards."

"She has reason to believe that, Chris." Morgan glanced around. "You didn't bring me a horse? What kind of escape would that have been?"

"A lousy one." He offered Morgan his hand. "Come on, we'll ride double to your stables."

When Morgan finally had his own mount again, and he and Christian headed for Royal Oak, Morgan's insides were churning. Jade wasn't going to believe he'd been in the tower. She'd think his explanation was just a quickly thought up excuse. And, other than taking her to Coffland, he couldn't prove otherwise. Even Christian's word wouldn't matter to her.

The ride to Royal Oak took forever in his estimation, and his worry over Jade's reaction had turned to panic when he finally pulled up in front of the manor and tossed Christian his reins.

Not bothering with amenities, he hobbled up the stairs to Jade's room. Since it was three o'clock in the morning, he knew she'd be in bed.

He'd only been gone for a day, but it felt like weeks, and he couldn't wait to hold her, to inhale her erotic scent, to feel her sweet curves molded to him, to kiss that lush, pouting mouth.

Then he'd have to explain.

Opening her door, he went inside. Maybe he'd slip into bed with her . . . and sleep for a few hours.

He grinned as he approached the draped fourposter. Who was he kidding? He'd never be able to sleep with her next to him.

He froze when he saw the empty bed. Damn it. She was probably downstairs—waiting for him—and that meant the explanations would have to come first, then it would be hours before they could . . . Ah, hell.

On his way back downstairs, he ran into Christian coming out of the parlor. "Is Jade in there?"

"No. Isn't she in her room?"

"Maybe she's with Wilkie, or perhaps Martha." Damn, was the entire household waiting up for him?

"She wouldn't be with her cousin at this hour," Christian stated firmly. "And the others won't be back until later today. They went to London for supplies."

"Jade must have gone with them."

"They'd already departed when I left to find you. She was here. Have you looked in *your* room?"

212

His room. That hadn't occurred to Morgan. She could be . . . "I'll check."

As he made his way along the upstairs hall, he noticed the door to his room was open. Maybe she *was* in there. Smiling now, he quickened his uneven stride, then shoved the door wider as he went inside.

His trunk was open, the contents tumbled. A card that had been in his coin purse lay on the bed.

For several seconds, he just stood there in numb disbelief. Jade couldn't have done this. She *couldn't* have. She wouldn't steal from him. She wouldn't forsake him. Damn it, they'd been too close. Too intimate. She *cared* for him as much as he did her. He knew she did!

But the reality before his eyes couldn't be denied. Jade was gone. His purse was gone.

"No!" he roared. *"Noooo!"* Then the pain came; a vicious, crushing pain in his heart that sent him to his knees. She'd betrayed him.

Jade hadn't been able to sleep. She couldn't stop thinking about Morgan. About what he would think when he found his money gone. She didn't have to study on it long. She *knew* what he'd think.

Turning to set a pan on the stove, her insides felt like they were splitting in two—and not just from her sore ribs. She was sick at heart.

"Can I help?" Wilkie asked as he sauntered into the cookhouse.

All the help in the world couldn't ease the pain in her heart. "You can put the utensils on the table."

"Can I cook, too?"

"Not this morning."

"At dinner, then." With a satisfied dip of his head,

213

he collected the eating utensils from a drawer in the sideboard and bounded toward the dining room.

Jade turned back to the strips of pork sizzling in the skillet. The smell made her just a little nauseous, and she knew the feeling was caused by her upset over Morgan.

Thinking again of the man who'd turned her life upside down, she wondered if his father had contacted Sawyer yet. Her gaze shot to the open door. What if he hadn't? What if Sawyer was still looking for them?

Her hand trembled as she turned back to the skillet. She could only pray Sedgewick would leave today so she and Wilkie could start packing.

As she worked, she thought about Morgan's kindness when he bought the food. Since the day she'd set eyes on him, her life had improved. First with food, then with clothing, then with the treasured memories of their lovemaking—something she'd never thought to experience. Because of her size, she'd been fully prepared for spinsterhood.

She stabbed a piece of pork and turned it over, remembering Morgan's proposal. Oh, she knew the words had stemmed from his determination to be honorable, but even now, the mere thought caused her to tingle. She found it extremely easy to envision what it would have been like to wake up to him every morning, to see his eyes softened by sleep, his boyish smile, and tousled black curls.

Just visualizing herself lying in bed next to him at night, feeling the touch of his hands and power of his lovemaking was enough to make her blush.

She gave herself a mental shake. Girlish fantasies were something *other* women had, not her. She couldn't afford them. She forced her thoughts back to reality. And the reality was . . . being married to Morgan would be like being married to her father. For all his kindness and compassion, Morgan was still a gambler, and she'd rather live her life alone and in squalor than in a see saw marriage to a man who loved cards more than her.

Willing painful thoughts away, Jade finished preparing breakfast. As she carried the fruit, scones, and eggs to the table, she glanced around the barren dining room, and firmly reminded herself what a man like Morgan had done to her life.

"Where is the tea?" Sedgewick huffed as he came into the room.

She glanced at her cousin as he took a seat at the head of the table. "It isn't ready yet, and what are you doing up at this hour?" Sedgewick usually slept past dinnertime.

He waved a hand. "Hurry with that tea. I have important business today."

So he'd roused himself early to go to London, but she couldn't help wondering if he could make it past the clubs before he paid for her father's release. It didn't matter. She was just glad he was going. "I'll check on it."

Hurrying from the room, sparing Wilkie only a passing glance, she made for the cookhouse. She was elated that Sedgewick would leave early.

With a steaming teapot in hand, she went back to the house and took her place at the table, then picking up her fork, she willed the meal over quickly.

But Sedgewick took forever as he carefully chewed each bite of food.

Wilkie, munching on a scone, set his fork aside. "Are we still going to get lost in the Colonies?"

"We are not going to get lost, idiot. We are going there to live. As soon as I can make the arrangements. When Uncle Fredrick is released, I will go to the docks to pay the passage and see how soon we can depart."

"Do you think it will be very long before we leave?" Wilkie looked oddly solemn.

"As soon as possible, I assure you."

Jade stared at her plate. Wilkie was going to be sorely disappointed when she told him her plans.

"Do I get my own room on the ship?" Wilkie asked.

Sedgewick snorted. "You can share with Jade. It is cheaper that way, and we will need all we can save when we get to the Colonies. If we are frugal, we may even have enough of Frazier's money left to buy a cottage."

"And how do we support ourselves after that?" Jade demanded, even though she had no intention of going. "Do you plan to go to work somewhere, Sedgewick?"

"Uncle Fredrick will provide for us as he has always done."

How typical. Leave the matters of survival to someone else.

Sedgewick rose and dusted crumbs off his breeches. "Your father and I will return on the morrow, as early as possible. See that everything is ready for our departure."

Jade kept her mouth shut as she watched Sedgewick walk out the door, his stride light and bouncy. It was obvious he was very happy. Of course, considering the way he idolized her father, she could see why.

She wondered what he would be like when he returned . . . and found her and Wilkie gone.

"Jade?"

She turned to her youngest cousin. "What, Wilkie?"

"We're not going to the Colonies, are we?"

She never ceased to be amazed by his insight. She placed her hand over his thin, frail one. "No, we're not. But we'll have much more fun on our own."

"Can Morgan come with us?"

Oh, God. "No. That wouldn't be a good idea."

"Then we won't have any fun."

"What's wrong with you, Morgan?" his father asked.

Morgan straightened from where he'd been selecting the clothes he wanted to wear on his journey to the Colonies the next day. "Nothing."

His father sat on the edge of the bed and frowned. "Liberty said you planned to leave tonight. Why?"

Morgan felt another surge of pain rush through him. When the reality of what Jade had done had sunk in, he'd left Royal Oak immediately. He hadn't even explained his hasty departure to Christian, but he hadn't needed to, either. Christian understood Morgan's desperate need to get away. "I . . . want to spend some time in town before the journey, at Madam Chesters." He knew he was giving the impression that he was going to sleep in the brothel, and that's just what he wanted. "It's going to be a long voyage," he added just for confirmation. "As you know, I've been a bit *incapacitated* and *incarcerated* lately."

His father had the good graces to look ashamed,

apparently remembering Morgan's angry tirade earlier that day. "What about the woman you asked to marry you?"

Morgan's heart gave a vicious twist and he clenched his teeth. "She turned me down."

"She didn't." There was such a note of disbelief in his father's voice, Morgan almost smiled. Then his father sighed. "What time does your ship depart?"

"Daylight."

"I'm going to miss you, son."

Morgan knew it would be months before he saw his father again, maybe even a year. "Why don't you come with us?"

"I've been thinking about it. But right now, I've got several commitments I can't put off. How long do you plan to stay?"

"A couple months. Possibly more."

Robert's gaze lowered to the floor in thought. "I should be caught up in the next few weeks, maybe I'll leave then." His eyes twinkled as he grinned at Morgan. "I've always wanted to see the place. Besides, I'd like to know how Clay and Amber are doing."

"So would I," Morgan said with complete sincerity. He'd only received one letter from his brother in the last months, and most of the contents had been about the prospects in the Colonies. Morgan missed his brother more than he cared to admit. And Amber. Nothing would give him greater pleasure than seeing that imp again. She was more like his little sister than his sister-in-law. "I'll be sure to tell them you're coming."

His father's gray hair bounced lightly as he nodded and moved to the door. "While you're about it, remind them that I'm still waiting for a grandchild."

"I'm sure they're doing their best, Father."

"Knowing Clay, I'm sure they are." His father chuckled as he left the room.

Morgan held onto his thoughts of his brother and Amber, but not for long. The moment his gaze landed on the bed, images of Jade's beautiful face swam before his eyes.

He tried to focus on the journey ahead and tried to feel the excitement. It just wasn't there. Since he'd walked into his bedchamber at Royal Oak and realized how Jade had betrayed him, he'd felt hollow inside.

Placing the clothes he'd selected on his trunk, he gave his room one last glance before heading downstairs to summon a servant. His gaze drifted again to the bed, and a rush of pain swept him. He'd never share that bed or any other with Jade.

He'd never share anything with her again, not her humor, her wit, her laughter, or her secrets.

But the worst of all, he'd never share her heart.

Chapter
19

Morgan stared out the window at the miles of rolling ocean, praying he'd made the right decision. If not, he'd caused himself and Christian a lot of grief for nothing. But all during the night, he hadn't been able to sleep for thinking about Jade and remembering how she'd been when he met her. She'd been upset because Fredrick had taken him. She'd been concerned about his phobia and injury. Yet, even though she hadn't had any food, she'd never mentioned selling Morgan's clothes or even his boots. She'd accepted her lot in life without complaint.

Those weren't the actions of a thief.

When that thought occurred to Morgan in the wee hours of the morning, he'd awakened Christian and begged off the journey to the Colonies. Morgan couldn't leave until he saw Jade again.

Christian hadn't been as disappointed as Morgan thought he would be. In fact, he'd grinned like a simpleton and told Morgan he'd see him in the Colonies *after* Jade and Morgan's honeymoon.

Morgan wished he could be as confident as Christian had been.

Turning back to his room above the docks, he picked up his coat and slipped it on. It was still chilly in the morning hours, but he wanted to find Jade as soon as possible. In his heart, he didn't want to believe she'd stolen from him, but if she had, he needed to hear it from her own mouth. *Then* he would leave for the Colonies.

Jade inspected the contents of her portmanteau. Hardly anything was there. A couple packets of dried beef, a small sack of flour, and a tin of lard. Enough to get by for a while. On top of that were a few of her meager clothes. Not much to start a new life.

A life without Morgan.

No, she wasn't going to start thinking about him again. It hurt too much.

Lifting the folds of her skirt, she went downstairs to make tea. Sedgewick had left yesterday for London, and he and her father would return sometime today. She wanted to be gone before they got here, but there was still plenty of time. If she'd calculated the journey right, she had another couple hours, providing they weren't sidetracked at a club.

As she pumped water into the pot, she remembered how peaceful it had been yesterday with just her and Wilkie. They'd played draughts, tossed horseshoes at pegs in the ground, waded in the pond, and baked gingerbread after supper. They'd had a wonderful time sitting in front of the fire telling stories, and she knew she was making the right choice by leaving Wentworth Hall.

She and Wilkie would be happy.

As she waited for the water to boil, she leaned on the sideboard, trying to think where to go. Stevenage was too close, and she didn't want to go to London. In either place, she'd chance running into her father or cousin.

Perhaps Bath. She'd always heard good things about the place. Maybe she could even work at one of the healing springs, giving towels to the patrons— if there was such a job.

She'd have to sell something to pay for a room, though. But she didn't know what. Yesterday, she'd returned the mare Sedgewick had stolen from their neighbor, and Sedgewick had Christian's gelding.

Even if her cousin hadn't taken Mr. Stanfield's horse, Jade couldn't have sold it. Christian had been too kind to her.

There was nothing. Not even something of Sedgewick's to sell—which she would have gladly done.

Sighing, she poured the steaming water into the teapot and added a handful of tea leaves. She'd probably have to sell Patience after she retrieved the mare from Christian's stables and rode her to Bath.

At the thought of the mare, she rubbed her temples. It wasn't going to be easy to get into Christian's stables, but she had no choice. She and Wilkie certainly couldn't walk all the way.

Carrying the pot and cups on a tray, she went into the dining room, where she met Wilkie as he came in from the hall. "Can I take my frog?"

"Why don't you leave him here with his friends at the pond. I'm sure there will be plenty of frogs in Bath." She hoped not, but with her luck there was bound to be.

He didn't look convinced. "Morgan won't be no trouble."

"Morgan? You named your frog *Morgan?*"

"Uh-huh."

"Why?"

" 'Cause I love Morgan and my frog. Can I take him, please?"

A low thrumming ache squeezed Jade's chest, and she set the tray down. It was just a name. She couldn't afford to dwell on it. "You'll have to find a small box to keep him in until we're settled. Now wash up, dinner will be ready soon." To her own ears, her voice sounded shaky. What had the man done to her? Even the mention of his name sent her into a dither.

When the noon meal was over, Jade headed for Wilkie's room to help him pack.

She had to bite back a smile when she saw the bare windows in his room and his open bag piled full of drapery cords and curtains. "What are those for?"

"Hammocks."

"What?"

He gave her a very serious look. "Pirates used hammocks to sleep on. I saw that in one of my books. I wanted you to have a bed."

"I see." Tears stung her eyes. Wilkie's thoughtfulness warmed her heart, and she knew she'd thank the Lord every day for the rest of her life for this precious being.

Blinking rapidly to clear her vision, she fingered the material sticking out of his bag. "There won't be much room for your clothes."

"I already packed those. They're underneath."

She felt another sting of tears. The bag was so small. . . . "What about your shoes?"

"I'm wearing them."

"Your draughts board?"

He looked away. "I don't need that. It's old."

Oh God, she was going to cry. Forcing her voice to remain stable, she nodded toward the game. "It's not that old. We can make room for it. Give me one of those curtains. I can put it in my bag."

"Truly?"

She touched his sweet cheek. "Truly, Will." Gathering the material against her chest, she made for her room, fighting tears the entire way. He'd been willing to give up his favorite game to see to her comfort. How could anyone ever repay that kind of love?

In her room, she took out one of the dresses and stuffed the curtain inside. Three dresses would be plenty.

She started to close the bag when she remembered her drawings. If she took them off the frames, she could take them, too. She had to. She certainly didn't want her father or cousin to find them.

Kneeling beside the bed, she reached underneath and pulled one out. The one of Wilkie. Then the one of her grandfather's worker. There were two other country scenes that she quickly removed from the wooden frames.

As she worked, she thought about the drawing she'd done of Morgan in the glen and wished she could take that one with her, too. The look of contentment she'd captured on his face could never be duplicated.

Another ache twisted her middle, and she stuffed the sketches into the bag and started dressing. She had to stop thinking about him.

When everything was ready, she carried her bag

down and set it at the foot of the stairs, then called out to Wilkie. "Bring your portmanteau. It's getting late. We need to go." She didn't want to chance seeing her father.

"I can't find a box for Morgan!"

That name again. She'd never get used to it. "Look in the study. I think there's an empty cigar box in one of the desk drawers."

As he darted across the hall, frog in hand, she headed into his room to collect his bag.

"I found it!" she heard Wilkie call as she set his bag next to hers in the foyer.

"Come on, then. Let's go."

"Go where?" a familiar voice asked from behind her.

Jade froze, her heart beating so hard she thought it would collapse. Why, *why* hadn't she gotten away sooner? Wanting more than anything to run, she forced herself to turn and face the man at the door.

"Welcome home, Father."

The tall, rail-thin man stared at her from the expanse of floor between the stairs and the door, his graying hair dirty and uncombed, his eyes looking almost too big for his gaunt face. "What is the meaning of this?" He gestured to the bags by the door, his voice every bit as hard and cruel as she remembered.

Sedgewick stepped in behind him and immediately assessed the situation. "Yes, Jade. Do tell."

She forced her chin up, but she was quaking with fear inside. Sedgewick's anger was nothing compared to her father's. "Wilkie and I are leaving."

Her father's eyes flared.

"Jade, I need some grass—" Wilkie stopped at the

door of the study, his eyes wide as he stared at her father's angry face, then his fearful gaze darted to her.

"It's all right, Will. But I think you'd better take your frog to the pond for now."

"But—"

"Go, Will."

He was still hesitant to leave her alone.

She touched his arm. "It's all right."

Reluctantly, he edged out the door.

Jade braced herself to face her father.

"Explain yourself, missy—*then* we will discuss punishment," he ground out in barely restrained rage.

Fear spiraled through her, but it was overshadowed by her burning indignation. This man had taken so much from her, and now he wanted more. Well, she didn't have any more to give! She didn't care if he beat her to death.

Crossing her arms, she stared him straight in the eyes. "Explain myself? *You're* the one who needs to explain! We've been through hell because of you, and I'm sick of it. I'm sick of being hungry. Of watching everything I've ever loved fall into ruins around me. Of watching my clothes disappear to finance another game. Of working my fingers to the bone while *he*"—she pointed a finger at Sedgewick— "waits to be served. You can beat me, you can whip me, or you can use your beloved strap, but *nothing* is going to stop me from going. Do you understand? *Nothing!*"

Her father stalked toward her, his eyes ablaze. "You insolent chit! How dare you speak to me in that tone." He drew his hand back to slap her.

Jade braced herself for the blow.

"I wouldn't if I were you," another voice stated calmly from the door.

Her father and Sedgewick whirled in unison, then gaped in surprised horror at Morgan's large frame filling the door.

The room went still, and the very air pulsed with the danger radiating from Morgan. He was too calm. Too controlled. And so very, very angry.

"What is the meaning of this?" her father demanded with false bravado. "You are not welcome here. Leave at once!"

Sedgewick inched slowly backward, clearly intimidated by Morgan now that his hands weren't chained.

"When I go," Morgan said in a deadly soft voice, "Jade and Wilkie go with me."

"Over my dead body."

"That can be arranged." Morgan's cold tone made certain her father knew there was no jest intended.

"What do you want?" Her father was a tall man, but clearly no match for Morgan. He retreated a step.

"I already told you."

"You cannot just come in here and take my daughter and nephew! I will have you arrested!"

"I'll buy them."

Jade's mouth nearly fell open. What was Morgan doing? He couldn't be serious. Could he? He'd better not be. Buy her, for goodness sakes. *Buy her!*

Her father watched Morgan for several seconds before the words clicked. He glanced at Sedgewick before returning his attention. "How much?"

Oh Lord, Jade moaned inwardly. She should have known.

Morgan didn't hesitate. "The deed to Wentworth

227

Hall, the markers you lost to me in the game, plus a hundred crown."

Her father's eyes lit with interest, but she knew he'd never give in that easily if there was a chance for a greater sum. "My daughter is worth more than that."

"Yes, she is," Morgan agreed. "But that's the only offer you're going to get out of me. If you refuse, I'll simply take her."

"You cannot do that."

"Watch me."

Jade wasn't just going to stand there and let them bargain for her. "I'm not for sale, Morgan."

"How well I know. If you had been, you'd have accepted my proposal."

"What's this?" Her father's eyes brightened considerably.

"I asked your daughter to marry me."

Her father whirled on her. "And you refused? Have you lost your mind? The man's worth a bloody fortune!"

"No, Fredrick, she hasn't," Morgan answered for her. "She won't marry a man she thinks will make her unhappy."

Sedgewick crossed his stocky arms and scowled at her. "Money can buy happiness, imbecile."

Morgan's eyes narrowed.

Jade clenched her hands. "Stay out of this, Sedgewick."

"How dare you speak to me like that." In his sudden burst of rage, Sedgewick overlooked Morgan's presence. Her cousin took a step toward her, his fists balled. "Someone needs to teach you a lesson in respect, bitch!"

An inhuman growl erupted from Morgan an instant before his fist slammed into Sedgewick's jaw.

Her cousin flew backward and crashed against the wall, then slowly slid down the wall in an unconscious heap.

"God's eyes!" her father wailed. "You can't—"

Morgan swung back to him. "Can't what, Fredrick?" Morgan's fists were still clenched, a muscle in his jaw throbbed wildly, while his eyes fairly shot sparks of blue fire.

Her father swallowed, then his gaze darted to Sedgewick's prone form, then back to Morgan. "Nothing. I . . . agree to your proposal."

Morgan reached in his pocket and tossed the payment on the floor at her father's feet with a vicious flick of his hand. "Jade, get Wilkie. Let's get the hell out of here."

Jade was torn between rushing to do Morgan's bidding and telling Morgan to jump off a tall cliff. But getting away from her father was more important than anything else at the moment. She'd inform Morgan of her thoughts on his *purchase* later.

Chapter
20

It took Morgan several minutes to calm down after they left Wenthworth Hall. When he'd seen Fredrick raise his hand to Jade, it had taken every ounce of control he possessed to speak rationally.

But when he'd seen Sedgewick go after her, the thin thread of control had snapped. If that bastard had been anyone but Jade's cousin, Morgan would have killed him.

Dragging in a steadying breath, he glanced at Jade. She was too quiet. Much too silent for someone as angry as she was. Wilkie hadn't said a word since he mounted Christian's sorrel behind her, either. In fact, he was so unusually quiet, he had Morgan worried.

Morgan hated uncertainty—and he damned sure didn't like being ignored. He focused on Jade. "We can ride all night in silence, beautiful. Or we can get the argument over with before we reach Royal Oak." He'd decided to leave her in Martha's care until the wedding since he wasn't about to leave her with her father. "We both know there's going to be one, so why put it off?"

"Don't talk to me, Morgan. Not ever again." She didn't look at him. Didn't even blink an eye. She merely kept her face forward and her small nose tilted upward.

Wilkie shifted in the saddle behind her, but he didn't say anything.

Morgan sighed. "Answer one question, then."

She still didn't acknowledge him.

"Did you steal from me?"

"No."

That was it. No surprise. No defense. Just a simple no. But it was enough. "I'd hoped—"

"Don't talk to me!"

She was certainly in a snit. "That'll be rather difficult since we're going to be living in the same house for the rest of our lives."

"You may have bought—*and paid*—for me, but I'm not going to marry you."

"Damn it, Jade. Money is the only thing your father understands. I didn't *buy* you. I paid to get you out of that household—and I would have paid a hundred times that amount to see that end. As long as there's breath in my body, you'll never live like that."

She still didn't look at him. Nor did she respond.

Wilkie did. He gave Morgan a secret smile.

Her cousin's approval increased Morgan's confidence. "Tell me, Jade. Are you really so angry at me for trying to make your life better?"

"Better? In what way, Morgan? You're just like the rest of the men in my life."

"I thought we'd settled this."

"In your mind, perhaps. Not mine."

Morgan was fast losing his patience. "What do I have to do to convince you I'm not like them?"

This time she did look at him. Furiously. "Swear to me you'll never pick up another deck of cards. That you'll never participate in a game of chance. That you'll never, ever, wager money for any reason. That's not so hard is it?" The last was hissed out between clenched teeth.

For just a heartbeat, Morgan considered saying the words, but he couldn't. Not because of any desire to play cards, but because he wouldn't allow their marriage to be based on terms and conditions. He wanted her love and her trust. Nothing less. "I won't do that."

"I didn't think you would."

"Damn it, Jade!"

She turned away. "Let me go, Morgan."

"No."

"Then we have nothing further to say to each other."

On that point, he agreed. Talking was useless. Kneeing his horse, he picked up the pace. Only time would make her understand, and he'd see they had plenty of that.

Jade sank deeper into the tub in her room at Royal Oak, trying to relieve some of the anger still coursing through her from last night. He'd bought her. Literally bought her! How could he have done that to her? How could he have been so insensitive? So cruel?

She didn't believe for a minute that he'd just been trying to rescue her. Morgan, like Father and Sedgewick, had a definite motive, but for the life of her, she couldn't imagine what. He couldn't possibly want to marry her that badly. Could he?

And why wouldn't he give her his word? If he was so bent on gaining her approval for this farce of a marriage, then why hadn't he promised her anything to see it through?

She would never understand him—and she wasn't even going to try.

Drawing the cloth up to her chin, she stared at the bubbles floating on the water's surface, planning her escape. Morgan wouldn't stay here long, he'd already told her that. He was going to London to procure a special license then to Ainshall to make arrangements for the nuptials.

She would leave while he was gone. Martha and Rawlins wouldn't watch her every move the way Morgan did. Escape from them wouldn't be difficult.

Confident now, she leaned her head back and closed her eyes, enjoying the soothing warmth and the heavenly scent of roses rising from the steaming water.

The door opened.

Jade jerked upright, instinctively bringing the cloth to her chest as she turned to see Morgan walk in, only slightly favoring his injured ankle.

Her heart kicked into uneven beats. "Get out of here."

He stopped for a brief second, then continued forward. "I came to tell you I'm taking you to London with me." His gaze slowly roamed her naked shoulders and her throat, then her face.

"Take someone else." The way he was looking at her made her insides knot.

He pulled a stool over with his foot and sat down beside the tub, his arm braced on the rim, his fingers just inches from her shoulder. "It would be difficult to fit them for your wedding dress."

It was extremely difficult to talk with him that close. "Save your money. I told you, there isn't going to be a wedding."

He gave her a slow, provocative smile. "There'll be one, beautiful. Mark my words." His gaze lowered to the cloth that barely concealed her breasts, and his eyes darkened. "Jesus, you're breathtaking."

Her heart was going crazy inside her chest. Every time he looked at her like that, she lost all reason. "Morgan, go away."

He leaned forward, his lips a breath away from hers. "No."

"I don't want you here."

Tauntingly, he brushed his lips over hers. "Yes, you do." He pressed his mouth to hers in a slow, carnal kiss that left her head spinning.

"Have I told you how good you taste?" He kissed her again, sampling her with his tongue, tracing her lips, then easing inside.

Heat rushed to her woman's place. Her nipples tightened. The power he had over her wasn't fair. She couldn't resist him when he was like this. She couldn't even think straight. All she could do was feel the softness of his mouth, the warmth of his tongue, and the frantic tingles racing wildly through her veins.

She leaned her head on the rim again, and he followed, deepening the kiss. Jade surrendered to the sensations setting her on fire. If nothing else, she loved the way Morgan made her feel. She would give him a good set down later. . . .

His mouth trailed across her cheek, then down her throat, before returning to hungrily assault her lips again and again.

The room disappeared in a swirling void, and she

was barely aware when he lifted her from the tub and carried her to the bed. Then he was there, leaning over her, covering her face and eyes with fevered kisses, then returning to ravage her mouth.

She buried her hands in his thick hair, pulling him closer, losing herself in his masculine scent, his wickedly soft mouth.

He tore his lips from hers and buried his mouth in the hollow of her throat, kissing her, nibbling, stroking her with his tongue.

She arched her head back and tightened her fingers in his hair. He knew just what to do to make her melt into a mindless puddle.

His hands stroked up and down her naked sides as he kissed his way down her chest, leaving a trail of damp fire in his wake. He nuzzled the valley between her breasts, then slid his lips over the rise of flesh until he reached her nipple.

He covered her with his mouth.

She sucked in a sharp breath, then moaned when he began to nurse her. Her nipple hardened against his tongue, and he circled it, then drew it deeper into his mouth.

Fire spread to encompass her entire body, and she arched upward, desperately needing more of the exquisite sensations.

He buried his face in her breast and fervently suckled her, turning his head from side to side as he tugged and caressed.

Her woman's place started to tingle, and as if he'd read her thoughts, he slid his hand across her belly then eased it between her legs.

The touch of his fingers caused another moan to escape her, and she lifted her hips, needing to feel the pressure of his hand.

With agonizing slowness, he slid his fingers over her, stopping to caress the folds, then to gently stroke her. He moved his hand up and down in an agonizingly slow caress.

The air was too heavy for her chest. She started laboring for breath. Her body began to tremble, and she tightened her thighs around his hand.

He released her nipple and softly kissed the underside of her breasts, then her ribs and stomach. His hand eased down her thigh, then around to encircle her bottom as he kissed his way lower, over her abdomen, over the mound that shielded her most private part.

Shifting his body between her legs, he lifted her hips, then covered her with his hot mouth, his tongue a spear of fire as it pressed against her growing need.

The pleasure was so intense, she gripped the coverlet for something to hold on to. She felt as if she were going to shatter.

He circled her with his tongue, then slowly drew the bud between his lips.

An explosion of sweet pain ripped through her body, and she arched into a bow.

He tightened his hands on her bottom and hungrily ravaged her, taking her higher and higher until she was sure she'd never survive the fall back to earth.

Then he was over her, filling her, and the sensations grew until she didn't think she could bear them another moment.

She erupted into flames.

Through the maelstrom, she felt him stiffen and thrust into her with such force, she screamed in pleasure.

Finally, finally, the world began to right itself and she could breathe again. She could feel the weight of his naked body over hers, the fullness inside her, the heavy beating of his heart against her chest.

A small part of her wished they could stay like this forever, but her rational side knew it could never be. Morgan was everything she feared.

Everything she wanted but couldn't have.

"Ah, *monsieur,* the gown, it fits *mademoiselle* like a lover's hand, no?"

Morgan grinned at the rotund woman with pink cheeks and an easy smile. He'd seen her yesterday, before he'd gone back to Royal Oak, and had ordered several garments for Jade. Even the material and design for her wedding dress. "Yes, Madam Bovier, it certainly does." His gaze roamed appreciatively over Jade's slender form molded by the ice blue satin he'd known would go perfectly with her coloring, and he couldn't help remembering the morning they'd just spent together. He'd made love to her four times.

"It's too tight," Jade mumbled.

Morgan arched a brow. The minx was determined to be difficult—when she was speaking to him, which had been very little since this morning. He ignored her protest. "Have the length adjusted a bit longer, Madam Bovier, then send it to Ainshall. Are the rest of her things ready?"

"Oh, *oui.* My girls, they put the last hems in as we speak."

"Good. Send them along as soon as they're finished, too." He took Jade's hand and drew her to her feet. "We should be going now. We have another stop to make."

She withdrew from him. "Where now?"

"You'll see."

"Morgan! You've got to stop this nonsense. I've told you and told you—"

He kissed her quickly, knowing that was the most effective way to overcome her stubborn streak. "Stop talking and start changing."

Madam Bovier giggled behind her hand. *"Oui, mademoiselle,* you much change quickly now." Ushering a mutinous Jade back behind the curtain, the older woman shot him a saucy wink.

He couldn't help smiling in return.

When Jade finally emerged wearing the royal blue riding habit Morgan had given her the day they went to the glen, he led her out to the boardwalk and down three doors.

She stopped abruptly as he started to enter the jewelers.

"Morgan, no. You've got to stop this. When are you going to get it through that thick skull of yours—*I'm not going to marry you?"*

"I'm not the one being hardheaded." He pulled her along behind him into the shop, then watched in amazement as her eyes widened with awe.

He checked a smile. If she reacted this way over a few baubles, he could just imagine her expression when she saw the Frazier jewels he would give her on their wedding day. They had belonged to his great-great-grandmother, and a single piece in the collection was worth more than all the items in the shop combined. Far more.

Giving her an appreciative glance, he was enthralled by the way the light touched her alabaster skin and shimmering dark hair. In that moment, he knew why he wanted to shower her with gifts like he'd never done for another woman—and it had nothing to do with the wedding and celebration and pomp. The reason was much more basic than that.

He loved her.

Chapter
21

Jade paced her room at Royal Oak, waiting for Morgan to leave. He'd said he would go right after supper—and that had passed more than an hour ago. Why on earth had he and Rawlins locked themselves in the study for so long? What were they talking about?

She folded her arms over her chest and thought about the ring Morgan had bought her. It was an exquisite emerald surrounded by diamonds that had cost so much, she could have purchased a cottage and lived for years on the staggering amount, but she wouldn't accept it. She had to make Morgan understand there was not and never could be anything serious between them.

She glanced at the door praying Morgan and Rawlins weren't discussing how to keep her confined. She had to leave today—tonight at the very latest.

The wedding was tomorrow.

As she'd done so many times over the last days, she envisioned herself as Morgan's wife. It wasn't a bad image at all. She liked everything about him, from his smile, to his laughter, to his fierce passion. She even liked his dogged determination.

But, just as she'd start to consider the possibility of throwing caution to the wind and marrying him, her mother's haunted eyes would appear before her, and Jade would again see the unhappiness and emptiness, and she knew she would never allow herself to live in such awful despair.

It could so easily happen. If she married Morgan, she'd commit fully to him, and she'd never be able to leave him.

Plopping down on the bed, she rolled onto her back and fixed on the canopy overhead, wishing with all her heart Morgan would have given his word that he wouldn't gamble again. She'd wanted him to agree so badly, she'd nearly said the words for him.

But he hadn't. Because he couldn't give up the game.

She knew he cared for her. She'd have to be blind not to see that, and he might even love her. But he'd never love her enough.

And she wouldn't settle for anything less.

The plod of hooves jerked her from her thoughts, and she rushed to the window, just in time to see Morgan ride out, his form erect in the saddle, his dark hair shifting against his collar with the movement of the horse.

Her heart gave a little lurch, and she placed a hand over her chest, telling herself she was glad he'd finally left. She was *glad,* blast it!

Glancing at the portmanteau that was still packed from yesterday, she thought about replacing her ragged clothes with some of the ones Morgan had bought, but she couldn't. She didn't want any reminders of him.

Each one would cause her pain.

She opened the door and headed downstairs, wanting to see where Rawlins and Martha were. If she planned to escape tonight, she had to know their whereabouts.

She found Rawlins in the parlor with his grandsons and Wilkie, just sitting down to play a game of whist. Hoping they wouldn't play long so she and Wilkie could get an early start, she went in search of Martha.

The aroma of baked apples and cinnamon wafting from the cookhouse told her where the elder woman was long before she reached the structure.

She peeked inside to see Martha, draped in a chest-to-knee ruffled apron, remove a steaming apple pie from the brick oven and set it on the windowsill to cool.

Jade's stomach fluttered. She loved apple pie more than just about any food she could imagine. "How long before we can eat some of that?"

Martha turned and smiled. "Half hour or so. I was just about to whip some cream to go with it."

"That has *got* to be sinful."

Martha laughed. "It is for those of us who have to worry about our figures."

"Then I'd better stay away from it."

"Oh, poo, child. You could eat a whole pie every day for the rest of your life, and you'd still look good." Her eyes twinkled. "Especially to Master Frazier."

Jade cursed the blush that warmed her cheeks. "Only if he likes *very* round women."

"Like my Rawlins does," Martha said tongue-in-cheek. "Oh, child. I am so happy for you and Master Frazier. He's such a good man, and you make such a lovely couple. And what beautiful babies you will have!"

Jade didn't know how to respond, but her insides gave a sharp twist when she realized there would never be a babe for her and Morgan. At least she hoped not. "I . . . think I'd better go check on Wilkie." Martha didn't know she'd just seen him.

The housekeeper waved her toward the door. "Go. I'll bring the pie and cream when they're ready."

Jade nearly ran from the cookhouse. She wanted to kick something—mainly Morgan.

Back in the house, she peeked in the parlor again to find all four males engrossed in the game, so she made for the front portico. There was nothing else to do until everyone retired.

Thinking of her coming escape, she planned her moves. After she collected Wilkie, they'd take Patience from the stables, then head for Bath. They'd have to find a shelter of some sort for the night, but they'd make Bath by tomorrow evening . . . or possibly the following day.

Once there, she'd sell Patience, find a room, and purchase enough food to get them by for a few weeks. Then she'd look for a job.

It was a good plan, so why didn't it feel right? She was afraid to consider the reason, because she strongly suspected it had something to do with a tall, black-haired, blue-eyed devil with a boyish grin.

"Pie is ready," Martha's voice rang out, and Jade nearly jumped out of her skin. But she was glad to have any diversion to keep her from dwelling on Morgan.

The pie was as delicious as it had smelled, and the

cream heavenly. Martha had even prepared hot cocoa to go with the fare. It took everyone several minutes to finish, each anxious to savor the wonderful tastes—herself included.

At last, when the dishes were cleared and the conversations dwindled, Jade yawned, pretending to be sleepy. The others apparently felt as tired as she affected to be, because a short while later, everyone headed for their respective beds.

Jade stayed in her room for more than an hour, battling exhaustion, making sure the household was asleep, and wondering why no one seemed concerned about watching her.

She quietly opened the door and crept down the stairs toward Wilkie's chamber, expecting to see someone step from the shadows at any moment.

No one did.

She stopped in the entry hall and listened for sounds.

There weren't any.

Was Morgan so sure of himself that he figured she wouldn't leave now? No. He was much too intelligent for that. So why wasn't anyone around? Could it be they were outside, waiting beneath her window? Figuring that's how she'd try to escape again?

The thought made her smile, and she couldn't help picturing Morgan as she'd seen him that night without his clothes. The man was intimidating . . . and beautiful, if a man that masculine could be called beautiful.

It was just one of hundreds of memories she feared she'd never be able to erase from her mind.

As she reached for the latch to Wilkie's door, she thought about the time in the glen, and how she'd wanted to savor memories of Morgan. But back then, she hadn't realized how painful they would be.

Now she did.

She took a breath to ease the constriction in her chest, then silently opened her cousin's door.

The room was empty.

Her gaze darted around in confusion. Where was he? He couldn't be gone. He'd never leave without her.

"If you're looking for your cousin, mum. He's in my room."

Jade whirled at the sound of Rawlins's voice. "What?"

The elder man looked embarrassed. "Master Frazier asked me to keep the boy with me tonight."

Jade clenched her hands. Damn Morgan to eternal hell! He knew she'd never leave without Wilkie. That sneaky, underhanded, arrogant, devious blackguard!

Not even pretending to be polite, Jade shoved past Rawlins and stormed back to her room. Morgan wasn't going to stop her. Blast it, he wasn't!

She paced and cursed Morgan until the early hours of the morning, when she finally fell exhausted onto the bed and succumbed to the pull of sleep.

But it seemed as if she'd lain there only a moment before Martha was in the room stripping her for a bath, sudsing her down, styling her hair, and stuffing her into the pale blue wedding gown.

"Oh, mum," Martha said in an awed voice. "You are stunning. What that gown does for you! It positively leaves me speechless."

Jade was speechless, too, but not for the same reason. The woman staring back at her in the mirror looked nothing like her. That woman was the spitting image of her mother. The same dark hair, upturned nose, and slender figure. The same haunted green eyes.

A hand clamped around Jade's heart and squeezed. She not only looked like her mother, she was being forced into the same life. Swallowing against the tightness in her throat, she turned away and picked up her cloak.

She couldn't allow Morgan to do this to her.

She wouldn't allow *anyone* to do this.

Morgan stood at his bedroom window at Ainshall, watching the parade of guests arriving for his wedding. His blue satin breeches and waistcoat felt too tight. The white lace dripping from his neck and sleeve tickled. His new stockings itched. About the only things that did feel comfortable were his black Hessian boots that had been shined to a mirror finish.

This should be the happiest day of his life. In a matter of minutes, he would make Jade his wife. She'd belong to him forever. She'd live in his home, share his life. So why wasn't he pleased?

He knew exactly why. He'd seen how unhappy she looked when she arrived with Rawlins a few minutes ago. She couldn't have been more dispirited if she'd been going to a funeral.

But what had he expected? He hadn't played fair, and they both knew it. He'd used Wilkie against her.

Even now, the underhandedness of his actions grated. He shouldn't have done that. He should have brought her to Ainshall and watched her himself. She'd never forgive him for using her cousin.

He'd never forgive himself.

"Morgan?" his father called as he opened the chamber door. "Reverend Jamison is here, and he'd like to speak to you as soon as possible. Something about the roses you wanted at the altar."

"Tell him I'll be down shortly. Where is he?"

"In the parlor."

Morgan nodded and turned back to the window, but he didn't hear the door close behind his father. Didn't hear him leave. Damn, he knew this would happen. His father had always been able to read him.

"What's wrong, son?"

"Wedding day jitters, I imagine."

"You never were a very good liar, not even as a child."

Morgan really hated the way his father could do that. "I thought I'd get better with age."

"You have to have a talent for it first. Now, what's the problem?"

Morgan didn't want to talk about this. "It's too complicated and nothing I can't work out on my own. Have all the guests arrived? The musicians? Grandmother's jewels?"

"You aren't very good at changing the subject, either." His father crossed his arms and stood there with that stern expression Morgan knew so well from childhood.

"Ah, hell. You want to know what's wrong? Fine, I'll tell you. *Jade Wentworth doesn't want to marry me.*"

"Is this another prank?"

"We both gave our word there wouldn't be any more, but the truth is, I wish it was a joke. Maybe then, I could better deal with her rejection."

His father moved to the bed and gripped a post.

"Let me get this straight. You've spent a bloody fortune on this affair. We have a houseful of guests downstairs, waiting to see you married, a king's ransom in jewels, and you're telling me the bride won't be here?"

"She's already here."

His father relaxed a bit. "Morgan, I'm not usually this slow, but you're not making sense. If she doesn't want to marry you, why would she be here?"

"She's going to marry me because I forced her into it. Damn it, I bought her from her father."

Robert stared at him in utter shock. "You've lost your mind, that's what happened, isn't it? That last prank was too much. You snapped."

"If only it were that simple."

"You *bought* her?"

As clearly as possible, Morgan explained what happened that night at Wentworth Hall.

Robert shook his head. "Her father was going to strike her? You were going to abduct her? This has got to be a prank."

"Even that would be simpler."

His father threw up his hands. "I don't know what to do."

"I'm afraid I do."

"What?"

Morgan took a breath and forced himself to say the words he hoped he'd never have to say. The only ones he could say. "I've got to let her go."

"Ah, bloody hell!" his father exploded.

A loud pounding startled them both.

Morgan looked toward the door. "Yes? What is it?"

The panel swung open, and Liberty walked in,

looking more disturbed than Morgan had ever seen
him.

A weight pressed down on Morgan's chest.

"What is it, Liberty?" Robert asked impatiently.

Liberty looked anxiously at Morgan.

Morgan turned his back to the men in the room
and gripped the windowsill, bracing himself for the
words he knew were coming, and he knew would
tear him in two.

Liberty shifted, then hesitated.

Morgan closed his eyes.

Another long pause stretched across the silent
room before the butler finally spoke.

"Miss Wentworth is gone."

Jade rode Morgan's horse hard toward Royal Oak, Wilkie hanging diligently to her waist. She had to get Patience and get away before Morgan came after her.

The smooth gait of the horse spurred her spirits, and she urged him faster. She wanted to get Patience before dark and leave the area.

She was still congratulating herself on her ingenuity. While everyone at Ainshall had been rushing around, getting ready for the wedding, she'd had a servant bring Wilkie to her, with the excuse that she needed to talk to him about his part in the wedding. The part Morgan had given him as best man.

Morgan apparently hadn't warned the servants at his father's home, because Wilkie was brought to her immediately.

She dismissed the servant, saying she wanted a private word with her cousin. It had only been seconds after the servant left that she had grabbed her bag, then she and Wilkie had climbed out the window and darted into the nearby trees to avoid being seen by guests milling about the grounds.

Jade's heart had pounded so hard, she'd thought she would be sick, but she'd anxiously motioned Wilkie toward the stables.

Her cousin had gone inside and told the groom he needed a horse saddled so he could fetch something for Lord Frazier. Jade had thought up the lie, knowing the groom wouldn't question his master's word.

As expected, the groom had complied instantly.

Dark had settled when they rode down the lane to Royal Oak, and Jade reined the horse into the trees to approach the manor from the rear. All she had to do was get Patience, and they were free.

When she could see the stables through the trees, she pulled the horse to a stop and waited as Wilkie dismounted and helped her down.

"Stay here, Will. I'll get Patience."

"What about this horse?" He gestured to the animal they'd taken from Ainshall.

"As soon as I return with Patience, I'll take that one and tie him to a tree in view of the house."

Lifting the voluptuous skirts of the satin gown she hadn't had time to change, she quietly made her way to the open back door of the stables, then, peeking around the corner of the weathered wood, she looked inside.

A groom was brushing Flame.

A disappointed sigh left Jade, but she was pleased to see Morgan's stallion had found its way back, or Morgan had gone after him. Either way, she was glad Midnight Flame was safe.

But how would she get the groom out of the way?

An idea hit her, and she hurried back to her cousin and the horse. "Stay here, Will. Don't make a sound." She took the horse's reins, then led the animal to the edge of the trees. Quietly, she turned it toward an area between the house and stables, then gave it a swift whack on the behind.

The horse whinnied, then bolted, its hooves clopping loudly as it raced through the stretch of ground that ran past the stable door.

The groom came charging out, looking around in confusion, then seeing the riderless horse, he gasped in surprise and raced after it.

Jade lifted her skirts high and rushed to get Patience.

Flame whickered in recognition, and she stopped long enough to give him a quick pat on the nose before opening Patience's stall.

There wasn't time to saddle the mare, so Jade grabbed a bridle and slipped it on, then led the horse out the back way. She would have trouble riding bareback, but she didn't have a choice in the matter.

Leading Patience to a log near Wilkie, she climbed on and straddled the mare's back, feeling decidedly wicked as she waited for her cousin to toss her the portmanteau then mount behind her.

Her only regret was that they hadn't been able to bring both bags, but that was something they would have to worry about later. They had to get away from Royal Oak.

Nudging the mare into a canter, Jade pulled the reins back and forth as she guided Patience through the woods and tried to think where they could go at this hour. She glanced around at the forest of trees and smiled. The glen.

Fleetingly, she thought about Morgan and how he might come there looking for her, but she had that figured out, too. She'd hide Patience, and she and

Wilkie would sleep in the cave. Even if Morgan came, he'd never look in there.

He couldn't.

It was spooky riding through the trees in the dark, and Jade wondered if she'd even gone the right way. Although she'd passed the graveyard and large clearing where Morgan had raced Flame, and they'd turned into the trees to the west of the meadow, it felt like they'd been riding for hours.

The mere thought of getting lost in the woods made her nervous.

"What's that?" Wilkie asked in an anxious whisper.

Jade didn't see anything. "What?"

"That noise."

She tilted her head, listening.

The distant sound of trickling water drifted on the cool night air, and she breathed a sigh of relief. "It's the spring." Kneeing the mare, she trotted toward the sound.

The moment they broke out of the trees into the glen, Jade was assailed by memories. Moonlight touched the circular gazebo and sparkled on the surface of the pond.

She could see her and Morgan as they'd been in the gazebo . . . and how they'd been in the water when Christian found them, how they'd made lov—

She turned away, refusing to remember any more.

"There's a cave behind the springs, Will. I want to take a look at it. You tie Patience in the woods, several yards in so no one can see her."

Sliding off the mare's back, she walked around the pool to the path that led behind the foliage and waterfall. The opening was there, just as she'd remembered, and she looked around for something to use as a torch, but when she glanced in the opening, she could see a silvery light at the other end. She ducked inside.

The long, narrow tunnel was dark, but the light at the other end led her way. About seven feet high, the tunnel ran only a score of feet into a wider area at the rear. The cavern was circular in shape, with walls that glistened with tiny specks of gold and silver color. In the center of the ceiling, a small opening emitted the beam of moonlight.

The cave was perfect for tonight.

"Come on, Will. This is it."

Her cousin came in, his eyes wide with wonder as he surveyed the cavern. "Is it a pirate's cave?"

"I don't think so, but you never know."

He ran a finger along a vein of shimmering rock. "I think it was."

Not wanting to destroy his illusion, she didn't say anything more about the unlikely possibility. "Why don't we gather leaves for our beds, then I'll fix us something to eat? Dried beef and scones?" There really wasn't anything else except a few peppermint sticks she'd thrown in as an afterthought when she'd packed.

Wilkie wrinkled his nose, but his gaze lingered on the cave. Then, as if he had to pull himself away, he turned for the entrance.

They gathered stacks of leaves to use as a mat and covering, then several twigs to start a fire. Once they were situated, Jade prepared their meager meal, remembering how she'd gathered radishes for her and Morgan to eat. Shaking off the thought, she handed her cousin the fare.

When they finished eating, Wilkie started digging in the sand around the edges of the cave.

"What are you doing?"

"Looking for doubloons."

Jade bit her lip to keep from smiling. They were miles from the ocean, and she doubted very seriously if ancient pirates would have ventured so far inland. But she didn't want to spoil Wilkie's fun. "Let me know if you find anything." She held onto her grin as she went outside to wash up.

The warm mist from the falls feathered her arms and she rubbed them while she walked down the path to the glen. Her step faltered when she saw the gazebo, and she suddenly visualized her and Morgan there, lying on her petticoats, making love.

Something sharp twisted inside her, and she looked away. But no matter which way she turned, she saw the places she and Morgan had been. Even the log she'd used to brace his injured ankle was there.

Then, unbidden, came the memories of their conversation about his gambling. She closed her eyes, hearing Morgan's words. *I'm not like your father.*

If only she could have believed that. If only it had been true.

She moved to the pond and again saw how she and Morgan had been in the pool when Christian showed up. She'd been embarrassed to death.

Christian. Now there was a friend to Morgan. Even he had been angered by her mention of Morgan's games.

Her brow furrowed as a thought occurred to her. Why would Christian have been angry? He should have been defensive, quickly making up a tale to exonerate his friend. For the first time, she concentrated on what Christian had said. *Who the hell told you Morgan was at a game?* He'd been upset, not fumbling for excuses.

She remembered another comment. *Morgan isn't at some game. Something must have happened to him. He would have been here.* She'd brushed the remark off as loyalty, but what if it hadn't been?

She hadn't even asked Morgan what happened.

And he hadn't bothered to tell her, probably because he figured she wouldn't believe him anyway.

That wasn't an appealing thought.

Her musings turned to Martha, and she recalled the housekeeper saying what a good man Morgan was. She wasn't even Morgan's servant, so why would she take up for him?

Jade closed her eyes and felt a swell of pain. She should have talked to him. No. She should have *listened* to him. But it was too late. She'd run away from their wedding and embarrassed him in front of his family and friends. She could never go back.

He probably wouldn't want her to anyway. Not now.

Or would he?

Yes, she decided. He would, if for no other reason than to give her the set down she deserved.

She crossed her arms and sat at the edge of the pool, wondering why she'd been such a fool. Why hadn't she been able to see Morgan's kindness and generosity? His patience and understanding? His gentleness?

He had protected her from harm on several occasions, and even at his angriest, he'd never raised a hand to her. And in her heart, she knew he never would.

She thought about what lay ahead of her in Bath. What lay behind her at Wentworth Hall. And what her life could have been like with Morgan. The ache in her chest caused tears to sting the backs of her eyes.

When she'd asked him to give his word he'd never gamble again, he'd refused, and she'd assumed it was because he couldn't give up the game. But what if it hadn't been? What if he'd had another reason?

She wanted to kick herself for her stupidity. Morgan was right, she was too blasted single-minded. Like a sparrow with a worm, she just wouldn't let go once she'd set her mind.

Now it was too late.

She lowered herself onto her knees and dipped her hands in the water to wash, but a realization hit her that caused her to sit back down.

Morgan would come looking for her.

All she had to do was wait.

But what if he didn't? What if he'd given up? How long should she wait? And what would she tell Wilkie? She couldn't tell him she was waiting for Morgan. If Morgan didn't come, Wilkie would be hurt.

She'd have to make up some excuse to tell her cousin, that was all there was to it. And she would wait two days. After that . . . she'd leave and never look back.

If Morgan didn't want her, there was nothing for her here.

A small voice told her she should go to him, but she was too ashamed. Too afraid of his rejection.

In a word, she was a coward.

Finishing her ablutions, she returned to the cave to find Wilkie sound asleep on a pile of leaves, his hand clutched tightly around a glittering rock.

She smiled and took off one of her petticoats to cover him, and remembered how gentle Morgan had been with him. Why hadn't she been able to see that sooner?

Because she was a fool.

Stretching out on the leaves beside Wilkie, she closed her eyes and tried to sleep, but it was a long time coming. Her mind was too full of memories and guilt and her own foolishness. She recalled seeing a patch of dawn just before she finally sank into a soothing black void.

"Jade? Wake up."

She blinked groggily and glanced around.

"When are we leaving?" Wilkie asked with a note of youthful impatience.

She forced her head to clear, and remembered she needed an excuse for staying. She brought a hand to her forehead. "I don't think we'll leave today. I'm . . . not feeling well."

"You're sick?"

The concern in his voice made her wince. "Not really sick, but I'd like to rest today."

"Maybe you should go to the doctor like me. Morgan would take you."

Knowing he was thinking of when Morgan took him, she smiled. "I'll be fine, Will. Truly."

"Can I swim in the pond?"

"Yes."

He jumped to his feet and raced out through the tunnel.

Jade felt just a bit insulted. So much for his concern over her well-being.

The day passed at a snail's pace, and she couldn't help staring at the trees in the direction Morgan would arrive. But he didn't come, and by the time she and Wilkie retired, the heaviness in her chest had doubled in weight.

She spent another sleepless night and prayed Morgan would come the next day.

But as that day too crept closer to evening, Jade knew he wasn't coming. She'd pushed him too far.

Feeling as if a piece of her soul had been ripped out, she lay down on the leaves and closed her eyes, willing herself to get some much-needed sleep, and willing morning to hurry so she could leave.

Morgan tossed a rock into the lake behind Ainshall, watching it plop and splash as it hit the water. He took another swig from the bottle of rum on the ground beside him, then picked up another rock.

He'd been drinking for two days straight, *two and a half,* but he didn't give a damn. Rum was the only thing that would ease the ache in his heart. Hurt caused by a green-eyed vixen who wouldn't even give him a chance.

Well, to hell with her! He hoped he never set eyes on her again. He slammed the rock toward the opposite shore, watching it fall short of the dusk-lit bank and sink into the water.

He tossed down another swallow, wondering if he shouldn't just drown himself in the rum and get it over with. Life didn't have a whole lot of meaning at the moment.

"Morgan?"

He didn't turn and look at his father. He just grabbed another rock and pitched it into the lake.

"Morgan, Wilkie's here."

Morgan's whole body tightened, and it took several seconds to drag in enough breath to speak. "Is Jade with him?"

"No."

He closed his eyes against the pain. Of course she wouldn't be. But why would Wilkie come without her? Had something happened? The thought propelled him to his feet. "Where is he?"

"The drawing room."

Morgan's concern for Jade grew claws as he darted past his father and sprinted toward the house, barely aware of the twinge in his ankle. What if her horse had thrown her, or she'd been run down by a wagon, or she'd been set upon by a highwayman?

He slammed through the back door, his blood pumping at a furious pace, his feet moving steadily toward the drawing room. When he opened the door, he saw Wilkie sitting on the settee, his hands folded nervously. "Where's Jade? Is she all right?"

"No."

"Is she hurt?"

"No. Sick. And you helped me when I was sick, so I took Patience and I came here so you'd help Jade, too."

Morgan's whole body went numb. "What's wrong? What happened? *Where* is she?"

"She's where the pond and gazebo are, in the—"

Morgan was out the door before he finished. She was at the glen!

"Jade?"

She came awake to some sound, one she couldn't

identify. Shaking her head, she tried to clear the fog from her brain. That was a mistake. The moment her thoughts cleared, she remembered the days she'd waited for Morgan. The days he hadn't come.

Pain squeezed her chest.

A noise sounded from the tunnel, and Jade blinked in the shallow dawn light filtering in from the hole above. She knew it must be Wilkie. He was probably pacing, anxious to leave.

Rubbing her temples, she took a breath and started to rise.

"Jade? Talk . . . to . . . me."

She froze for a heartbeat, then whipped toward the cave opening.

Morgan stood in the entrance, his hair tousled, his clothes dusty. His features were tight. A pulse beat rapidly at the base of his throat, and there was a look of sheer terror in his eyes.

Terror? Then it hit her. *The cave.* "Morgan, get out of here!"

Trickles of moisture ran from his temples to his jaws. His hands were clenched at his sides, his chest rising and falling heavily, his face deathly pale. "Not . . . without . . . you."

She sprang to her feet and hurried past him to the entrance. "All right. Let's go outside."

He didn't move.

"Morgan, come on."

He still didn't move.

She stepped around to face him—and gasped at the look of stark fear. "Morgan!" Oh, God. She had to do something. "Wilkie! Help me!"

He didn't answer. Didn't come.

Morgan started to shake.

Panic spurred her into action. She placed her hands on either side of his face. "Morgan, look at me. Do you hear me? *Look at me!"*

His gaze fixed on hers, and she saw a flicker of reason, but it receded quickly. Fear grabbed her. She had to get through to him! "Don't you dare take your eyes off mine after all you've done to me," she hissed, hoping he'd become angry at the blatant lie.

He didn't flick an eye.

She was starting to panic. "Morgan, walk. Do you hear me? Walk. No, don't look away. Just put one foot in front of the other." Slowly, she eased backward toward the entrance, holding her hands steady on his cheeks, forcing him to follow. To focus only on her.

She became aware of his increasing trembles, the ticking pulse beat beneath her palm, harsh rasp of his breath, and the faint scent of rum.

He'd been drinking. Was probably even drunk. He'd never have gone in the cave if he'd had his wits about him.

Taking each step slowly, willing the opposite opening to appear quickly, she kept her eyes fastened to his.

When she at last felt the spray from the falls, she thought she would burst into tears with relief.

The instant Morgan stepped out of the cave and saw the light, she felt the change in him. The muscles in his jaws relaxed, and his eyes began to focus.

Dragging in great gulps of air, he collapsed against the rock wall and pulled her to him.

For several minutes they just stood there, and she closed her eyes, listening to the beat of his heart and rasp of his breath as it grew increasingly calmer.

Finally, he bent his head to her ear. "I guess . . . you're destined to . . . save my life."

"Or end mine. I was scared to death."

His arms came around her, and she felt the tremors still running through him. "That makes two of us."

She shoved away from him, suddenly angry at him for putting her through such an ordeal. "What are you doing here? Why were you in that cave? Curse you, Morgan. Don't you *ever* do that again."

"Wilkie said you were sick."

"Wilkie?" She glanced around. "Where is he?"

"At Ainshall."

"But—"

He placed a finger against her lips. "Jade, we need to talk."

She felt her lips tremble against his fingertip, and she forgot all about Wilkie, about everything but the ache in her heart. "I know."

Slipping an arm around her waist, he led her to the gazebo and they both sat down.

For several seconds, he just sat there, staring at the plank flooring.

"I am a gambler, Jade. And I enjoy it. I love the challenge, and the thrill of victory, but I'm not obsessed by it. I never have been. It's a pastime. A way to while the hours, but the games could never mean more to me than you do—and if it takes a vow from me for you to believe that, then you shall have it."

Her heart started pounding in her ears. Oh, how she wanted to believe him. "Why didn't you give me your word when I asked?"

He leaned back and rested his head on a post.

"Because I wanted our marriage to be based on trust, not conditions. But none of that matters anymore. Nothing does but being with you . . . on *any* terms. Jade, I swear to you, I'll never—"

"No! Don't promise me you won't gamble."

He turned away, his jaw clenched tight. "There's nothing else I can offer."

"Yes, there is."

His gaze met hers, and she felt a swell of love so great; tears stung. "The only promise I want from you is that you'll love me for eternity."

A sheen of moisture brightened his eyes, and he slowly reached out to place his hand on her cheek. "Ah, beautiful, I'll love you a helluva lot longer than that."